The author began his working life in advertising becoming an account executive. He draws on his experience in this field in the plot of this novel. He went on to become a minister of the Church of England taking a close interest in Judaism. Again he brings this element into the book demonstrating how Benjamin Traumann grows in maturity through the Jewish religion.

As one who appreciates the contribution of Judaism to the human race, I dedicate this book to all Jews from the earliest times who have given so much in many fields from literature, art, music, philosophy and psychology. One person I must mention is Rabbi Jonathan Sacks whose deep wisdom is reflected in many books.

T. Denis Desert

NASHOTAH PEAK

AUSTIN MACAULEY PUBLISHERS™
LONDON • CAMBRIDGE • NEW YORK • SHARJAH

A CIP catalogue record for this title is available from the British Library.

ISBN 9781398467750 (Paperback)
ISBN 9781398467767 (ePub e-book)

www.austinmacauley.com

First Published 2022
Austin Macauley Publishers Ltd®
1 Canada Square
Canary Wharf
London
E14 5AA

"Life," said the MAN, "is a pretty tricky."

"Pretty tricky. Pretty tricky," agreed a bug hiding under a hot rock.

"Pretty tricky. Pretty tricky. Pretty tricky," came in just about every bug hunkered down under hot rocks on Nashotah Peak. The MAN stroked his thick beard and nodded his head and sighed.

"Guess it's damned pretty tricky. Damned tricky, tricky – 'tricky' – 'tricky' – 'TRICKY'."

I guess he was damned right about that. Life can be mighty tricky. Okay. It can also be mighty full of surprises that put you on your feet and get you walking tall. I reckon that's just about how it's been with me. Some things way back have left me right on my face howling in a pain that just about tore me right apart. Then the wind changes bringing that certain something that makes you feel someone. That's how it is. So if you've figured that out, you just don't get to making life to be just a can of worms or hopefully a jar full of honey. No, sir, life's a mixed package. You get a bit of this and a bit of that and so on. I guess that's just how it's worked out for me.

So let me say who I am. I'm Benjamin Traumann, a Jew born in the good old USA with Uncle Sam smiling down. Fine. Let me make it clear I'm a whole lot proud at being Jewish. Real proud. So why am I writing all this stuff down? I'm getting all this down at the suggestion of Mom. Mom? More about her later, much later. Now I've got a hunch that folk if they're really going to know whom they are, need to know where their family came from. Their roots. So what of the Traumann's?

We came from right the other side of the pond across to quite a town in Germany, Mainz. There were a whole lot of us Jews who had pitched their tents there over the years. So it was that the Grossmanns and the Traumanns got together and built up a mighty fine optical business, G undt T So they produced anything from eyeglasses, microscopes through to telescopes and so on. They sold stuff all over Europe and the States. They made it big. The two families kept together and the young members got under the chuppah together and raised good Jewish families. I guess they all enjoyed living in a promised land flowing with a hell of a lot of milk and honey.

But it didn't stay that way. It so happened that this Austrian guy, who didn't make it at art school, decided to ease his way into politics. He couldn't paint too well, but somehow, he could speak and folk listened. He got men into uniforms and setting up parades and that sort of thing. Everyone, except us Jews, thought he was one hell of a guy. It looks as if he was not too keen on us Jews and made us wear yellow stars. What the hell? Things got hot in Mainz and the goys started treating us like we were not too human. It looks like the Grossmans with the Traumanns got to looking ahead. They transferred assets into Swiss banks and set up a branch of the company over in the States in the City of Chicago. I figure it was a pretty bad time for us Jews. The pot of honey had become one heck of a big can of worms. You bet.

So things got worse as the goys yelled at us on the streets and hurled bricks. It seemed that Catholics got it bad with nuns and monks turned out of their places. Then came what was known as Kristallnacht. Mobs went around smashing the windows of our Jewish shops and torching our synagogues. It so happened that the main synagogue in Mainz was full and my ma and pa, newly married, were there. Ma it seems was pregnant with me. You can guess the congregation panicked when the flames got a hold. They fought to get out. I guess some just didn't make it. But my folk got out and made it back to their place. I reckon they were shaken real bad.

***

The Traumanns and the Grossmanns decided it was time to hotfoot it to the States. They piled into automobiles and got going fast. They sailed through checkpoints assisted with handouts right across the country into France to Le Havre to board the Normandie. They berthed at New York and headed for the windy city, Chicago, and pitched their tents right there.

It looks like the Traumanns and the Grossmans had got things lined up well ahead. They'd got themselves an agent who made the right contacts. Pretty soon, they got the business going and with the war getting going in Europe, optics were in demand. So G & T optics got off to a mighty good start, and the family soon made a pretty strong mark in the Jewish community.

But there was a problem. Pa was not into optics or business. It just wasn't his line of country. Back in Germany, he'd enrolled in some sort of art academy and was getting somewhere. It so happened that there were quite a number of cousins around who were into the business. So Pa slipped out of things and enrolled in the Chicago Academy of Art. It so happens, I got there myself way ahead. So Pa spent his time painting and going up around the lake sketching and whatever.

Well, as just about everyone knows, the Japs hit the US fleet at Pearl Harbour in 1941, but what just about what no one knows I gave my ma a bad time getting into this crazy, tricky world. Ma's hips were not exactly designed for childbearing, it seems, and she nearly ended, with me, in a long narrow box. She then, so I'm told, got pretty strange sitting around and doing just about nothing. They got in a nurse, Rebecca, to take care of me. But Ma didn't get better. She got into black moods, screamed at me and then push a cushion over my face and try to finish me. It sticks with me right now. Then she'd get good days and say she was real sorry for being such a wicked mother. She'd pick me up and kiss me and give me nice little presents, a cookie or something.

It was pretty bad time for me as a kid. Sometimes she was okay and sometimes she went bananas and treated me real bad. Then I got it figured out. On bad days, she'd just sit there with her shaved-head covered in a scarf made of some dull woollen stuff that looked as if it'd been around for a hell of a long time. But on good days, she'd have on a wig with the golden curls and she was real nice to me. So I got to figuring out, as kids do, that the woollen scarf must have something in it that was bad. A dybbuk? But the golden wig had something in it that made Ma feel good. Was that how it was?

Now some folks think that young kids just don't make things out. They're damned wrong – my god, they are! So I worked out that what I just had to do was to get hold of that evil kerchief and destroy it. So I just had to wait for an opportunity. Ma was sleeping late. So I slowly opened her door and crept in. On her dressing table stood the stand with the golden wig. That made me feel good. Just by the stand was the bad dark blue kerchief. I moved slowly across the room with my heart thumping hard. I reached out and took the kerchief holding it well away and crept out. What was I going to do with it? The trash can! I slipped out to the backyard, eased the lid off the bin and slipped the evil thing in. I did a dance, skipping and jumping around. I'd saved Ma from the demon in the scarf. I felt real good and slipped back in again.

I reckoned that I had got the dybbuk in the trash bin and from now on Ma would be real nice. But I was just about as wrong as anyone could be. My guts get knotted up now just thinking about it. Ma came out wearing her golden wig. "Vat done vit it? Vat done?" she screamed glaring at me. "Vat says Torah? No steal. No steal. Fater vill beat – yah?" Then she hurled the contents of the chamber pot covering me with cold piss. God, I can feel it now – the foul, wet stuff soaking me all over, running through my eyes, down my neck and right down into my clothes. "Tief! Tief! Tief!" she yelled. I had got it badly wrong. Something snapped inside me deep down. That dybbuk was not in that cloth – it was right inside Ma. No way could I get it out. I slipped back to get the cloth from the bin. I brought it back and pushed it right down into the upholstery of Ma's chair.

Pa was a switched-off sort of a guy. Maybe Ma's condition had put just a bit too much strain on him. Maybe he just found getting keyed into the new world was a bit too tough. Whatever it was, he, like Ma, had never got too easy in English. Life for him was just a damned great burden. He'd just sit there in a chair, gazing into space with his brow all wrinkled up and giving out these great soul-sighs. At times, I'd come and sit at his feet and look up at his sad face. Sometimes he'd look down with his brown, sad eyes and maybe give me something of a gentle smile. I liked that and would beam right back.

That evening, after I'd taken Ma's kerchief, when Pa came in Ma gave him a mighty queer look. I couldn't make too much of it but felt mighty uneasy. What Ma told him I just couldn't figure. Pa just stood looking helpless. Then Ma, who had lost a hell of a lot of weight, blew up. She stormed around yelling words I couldn't make out and kept pointing at me. I wet my pants. "Yitzack Traumann – joke – dreamer," she screamed at Pa. I knew she was making fun of him. She just went on and on and just didn't let up. Then suddenly, he snapped. He threw back his head and gave out this terrible cry like some animal or lost soul. Maybe the dybbuk had got somehow into him? That sound never left me. Years on, I saw a picture by that Munch of some guy screaming out from his depths. That's how my pa cried out, like a trapped creature in black despair. Ma put her hands over her ears and bolted back to her room. Pa fell to his knees, drew me into his arms, and we both sobbed together.

What then? Ma went into one of her long, deep depressions. She let everything go and started drinking stuff out of bottles and smoked a lot. Rebecca came in every day. She got things in order and was real nice to me. She played games and told me stories – real nice stories that made me laugh. She got me speaking English just a bit better. She really got me going and taking me out for walks. I guess that she came from one of the poorer Jewish families.

Anyway, Rebecca would take me out every day. One thing she did was to put up a mezuzah by the door. I daresay Pa agreed. She got me touching it as we went out and came back and got me saying something. I guess that I didn't understand what the hell it meant, but I can still say the words, "Hear, O Israel: the Lord our God, is Lord is One." She'd take me to the park and talk about what we saw there. There were trees and plants, birds and ponds with fish. She knew just about everything. She'd tell me the names of things and where they came from. She'd tell me stories of how things came to be and about God – blessed be He. How God made everything and how He made us. I'd listen wide-eyed and ears a-twitch. She would bring some old black book out of her bag and show me the pages. I could see that the writing was different from anything I'd seen before. She told me it had belonged to some uncle way back in a land way over the sea. It was a special book written in the language of our people God knows how long ago. She said it was the Bible and contained all a good Jew needed to know. We'd sit on a bench for hours as she read to me from the book in words I couldn't get. Then she'd tell me all about it.

One of the stories just grabbed me. The one about a baby that got put into a basket on a great river and was found by a princess. I'd get Rebecca to read it time and again until I knew it by heart. Then she'd tell me about people called Israelites who crossed a sea into a place that was just nothing but sand. But God loved them and was always with them and made sure they were okay. She said I was an Israelite – Jewish – and that made me different from other folk – special. That sounded okay. Rebecca did a damned lot for me.

What then? I guess Ma got to hitting the bottle hard. She began to fade right out of my life. I knew she was in her room, and she stayed right there. Rebecca couldn't take me out so much, and I missed that. She had to be something of a nurse. She was at it all day carrying and fetching, but she never got into a hassle. She always had a smile and did all she could to keep me amused. In time, Rebecca came to live in and that made me feel a whole lot better.

The medical people started coming most days, as Ma got worse. One day, I was sitting looking out on to the backyard. It was spring with nice warm sun and shrubs and things bursting into flower. It gave me a nice, good feeling inside. I felt okay. Rebecca came in, picked me up and gave me a hug and a kiss. "Now then," she said, "you've got to be a great big brave Jewish boy. Your Ma's just died." Something went inside me. I just screamed and screamed. I beat Rebecca, scratching and punching her until she just had to let me go. I rushed sobbing across the room, threw myself into the deep chair, pulled out the kerchief, buried my face in it and howled and howled and howled.

Things got mighty confused after that. Rebecca got out a little black book and started making weird noises. Pa came and went like a ghost. Folk came and went. Curtains were drawn and the house became dark. I had bad dreams and wet the bed. It was a real bad time. I started imaging things and hiding away in dark corners. I started sitting in Ma's chair and imagined scary creatures with teeth, claws and horns. I looked into dark corners and got to seeing some semi-human creature all curled up. It was thin and clothed all over with some dark, tight-fitting garment. Its eyes glittered with a strange light glowing red, blue and then green. It eyed me, and it scared the life right out of me. I hardly dare moved. My little chest went tight and my belly turned to ice. The skin of my face went tight and pricked uncomfortably.

Then Rebecca would come in and throw open the curtains and let in the light. The creature would then vanish right away, Rebecca would take me up and give me a real big hug and take me off to the park where spring flowers were bursting out just about everywhere.

I guess you might think it odd that my grandparents didn't figure too strong. I figure it out this way. Somehow, my pa Isaac and my ma Ruth were a big disappointment to the Traumanns and the Grossmanns and so they kept their distance. The old folk had been pretty good at getting their act together in the States, but somehow, their children just hadn't transplanted too well. The new soil didn't suit. I don't know. Sure, they saw that the young Traumanns didn't go short of bucks. I guess they arranged for Rebecca to come and put her on the payroll, but to me, they were vague shadows as a young kid. They appeared now and again and then disappeared for quite some time.

Sometime after Ma's death, the Traumann grandparents started to put in something more of an appearance. They came around in their ritzy limousine and took me out for a drive with me sitting in the front between them. We'd head for the big lake. I guess those trips made quite an impression on me just sitting and driving around that great expanse of water. I got to wondering if this might be the water that Rebecca told me about that God parted to let our people go. It was a new world to me. All I'd ever known was the backyard and the nearby park – but this…! It just bowled me right over.

At another time, they drove me into what I suppose was an industrial part of the city. Grandfather drove through some gates and into the parking lot. He swung me up on his shoulders. I can hear him say in that strange voice of his, "Bennie, my boy, von day dis vill be yours." I guess I just looked and wondered what the hell I could do with that mass of buildings. Did Grandfather expect me to live there or something? I didn't feel too interested.

I suppose the grandparents started coming around every week or so. Maybe I didn't take to them too well. Perhaps they were just a bit too strange. Who can tell? However it was, the relationship didn't gel too well. They came. They took me out in the limo. They talked their talk in words I just couldn't figure out. They brought me back and off they went until the next time. They were figures from another world.

Rebecca wasn't sleeping in anymore, but she carried on as a sort of house-nurse maid. She got meals for my pa and fed me. She put me to bed and then disappeared. In the morning, she arrived to get me up and spent time looking after me. It went on like that for the hell of a long time. We had those walks in the park, and she told me those stories about our people from a heck of a long time ago in some place a long way off. It felt good when she was around. As I've said before, I owed just about everything to Rebecca. She was my ma – my proper ma. She made me feel I belonged to these very special people – Jewish people, different people. We were not like other folk we saw around; there was nothing special about them. But we were special, and I was one of the special people. It made me feel good. Rebecca gave me something to hold on to. [c. 1946]

I suppose it was around this time when I was coming up to five that Pa started to look a little more human. I would look at him, and now and again, he would look at me and give just a whisper of a smile. He looked pretty big to me but, as I came to see later, he was small. He was dead thin with one of those drawn-in faces that shows just about every fragment of bone. His eyes had a haunted look that seldom looked at any place in particular. He had a thick head of black hair, but his beard was thin and wispy and pretty untidy. I used to look in the glass and just hoped I wouldn't get to look too much like him with that thin beak of a nose. I got to examining my own nose carefully. I didn't like what I saw. It was too big for my face and like Pa's, dead thin. So I got to sticking my fingers right up my nose to try to make it fatter. Rebecca caught me at it one day and laughed. "What are you doing, you silly boy?" she asked.

"Don't want a nose like Pa's," I came back. "I want a fat nose."

"Bennie," she replied, "your Pa's got a nice nose and a nice face." That's when it came to me that Rebecca liked Pa, and I began to feel a touch of jealousy.

Now you will be getting to thinking that Pa didn't look too human. I guess that infant observations are often pretty accurate. He did have this long, thin face, not quite a death's head but damned close. I fancy that he had gone through quite a lot when young. By this time, he'd be no more than his early thirties. But somehow, he began warming up just a little and beginning to give me a shy little smile and a touch on the shoulder. I guess that Rebecca was having something of an influence on him.

After a while, Pa started playing this little silver flute. It fascinated me. The flute was small and looked carefully made. He would sit there in the big chair where once I had hidden the kerchief and play for hours. He played soulful, plaintive melodies. They brought up sad memories, but somehow, they made you feel better inside. All the grief and bad memories floated up; the notes wrapped themselves around the hurt feelings and made them better. Rebecca would come and curl herself on the floor against the chair. Tears would flow down her cheeks and a smile would touch her lips. Then Pa would stop and a great silence would follow, a silence I shall never forget. It was a good, healing, bonding silence and the three of us just sat. Pa's sallow cheeks began to be touched with colour, and for the first time, I began to feel warm towards him.

Rebecca would get up, place here hand gently on his shoulder and recite, "Those that sow in tears shall reap in joy." I wondered what the words meant, but they stuck in my mind.

I suppose you can guess how things progressed. The day came when Rebecca took me out into the park. It was the early part of the fall. The air was still warm and cosy. The trees were getting tinged with yellow and gold, but that deep impossible red had yet to come. I'd learnt to look forward to that magic each year. I just loved to sit in the park at that time and imagine all the trees on fire against the deep blue sky. Then I'd rush through the piles of fallen leaves kicking them up in the air. It was magic. It's maybe that with most folk they lose that sense of magic. Maybe it gets lost by seeing too many falls as the years go by, or perhaps getting caught up with the damned-all of everyday, the kid inside them gets pushed out. Somehow, I've managed to keep just a bit of that spark.

There was this small lake in the park. Ducks abounded there and came up squawking for crusts of bread. But what I liked best were the fish. There were great golden carp living deep down in the murky waters. Monsters! You had to go out on this rickety wooden bridge and throw in hunks of bread. The great creatures came up out of the mud. First, you'd see bubbles and then a swirl followed by the first sight of the beasts. Then a head, like that of a monster, would break the surface. They had great thick lips with mouths large enough to swallow me whole. And the eyes – great yellow-gold eyes that stared up at me in a fishy way. Frightening eyes. They gave me bad dreams. I'd be in some great dark room. The eyes would start to come – many eyes just looking at me. Sinister eyes. I got the feeling they were making some terrible plot against me to upset my little life. They fascinated me those eyes but also made me feel uneasy.

And Rebecca? I got carried away with those fish. You know how it is when you get a talking and thinking. You get down some sidetrack or other. That's just how it is. It so happened that the time came when she took my hand in hers as we sat on a park bench. "Now, Bennie," she started, "how would you like me to be your ma? Your real ma?" I suppose I'd been turning things over in my mind as kids do. Folk don't get to realise what goes on deep down in the minds of kids. They're a darned sight more cute than folk think. Somehow, I'd begun to see how it might be between Pa and Rebecca. As I've made pretty clear, I'd never been too close to Pa and Rebecca was the only adult who'd meant anything to me. I just wanted her to myself. I just didn't want to share her with Pa or anyone. I just sat staring out over the park watching leaves falling and turning what she had said over in my mind.

"Things will be just the same," she said quietly. "I'll be with you all the time and I can be a real ma to you. We can be a real Jewish family and do all the right things I've told you about."

"You mean that we can have a real sukkah in the yard at Sukkot?" I asked. My heart warmed at the thought.

"Of course, we can," she replied. "And we'll have a special menorah at Hanukkah. We'll keep Shabbat properly and do everything a proper Jewish family does. It will be wonderful, you just see." I sat thinking it over. It sounded good – okay. Rebecca continued, "Then when you are a real big boy, it will be time for your Bar Mitzvah. That's when you will have to learn what it means to learn how to be a real Jewish man. And then we'll have a real nice party – you see if we don't!"

Rebecca had that nice, positive reassuring manner of the sort that could turn a disaster into a jubilee. Deep down, I could feel that everything was going to be just fine. Rebecca would see us through. She'd make a proper Jewish family of us. I got to thinking that maybe I could share her with Pa so she could become my ma.

That fall was followed by a long, cold, bitter winter. Just about everything froze up. The house was full of draughts, and Rebecca made me wear thick undergarments. They made me itch like mad. It was still good in the park. She'd take me out in the frost and snow. I would think about the golden fall and now the magic of a white world with icicles hanging down from the trees and with thick ice over the lake. I looked at the ice and thought of those monsters deep down in the green water and wondered how it was with them. Rebecca said that like a lot of creatures they were asleep in the mud. "What if they don't wake?" I asked.

"Sure they'll wake up okay. You just wait and see. As soon as the ice melts, they'll come up and ask for bread. You just wait."

"Do the animals go down into the mud?" I came back.

"I guess they wouldn't like that too much, Bennie. They just find themselves a nice little hidey-hole and curl up all nice and snug and have a good long sleep. Then come the spring they'll wake up and get busy starting their families. Just you wait and see."

The spring came, the ice thawed, the golden carp came up for their bread, the little grey squirrels came out of their hidey-holes and got busy getting their families going. The birds too started singing their songs and building their nests, just as Rebecca had said. It was one of those springs when it heated up fast. The winds blew up from the south and stayed that way. Women got out their summer frocks and men rolled up their shirtsleeves. It was just great. Folk went around looking real happy and saying, 'Great weather!' Everything was moving and bubbling over. Flowers were bursting out all over the place and birds, animals and all creatures were going crazy with excitement. It was great.

Pa got out that silver flute and started playing lively tunes. Wonderful tunes that got my feet a tapping and eyes a sparkling. I did a little dance, and Rebecca clapped her hands in time. I dance around the room, waved my hands and just laughed and laughed. It was a great moment. "Bennie," she said, "you'd make a fine Hassidic!" I just couldn't figure that one out.

Pa never really laughed. I guessed his poor heart just wouldn't let go. At least he managed to play that happy tune. But when he'd put down the flute, he'd say, "That was good, Bennie. That was good."

Rebecca? Yes, as I was saying, she had hinted that she and Pa were going to get married. Then came this terrific spring when life was just bursting out all over the place. That's when preparations got started. I would have been around six or so at the time. I got fitted out with a fine new suit. A proper suit in a real grown-up style. It made me feel swell. They told me that it was in something they called English tweed. It was not too easy to get at the time. I guess it was soon after the war and some things were hard to get. I knew that things had been happening somewhere or other and men in uniform made their appearance. I thought they looked real, good and maybe I'd become a soldier one day. But I was glad to have this swell suit. I guess the Traumann grandparents picked up the tab. I remember Grandma saying to Grandpa, "Remember, Solly, one day Bennie will be sitting in your seat." It stuck in my mind. But like a lot of things, kids don't figure out; it just buzzed around.

The wedding day came. It seemed a swell do to me, but I reckon by Traumann standards, it was somewhat low key. It took place in the grandparents' place. It was big pad in some swell neighbourhood. The spring continued fair and warm. On this big lawn, they had set up this large, decorated canopy. I got pretty excited and did my spring dance. I banged into one of the supports, knocking it loose. Grandma gave me a shake and someone had to do a fixing job.

Folk started to arrive. It looked like a crowd to me. The man they called the Rabbi came dressed in black with some sort of hat on his head. I didn't like the look of the guy. Pa stood there looking uncomfortable. His face looked thinner than usual and sallow. He had on a very dark suit and something like a shawl over his shoulders. I'd never seen that before. He had on the back of his head a little black cap that didn't look too secure. I couldn't keep my eyes off it. Would it fall off? Pa kept messing about with it as if he were not too sure either. Rebecca came in. I didn't recognise her at first. She wore a white gown and a veil. She looked at me and gave me a smile. I suppose the whole thing went right over my head. I knew, whatever it was, that this had to happen if Rebecca were to become my ma. Something was poured into a glass. I felt hot. Would I get some? No. It was just for Pa and Rebecca. Perhaps they needed it more than the others? Then Pa, I guess he was dead nervous, dropped the glass. I felt sorry for him and looked away in confusion. But no one seemed to mind. Pa then stamped on the glass shattering it in pieces and everyone shouted out something I couldn't figure out. They all clapped and looked real happy. Then we went into the house for the reception. It was noisy. I ate too much. There were no other young kids around. I went outside and was sick. I felt dead and cold inside. I felt alone – unwanted.

I once heard it said, you live your life forwards but get to getting the hang of it backwards. It took me some time to figure that out. I guess that it would save a whole lot of trouble if we got to understanding what the hell it's about at the time, but it just don't seem to work like that. Looking back at the time I was a kid is just a hell of a jumble. This happened and then that with great spaces in between. Folk you got to thinking were there for keeps get snatched away. As a kid, I just didn't figure it all out. After Pa's marriage to Rebecca, I got to calling her Ma. But things started to drift away. Ma appeared to lose just a bit of interest in me. Maybe she was just taken up with her new life as Mrs Isaac Traumann. But as a kid, I just felt left out. I just didn't matter too much.

It was a tough time for me. I got sent off to some school. It was the first time I'd had real contact with other kids. I didn't care too much for it. In my first years, I'd been alone in an adult world. Now I was plunged right into this scary world of kids. Kids who pushed you around and made trouble. That first day at school was hell. It got so that I wet my pants and got sent out to clean myself up. The other kids came out and laughed. "Bennie wetty," they crowed. An older boy came in.

"Look he's a Yid! He's a Yid!" he called out. "He's got a bit off his thing – that's why he pissed himself." They then turned and pissed on me.

I stood there a hell of a time. I was cold and wet and dripping with their foul piss. I tried to figure out what they meant by Yid. Something to do with my thing Was it bad to be a Yid? Why was I different? I didn't like that. I just wanted to be like the other kids. I wanted to be one of them and play with them. That's all. I couldn't make it out.

Ma was real kind when I got back. She listened to me as I sobbed it all out. She put her arms around me and gave me comfort. That was good. Then she bathed and changed me and held me in her arms for a good long time. "What's a Yid? And what's wrong with my thing?" I asked.

"It's what they call us Jews," she explained.

"What's wrong with my thing?"

"There's nothing wrong. It's fine. It's okay. It's just that God told our father Abraham to have this bit of skin taken off boy babies' things. It's something to be proud of. It shows you're special – a Jew. So just you don't go minding what those boys say. Don't forget you're a Jew and just about the best sort of human being to be." I didn't feel too certain about that.

Ma helped me to feel better – okay. That's how it was with her. She made me feel big when I was feeling pretty small. Okay, I still got it from the other kids at school.

It still made me feel not too good. But deep down, I felt okay and comfortable about being Jewish. I figured the other kids couldn't go right back God knows how long to Father Abraham.

The years after that get something into a blur. I moved around schools and worked up the grades. I never felt I belonged. Okay, there were other Jewish kids around, but somehow, I was the kid who walked alone. I watched kids playing their games but was not asked to join in. I got on learning what I had to learn. I got the feeling I did well. But it just wasn't a time I looked back on with satisfaction. I just didn't make friends with goys and didn't come too close to other Jewish boys around. School was just a place where I had to go and learn and then come back to Ma.

Ma was always there waiting for me with a great hug and a kiss. "Good day?" she'd ask. And then draw out from me what I'd learnt and ask me a whole lot of questions. She was pretty sharp and got me thinking about all sorts of things. It was just no good taking in facts and passing examinations. You had to get deep into the meaning of things. Facts were facts, but they just had to lead you into seeing beyond them. "You have to use your imagination," she'd say.

I guess I must have been ten or more at the time. We'd been doing quite a bit on the earth's crust and that sort of thing. I got out my book of maps and pointed out the Rift Valley. She knew something about that. "Maybe here, way down in East Africa, is where Adam and Eve crept out of the dust. Maybe they went right up the valley and crossed right over until they got to the Promised Land. Don't you think that's just how it happened, Bennie?" I smiled at the thought and nodded.

We had a good number of talks like that. Maybe Ma hadn't got too much education, but she knew how to think – she had ideas. She'd arouse my curiosity. I got the facts at school, but Ma taught me how to use them. We figured out that if all folk went back to Adam, then just about everyone had to be related. That's just how it had to be. We got to thinking about Father Abraham and God's promise to him that God would bless 'everyone' through him. This just had to mean the promise was not just for us Jews but the goys as well. Fine, but what was the point of keeping a kosher kitchen and boy babies getting circumcised and that sort of stuff? Ma always managed to work out some sort of answer that made some sense. After all, she had come from a family of rabbis. Sure, it was that God had to have just one special people to learn his laws and keep them so he could bless other races. Why can't goys see this? Maybe it's just because they can't see too well.

Pa had taken to going to the synagogue on Shabbat. As I grew older, he'd take me with him. I guess his Hebrew wasn't of the best. Maybe he'd just forgotten it. He'd just stand there looking into his prayer book, mouthing things silently and turning pages just too often. But he went and I guess that pleased Ma. I got to ask her why women didn't go to the synagogue as much as men. She came back with, "Because men need to pray more!"

The best time of all was Sukkot. That comes at the end of harvest when Jews just about everywhere go crazy thanking God for the blessing. It's a great time for kids and adults. We put up this light shelter in the yard called a sukkah. Ma told me that it was a reminder of our time in the wilderness when we just had to live in tents and that sort of thing. I'd go out and sit in it for hours. We'd even eat a meal out there. It was fun. Some of the local kids came and wanted to come in. I told them to scram. But Ma would come out and invite them in. I was just mad. She said Sukkot was for everyone. So she brought the goy kids in and told them all about it. She'd tell me, "Remember, Bennie, that the Almighty, blessed be He, pours his blessing on us so we can share it with the goys. We have to learn to share what is given to us. Good Jews learn to share. You keep your blessing to yourself and you just lose it." A pretty hard lesson for a kid to learn. You just don't want to let some goy get some of the candy.

Ma was a great teacher. She didn't ram her stuff down my throat but let me work things out for myself. She'd throw out a question and got me to work it out. "What do you think the Almighty gave us the Promised Land for?" she'd ask. I'd come back with 'so we could have a real nice life'. But she would get me to see that the land had to be shared. The stranger within the gates had to have a place too. She majored on Jews being a people who shared and didn't snatch. Somehow, through Ma, I started to get this deep feeling that I was not just a kid floating through life on my own, but I belonged to a people with, yes, a past, present and a future. I got to feeling real proud of being a Jew, and I didn't care a damn about what the goy kids said. I was a Jew, Bennie Traumann, and that was it.

I guess, as a kid I tried hard to do as she taught me. She used to make up these pretty good packs of food to take for the break at school. I got to sharing with the other kids. They thought I was just crazy and snatched the stuff out of my hands so I ended up with nothing. I got real sore. Now if the other kids had liked me for sharing. Fine. But they just got the lot and laughed at me. So what was the point? Sharing got me nowhere, so I got to eating the whole pack before I got to school.

So that's how it was when I was a kid. Ma was my fixed point. Pa was not really switched on. He'd just smile that sad smile of his and maybe pat me on the head. I reckon that there was something inside him that was just a bit too dead. I got to wondering if Ma wore a wig. I guess she did. She came from a pretty strict family so that's how it was. Pa would take out his silver flute when the fancy took him. Mostly, he'd play these sad, sad tunes that sounded nothing like the stuff I'd heard over the radio. Sometimes Pa might take me on his knee – I was pretty big by now. He still spoke with a thick accent. "Von day," he'd say, "I vill learn you this. Ja?" Somehow, he never got around to it.

Once, he told me of a place a long way off that had been home to him. It was a place of woods, valleys and rivers. There were little old towns with old wooden houses that had been there for just about ever. There was a shop, Grandpa Traumann's shop, where folk came for spectacles. There was my great grandfather with a long white beard who played the silver flute that had been in the family before Noah got into the ark. It was a damned nice little flute and felt nice. The silver was soft and worn with the touch of finger and lips over the years. The flute was sad with all those melodies that spoke of the bad times of the people of Israel.

I guess the house they lived in this far off land was pretty nice. It must have been big too. Just about all the Traumanns lived there and God knows how many kids. But it sounded great. Shabbat was really something. They had this great room with a great table. The old lady, Pa's grandma, would set up the table with a fine linen cloth and the Shabbat candles with the Kiddush cup and challah bread. It sounded real good. Ma was good at setting up the table for Shabbat, but somehow, I guess it was just nothing compared to the table Pa knew way back.

I reckon I felt just a bit sorry for the goy kids. They just missed out on all the family fun we Jews had. There was Shabbat on Friday going on to the next day at sundown. It gave me something to look forward to. We just sat around the table. It felt like being right in heaven. Ma made it real special. There were the candles and the prayers. Even Pa had his part. He had to say what Ma called the Kiddush prayers over the bread and wine. Ma did most of the talking, but Pa just sat smiling and putting in a word here and there. I got to wondering what the Christians did on Sundays. I see them going off to their churches looking pretty uptight, and when they came back, they didn't look too happy. I felt real sorry for them and was mighty glad I was Jewish.

Sometimes when Pa got me to himself, he'd start telling me something of where the family had come from. Okay, I've touched on this earlier, but I'd like to get it down as Pa told it. Our roots go back to this cute little town in Germany. Maybe I'd get there when I grow up. Maybe. It was all narrow street and these wooden houses and so on. The Traumanns and Grossmanns with the other Jewish families went to a little old synagogue with a little old rabbi with a long white beard. He taught Pa and the other boys Hebrew and how to be a good Jew and keep the Torah. Rabbi Moshe Capplemann just oozed goodness and kindness. He made a big impression on Pa. Pa said that the boys just couldn't wait to get to his yeshiva and learn how to be good Jews. The old rabbi never had to raise his voice or use a stick. The kids just ate right out of his hand. I guess this all happened somewhat after what they called the Great War. Folk were feeling pretty sore and maybe confused. The rabbi got to quoting the ancients. "Who is the true victor?" he'd throw out.

"The one who makes his enemy his friend," the boys would come back. I guess, maybe, that was asking just a bit too much. Just think of it. There were these Jewish German boys beating the hell out of British, French and American Jewish boys. Can that make sense? Just think – two Jewish boys facing each other with bayonets fixed trying to send each other to Abraham's bosom! What sense is in that? I guess it's just as crazy as you can get!

Pa told me how things got bad. The currency just went plumb crazy. One day you could buy a pair of Traumann spectacles for five dollars, or whatever, and the next day, it was it was up to fifty. There was this day when my Pa had his life insurance mature. It had been for good money. He went to the office with a sack to collect the dough. What did he decide to buy with the payout? Strawberries and cream! That's right – just think of that all those years of paying premiums and hoping for a big pay off just to buy strawberries and cream! What did he get in the end? Prices had soared right up so he could only get the strawberries! So Grandma kept the fruit for Shabbat. They each got at most two strawberries. They tasted real good, but they had cost a whole lot of dough.

I guess that it was dough going crazy that got folk screwed up. I guess that when the dollars get short even good folk get a touch edgy. But in this nice little neighbourhood where we Jews rubbed along well with the goys, the barriers started going up. The goys took to walking on one side of the street and we Jews on the other. There were some sinister guys around in brown outfits and crooked crosses on their arms. Things got real bad. The younger Jews got together and started training in self-defence. Shabbat came. Jews were flocking to the synagogue and passing through the town square. The men in brown shirts were waiting. They started shouting and throwing rocks. The young Jews took off their jackets and went in with everything they had. Pa was in the middle of it. The Jewish boys just about finished the goys. Bones were broken. The cops came and arrested the Jewish boys. The trail was just a phoney. They even got this Jewish boy – I reckon he was just about as non-kosher as you can get – to testify against the other boys. A whole lot of them got sent to jail. You can guess how the Jewish community felt about that.

Rabbi Capplemann got the men together and tried to let the steam out of things. He reminded them, so Pa told me, of how Jewish people had always suffered at the hands of the goys. "Look how it was in Egypt," he told them, "but our people trusted in the Almighty, blessed be He, and what happened? He delivered them through Moses." He just told them to bear the injustice, and he said prayers for the goys in the synagogue.

Just think of that – he prayed for the goys! I guess that made some of the men feel pretty sore, but he just reminded them that we are all sons of Abraham, and we Jews had to act like his sons even if goys didn't. Pa seemed to dig all this stuff out of the past. Maybe he just had to get it out. I drank it all in.

I suppose it was around this time that the old folk died. Maybe they were finding things just a bit more than they could stand. Rocks were thrown through the windows of Jewish businesses. Shutters were put up. Goys scrawled yellow stars all over the boards and wrote up 'Jewish swine'. Trade got bad. A few goys kept going to Traumann's, but they came at night so the other goys wouldn't see them. There was only one who'd come by day. He was the protestant pastor. Pa said he'd never forget him. His name was Rudi Gutenkirche. He was even on good terms with our rabbi and sometimes seen around the synagogue with him. He was big guy and had to get his head right down to get into the shop. Pa said he had these bright blue eyes and a great mass of yellow hair and often gave out this great deep belly laugh. He'd known Pa from just after his Bar Mitzvah and would often greet him,

"How's the Bar Mitzvah boy?" It became a little joke between them and stuck even when Pa was in his teens.

The pastor came to a bad end. It must have been around the time when this guy Goebbels started leaning hard on some Christians. He made them read his version of the scriptures and to put up swastikas in the place of the cross. This pastor just wouldn't go along with all that. His folk were right behind him. One day, he got to hear that a bomb had been put in the church. He searched until he found it. He got it out just in time. The next day, two guys called from some place, pushed Rudi's wife and kids out of the way and left him with a lump of lead in his head. Pa and everyone else felt real bad about that. And do you know what? The rabbi said Kaddish for him. I guess not too many goys get Kaddish said for them.

Pa got to telling me how things got worse. Some of the Jewish families started selling up and going someplace else. Grandpa Traumann got to saying that this was not good. He, with the Grossmanns, had a good business and things were picking up. The family had lived in this little old town for a hell of a long time. Okay, the States was a good place for Jews to go to, but what the hell, he was just not going to let a bunch of thugs drive him out. He'd sweated hard building up the business, and he was just not going to let it go for a few dimes. The Grossmanns felt the same.

Pa didn't get to mentioning brothers and sisters. I guess they were around, but maybe something bad had happened. Getting educated was tough for the Jews. They had something of a school attached to the synagogue. The rabbi saw to it that the boys got something of an education. Pa started working in the business, but there was no chance of getting qualifications. The Grossmans were a pretty important people. They had dough salted away in Swiss banks. If you had dollars at your fingertips, then you could buy folk off and get favours done. It was time when plenty of favours were needed. So it was my Grossmann Grandpa that had a word with the matchmaker. It was not a good time to get married and raising a family – but hell, when is? I guess that Pa was somewhere in his middle twenties when he got under the marriage canopy with Ruth Grossmann, smashed the glass while they shouted 'Mazel tov!'. But I guess that not too much good luck came their way.

It was some years before Pa got to telling me what happened. I fancy it was just around the time I was coming up to my bar mitzvah. Pa had gone to the synagogue around Pesach time. It was packed. A truck pulled up outside and these guys in brown outfits poured out. They burst in. Rabbi Moshe protested. A shot was fired and the old man fell down. Firing broke out and men and boys were falling down. Pa panicked. Maybe it was the panic that saved him. He made a dash for the rabbi's office. He knew it well from a kid. He was out through a window and out on the street. He kept running back to the shop. The Grossmanns had this big Mercedes limousine. There it was with the engine running. They were all inside just waiting for Pa. They pulled him in and Grandpa Grossmann let in the clutch.

Anyway, I've been all over that stuff before and how they went over to the land of the free in the French Liner, the Normandie. But I guess what happened and to getting the hell out of the synagogue left a pretty deep scar on Pa. I figure it must have left something of a scar on Ma too. I guess that there are some hellish experiences in life that throw the psyche right out of balance so that you just don't get back to where you'd want to be. Maybe that's just how it was with my folk – they'd just suffered a hell of a lot too much.

That's just about how it was with my folk. They'd just gone through too much. Pa got shut in on himself, and Ma slipped off the rails. It may be that the old folk got on much better. The Grossmanns had a sharp eye on the weather and could see the storm coming. They got their dough in secure places and brought a whole lot of jewellery with them. So along with Grandpa Traumann, they got the optics company set up pretty fast. With the war in Europe heating up, they got a whole lot of contracts. They made it big – fast. But somehow, Pa didn't get in on the scene.

The world of optics and business just didn't grab Pa. Somehow he met this Jewish art teacher Abe Grosnevski. Pa had got into art back in Germany so Abe got him to enrol at the Chicago Academy of Art. I guess that Grandpa reckoned it would be best for Pa to paint and that sort of thing rather than just hanging around looking sick. A studio got built in the backyard. As a kid, I thought his stuff looked pretty good. Some days, he'd get himself a cab and go up on the lake sketching and then work up his stuff into a great canvas. I'd just sit there watching him covering great areas with paint laying on great brushfuls of colour with shapes and forms appearing just like magic. It was quite something. At times, he'd work with a fine brush so that nothing seemed to be moving. That's when I just got fidgety.

Pa didn't talk too much when he was in the studio. But when he stopped to fix himself a coffee, he'd put his arm around my shoulder and we'd just stand looking at his work. At one time, he was working on a white-boarded shack at the edge of the lake. The sun shone so brightly that I had to screw my eyes up just looking at the painting. "You know vot I vant to do, Bennie?" he asked. "I just vant to paint light fallin' on a vite vall!" Those words stuck right in my mind, but I didn't understand what he meant. I guess it's becoming clear now.

I'm sure you can see I owed a hell of a lot to my stepma, Rebecca. Somehow, she never got to having kids of her own. I guess that suited me fine. I got a whole lot of her attention. She'd spend a heck of a time telling me all sorts of things. Somehow, I reckon her family had come over to the States way back. It seems her family came from Poland somewhere around the turn of the century. They did tailoring and things like that. Maybe I felt that the Traumanns were just a bit above them on the ladder. I picked up a bit here and a bit there and stored it away until it came together.

So Ma got to teaching me all the proper Jewish things and made sure we lived a proper Jewish life. Somehow, I got the feeling that Pa wasn't any too fussy. He just went along with it all. I got to giving Ma a hand in the kitchen. There was this time when I got to putting meat down on the dairy side. Ma was cool most of the time, but boy, you'd just about think that the Almighty, blessed be He, was going to blast us right off the face of the planet! She really took off and got angry with me for just about the first time. She snatched up the meat and threw it straight into the garbage bin. Then followed a hell of a lot of scrubbing. But when she'd finished, she just put her arms right around me and showed that everything was okay, at least by her, but I was just not too certain how the Almighty felt about it.

"But, Ma," I asked, "'why do we have to do all this stuff?"

Ma washed her hands carefully and got down her Bible. She read a passage about not boiling a kid in its mother's milk. "That means," she explained, "we Jews just mustn't mix up meat and milk. It's just not right. So we just have to keep one part of the kitchen for meat and the other for milk and stuff like that. That's just how it's got to be."

"What about the goys? Do they keep kosher kitchens?"

"No," she came back, "it's the way the Almighty, blessed be He, shows we Jews are special."

Somehow, I felt all that sounded just a bit too screwy. It just made a whole lot of trouble for us Jews, and it just didn't add up to too much. Why the hell would anyone want to boil a kid in its mother's milk anyway? Jeepers – if boiling a kid in its mother's milk caused the Almighty a problem, then why not boil it in milk that just didn't come from its mother? Wouldn't the Almighty be satisfied with that? I figured out that He just couldn't be as hard to please as all that! I pressed Ma on all this, but she came back with something that I just couldn't make out and closed it with, "Well – keeping kosher kitchen is just the way we Jewish women please the Almighty." I just had to leave it at that.

I was just coming up to thirteen and getting ready for my Bar Mitzvah. The Traumann grandparents were always on about it. "Don't you forget, Moshe Ben Yitzack, you will then be a man and do all the things a man can do," they reminded me. They kept on about me going to college and then joining the company and making it big. They had great plans for me as Pa had dropped out of things. They reckoned I was pretty cute and for a time the ideas of becoming head of T & G's began to grab me. Anyway, I started preparing for the Bar Mitzvah. I had to go around to the rabbi to learn about the Torah and how to be a really good Jewish man.

I had a personal interview with the rabbi. He told me I just had to stick to Jewish ways and not slip into the ways of the goyim. Being a Jew was something to be mighty proud of. It helped you to hold up your head in the world and look other folk straight in the eyes. He reminded me of the four species of sukkot with the lulav palm branch. A Jewish man had to have the right character and to be straight like the palm. "Just look at these goyim. Sure, some of them are nice people. But they have no history like us. They just don't know who they are. But we do. We are a people with a history, and we know how to live on the face of the earth. So just you see to it, Moshe ben Yitzack, see you marry a good Jewish girl who keeps a kosher kitchen and knows how to keep Shabbat."

He then gave me a funny look and made me feel real uneasy. "There is something I must tell you," he continued. "Good Jewish men must keep themselves pure and clean." I squirmed on the hard seat and coloured up. "You know the place where you have been circumcised. Now a good Jewish man just doesn't touch himself there unless he has to pass water. Yes? You understand?" I guess I didn't. Why the hell should a guy touch himself there unless he wanted to pass water? Then the rabbi got down the Torah and started telling me about some guy way back called Onan who touched himself in the wrong way and the Almighty, blessed be He, was mighty angry with him. I just couldn't figure this out. Maybe I'd been touching myself in the wrong way and just didn't get to know. Hell. Would this be held against me and I'd get it in the neck like Onan? I just couldn't figure this out. What the hell did the rabbi mean that if I got to touching myself in the wrong way that this holy stuff would come out and the Almighty would get real mad at me like Onan. I just didn't get it. Okay, you had to touch yourself there to go to the toilet but not to make the holy stuff come out.

I just wanted the rabbi to shut up, but he kept on talking about the bags under my legs. He told me that's where the holy stuff comes from. He said they held the seed that made good Jewish babies. If I touched myself in the wrong way, then the holy stuff would come out, and if I go to doing that, I would just go crazy – mad. That just wouldn't be too good. Then he went on about sometimes they'd be just too much seed in the bags, and at night, it just had to come out. That was okay. That was natural. Then he went on to tell me of this boy in his yeshiva group years back. He just hadn't been told about what might happen. He got wet in the night and hanged himself. That was bad.

By now, I was dead uneasy. I just wanted to get out and use the john. But the rabbi just had to go on. He told me about some goy women who liked to get hold of good Jewish men and make them impure. They'd get them to do wrong things so the holy seed gets spilt out inside them. That was dead wrong. I just didn't figure this stuff too much. Then he went on to say that these goy women could pass on some real nasty infections and you could get real sick and maybe even go crazy. That was it. I got out and made a dash for the john and passed a whole lot of water, but I got to wondering about this holy stuff.

A few days on, I made my Bar Mitzvah. I'd hit my thirteenth birthday. I felt real good as I put on my tefillin and my tallit. I was getting to be a real man, a real Jew. Great! I was just in a whirl as I went into the synagogue with Ma and the family all around me. I'd been going over the scripture I had to read. I knew it just about by heart. But when the time came, the Hebrew words looked one hell of a jumble. I found myself shaking and my throat went dry and croaky. Somehow, I stumbled through and someone gave my arm a squeeze as I stepped down. Then I had one hell of a party afterwards at some fancy hotel. I had to get up and say something. God knows what. Ma had given me some things I should say. The grandparents had opened a bank account and paid in a whole lot of dollars. Pa gave me the tefillin and the tallit.

Gosh, I was in quite a whirl after all this and real glad to get back home and get to bed. I got down to pray and thank God, blessed be He, for just about everything. But then what the rabbi had said about that guy Onan came into my mind. My thing started to grow and my heart started to go wild. I kept telling myself not to touch my thing. I was stiff and poked right out of my pyjamas. I tried to push it back in. But I kept on touching it. Touching it in the wrong way. Then hell – hell – the holy stuff started shooting right out sending the seed just about everywhere. I shook hard. There was I, a bar mitzvah boy, doing something real bad. Something real Jewish men just don't do. The Almighty would be mighty angry. Something real bad would happen. I sobbed out loud. I guess Ma heard. She came in quietly, hugged and kissed me and got me into bed. Maybe she guessed what had happened. She gave me a last kiss and said, "Okay, honey, don't you worry – you'll be fine."

After that, it was just hell. Night after damned night, I got to touching my joey in the wrong damned way and spilling out the holy stuff. I got real screwed up. Okay, I guess, just about most kids get to doing it. It gets something like a compulsion. The more you try not to so some damn thing like that, the more you just have to do it. For some guys, they just don't care a damn, but if some religious guy tells you it's just wrong, then you're in real trouble. That's how it was with me. I'd made my bar mitzvah promising to be a good Jewish man and there I was committing the sin of Onan. I suppose Ma could see the trouble so she used to come and sit on my bed until I went off. But I reckon she just couldn't keep doing that all the time, and I got to doing it until it drove me just nuts. The more I tried and struggle not to do it, the more I just had to do it.

I suppose this thing got right on top of me, and I started slipping my grades at school. Grandpa Traumann started breathing down my neck and told me that I'd just never make it to the board at T & G's. I just couldn't get this damned thing out of my hair. I got screwed up and just moped around. I figured I might be going real crazy. The kids at school started nudging one another and gave me queer looks and grinned. But Ma somehow was pretty kind, but I just couldn't come out with it. She got me to take long walks to tire me out. We'd go to the bridge over the lake and look down at the fish as they came up for bread. I just couldn't stand looking at these creatures as they came up with great googly eyes looking just like the rabbi with those great thick glasses of his. How I got to hating that damned rabbi.

My thing kept perking up all the time. I just hoped Ma would get to seeing it poking up through my pants. I kept looking to make sure the flies were done up. Ma was getting real worried. She'd put her arms around me and ask if I were okay. "There's something causing you trouble," she'd say, but I'd just push away and clam up. I felt real close to Ma, but she just wasn't going to get this out of me.

I got real mad with the rabbi. Why the hell did he have to tell about that guy Onan and all that stuff. Why didn't he keep his damned trap shut and stick to the religious stuff about going to the synagogue on Shabbat, marrying a good Jewish wife and so on. Why the hell did he have to talk about THAT? I used to get myself worked right up into a hot rage. I'd look around for something to kick or smash. One time, I went out to the place where Pa did his painting. He had a canvas of an old man in his shawl and tefillin. I just put my foot through it time and again until it just hang is shreds and the stretcher was splintered. I spat on it and then pissed on it. Pa and Ma said nothing, but they just knew it had to be me.

The great sin took over my life. It just kept buzzing about like some hell of a fly that drives you crazy. Kids at school started coming up in the yard and shoved me around and said, "What's the trouble Jew boy?" And they'd start sniggering. Then they got real nasty. "What do you do – dirty yid? You'll go crazy if you do that. Crazy yid." They'd keep on until I could stand it no more, and I'd fly at them with my fist hitting out. Then they'd grab me, get me to the ground, pull off my pants and expose me and fall about laughing. So these goy kids gave me hell, but the other Jewish kids kept right out of the way. I guess they didn't want too much to do with a kid who spilled the holy stuff. But it was that rabbi's fault in telling me about that guy Onan from way back. If he'd kept his trap shut, I'd been like all the other bar mitzvah boys and been a real pure Jewish man.

I just hated myself and what I was doing. Things didn't get any better. I just wanted the damned thing to go and leave me alone. One Shabbat in the synagogue, the rabbi started talking. I guess I hadn't been following him too well until he got on about sin. I sat up. It must have been around Yom Kippur. Anyway, he said that some rabbi way back said that sin started off as fine as the thread of a spider, but it got to growing so much that it ended up as strong as a cart rope. That stuck in my mind. That's just how it was with me. I just couldn't stop it. It just kept on growing and growing until it was one hell of a cart rope. The rabbi went on what could be done when sin got like that. My ears tingled. "First, you had to remember the hesed of God, blessed be He. God was well disposed to us even when we do wrong. But you just had to struggle like that time Father Jacob had that struggle at Jabbok. You had to learn to struggle real hard with that evil yetzer. You had to take it to the school of Torah, teach it a lesson and show it who was boss. Not easy but that's what a real Jewish man had to do." Those words stuck real hard. I got the message as a young kid who had just made his bar mitzvah. You just can't go blaming some other guy for what you did wrong, you just had to pick up the ball and run with it like a good Jewish man. I guess for me that was one hell of a turning point.

So that night, I got out my tefillin, bound my hands with the thongs and so on. It was pretty tricky. I stood and recited the Shema with some care. I got into bed with my hands bound and tried to keep my mind on something good and holy. I thought of the lula branch at sukkot. I guessed I'd have the straightest branch in the synagogue at the next sukkot. I'd be a good, upright Jewish man for keeps. Then the terrible feeling like a black wave started to swamp me and drag me down. It was like Jonah being swallowed up by the deep and getting dragged down into the weeds. The sheets of my bed got twisted up as I threw myself around. I just wanted to get rid of the sin, but it just wasn't going to give in that easily. I couldn't get my hands free to touch myself. I was stifling and sobbing. I just hoped I wouldn't be heard.

But Ma heard. She came in and just stood by my bed in the dark. It was great to have her just there. She stroked my head and put her arms around me and held me real close. I guess, I've never had too much peace in my life, but that was a great moment. She said nothing. She didn't have to. She just kept quiet and held me for a long time. I guess I must've gone off to sleep. Next morning, I found that my tefillin had been taken off and put away. My bed had been tidied up and smoothed out. I felt as if I'd been made new – cleaned up inside. Had that damned cart rope been cut? Maybe. I have to admit, the sin didn't go away just like that, but somehow, I showed it that I was boss.

Well, I guess that things were not so bad when I'd faced the problem with the holy seed. Okay, it got split from time to time, but it had lost its terrible grip on me. I figured that if the Almighty, blessed be He, had made us that way, you just didn't want to go around wasting the holy seed. But if it happened, He wouldn't go holding it against a guy too much. Maybe the rabbi who'd got me ready for bar mitzvah just made too much of it.

Ma was one of these bright little bird-like women with a great and easy smile. She had this thin, agile figure. Her face was like the shape of an almond with fine, high cheekbones and just about the brightest and blackest eyes you've ever seen. While she could be bright and chirpy, she knew how to keep dead quiet. You know how it is with some folk. There are those who are so dead still you get to wondering if they've died. Then you get the others who rush around like the fly with a blue backside. They just go buzzing around and wearing folk out. But Ma knew just when to keep quiet and when to move fast. She had a sort of presence you just can't quite figure out. She was right in tune with everyone and everything around her. Looking back, I can see that I was a real hard kid to handle. But somehow, she knew what was going on inside me. She knew just how I felt and how to handle me. She never put on the screws or quizzed me. She just let me be myself. I figure that she was dead right for Pa too. Most of the time, he was quiet and switched off. But she never harassed him or gave him a bad time. She just let him be, let him go off and paint in his studio. That was okay. She was just content to let other folk just be themselves. I guess there's not too many around like that.

As I got into my teens, I got to going out with Pa on some of his painting trips. He didn't drive, so we'd get a cab to some place or other up on the lake. He'd set up and start making sketches in watercolour. I reckon he was pretty good. He was more or less self-taught, but he had this friend, Abe Grosnevski, who had come from Poland way back. Abe, as it happened, taught at the Chicago Academy of Art so he knew what he was about. I figure he gave Pa quite some help. Abe would come out with us at times, and he'd set me up sketching rocks, tree stumps and bits washed up along the lake. He'd make me draw with this great thick pencil. I can hear him saying, "Now, Bennie, my boy – let's see you doing some real bold sketches. If you're going to be an artist, you've just got to be real bold – bold. Just you go for the form and don't worry too much about detail. Be bold." So that's how old Abe got me going on art. Out there on the lake, I just got carried clean away. I reckon it did me a whole lot of good. Abe got to coming out with us more often than not.

I learnt a whole lot from Abe. He got me looking at things in the right way. "Bennie," he'd say, "I just don't vant to see fancy technique. Fancy stuff sell maybe. Folk that don't know think it's good stuff and pay fancy prices. But there's nothing under the fancy paint. Nothing. No real drawing. The picture says nothing – so I just don't vant to see you doing fancy stuff. Okay?"

He then went on to tell me of this Jewish artist from Russia named Chagall. He'd painted this picture of Christ on a cross with a tallit around his middle. All around terrible things were happening to Jews, a synagogue in flames, a man with the Torah – all hell taking place. "Now that's a bold picture," said Abe. "It's got power – feeling – it makes you think – it takes us into the pain of our people. Yes? You must come and see it at the institute. It will help you be a real artist." I saw it. I just stood there shaking. I wanted to cry out – howl. But I was struck dumb. Abe just left me there. God knows how long I stood there just shaking. The pain and suffering of us Jewish people – okay. That work carried me right away with tears running down my face. It was then I decided that I was just going to be a painter and not some stuffed shirt guy of the board of T & G.

I guess that experience with Chagall's *White Crucifixion* was life changing. From that point, I took in mighty carefully all that Abe passed on in those trips up the lake. He made me look at things real hard. "Get right into the feel of that rock – get to know what it is to be a rock and get it down on the sheet." He went on to tell about some old rabbi when he was a kid getting ready for his bar mitzvah way back in Poland. "He had eyes that could see deep down and what was real." He told me about how the rabbi would go over a passage in the Torah and ask questions. He would tell us what rabbis in the past had said but that the real meaning lay in the white spaces, the gaps, between the Hebrew characters – that's where the truth was to be found! So Abe went on that it was the same in art that we had to look at the spaces, the gaps, between objects. It was the gaps that made the work come to life. I wondered if this is what Pa meant when he said that all he wanted to paint was sunlight falling onto a white wall.

My Traumann grandfather was getting pretty worried about me getting caught up with all this art stuff. I reckon he was dead concerned that the family stake in Traumann and Grossmann Optics was slipping away. Okay, I was getting better grades at high school. But if I was going to get to the board, I just had to get to somewhere like Harvard or another Ivy League place and get myself a really good degree. He could see that the younger Grossmanns were forging ahead and our family was getting sidelined. Grandpa had put in a whole lot of technical knowhow into the company, but the Grossmans had it where business came in, and he just didn't want that side making all the running. He'd written off Pa and left him to paint his pictures, and he just wasn't too happy to see me going in the same way.

"Bennie – Moshe ben Yitzack," he'd say. "You'll never make a businessman dreaming all day painting pictures. You'll just have to get down to those books unt von day you have a nice place up near Forest Lake. Just you think of that. You have a fancy Cadillac, and when you go to the synagogue, you get a nice seat and the rabbi will treat you nice. You'd like that, Bennie? You von't go letting your grandfather down and letting the Grossmanns make the running?"

I just said nothing, but Pa came out strong. "Father, you just get to leaving the boy. He vill be vat he vill be. He vant to paint picture – he vill paint picture. He vant to be businessman – he be businessman. Okay? You forget dose bad days? Broken vindows? Shootings? Killings? The synagogue on Yom Kippur? Rabbi Capplemann? You forget fire? Getting out of Germany? You forget? I tell you, Bennie, my boy, vill be vot he vont. Grossmanns vant business? Okay. They get it!" I just couldn't believe what I was hearing. Pa was making a stand for me. I guess Grandfather got the message. He stopped coming around too much and just let us go our own ways.

I guess around this time, I was coming up to seventeen. That's when Ma started to get sick. Doctors and nurses started coming around and trips were made to the Jewish hospital. Pa arranged for someone to come and live in and hold things together. Things got pretty bad. It was like the time when I was a kid and my own ma got ill. In those days, I didn't feel too much for that overweight, damned tricky woman, who'd brought me into the world.

But this time, it was a whole lot different. Ma had seen me through and got my feet on the ground. She helped me to feel I belonged to some place. She made me feel I mattered – I was someone. Pa stopped his painting trips. He just sat in his studio in the backyard. He'd have his brush in his hand, but he just didn't get the paint on canvas. He just sat there with a deadpan look on his face and his eyes squinting through his thick lenses. But I guess he didn't see too much.

I reckon they operated on Ma. It looked like things had gone too far. She was brought home and a nurse came in just like the old times. This time, I was allowed into the bedroom with its sweet-sick smell. I just wanted to be there all the time. I'd just sit there and hold her hand. She wore a bright red headscarf. Her neat black wig with its glossy hair stood on the chest. I guessed that's how her own hair would have been – neat, thick and glossy. As a kid, I would ask her why Jewish women shaved their heads. She'd just say, "It's custom, just custom. That's how the men like it. Custom." So I'd sit and hold Ma's hand. She'd get me to say prayers – maybe a psalm or the Schema. There's one psalm she'd get me to say time and again – "Blessed is he that considers the poor and helpless: the Lord will deliver him in the day of trouble: and if he lies sick on his bed the Lord will sustain him; if illness lays him low you will overthrow it." It was just as I was saying these words that I heard her give a little sigh and her hand went limp. I knew that the breath had gone out of her body. Ma – Rebecca – had gone into the bosom of Abraham. I kissed her and said Kaddish. I had just about everything to be thankful for. Ma had made me. I went out and nodded to the nurse. She had been waiting for this moment. She went in and did whatever had to be done.

Things went numb after Ma's death. The day we placed her into the ground was cold and wet. It was spring. The driving rain and wind battered us around. We got wet and muddy. Abe came along with the Traumanns. I just thought of Ma lying there in her simple wooden box. They lowered her down into the grave. It was just a bit too narrow even for Ma's narrow coffin. The diggers had to get out their spades again and clean some more off the sides while we kept on saying Kaddish. Once more, the box went down. This time, it cleared the sides and got down to the bottom. There must have been inches of water down there and the coffin floated like a boat. I thought of the ark of Noah that Ma used to tell me about when I was a kid. The spades were handed around and slowly we shovelled in the heavy soil. First, it splashed into the water raising the level with the box. Then we got to getting the soil on to the coffin until it disappeared. I kept my eyes closed until the grave was filled in. I just felt – God knows how I felt – just empty – empty – nothing. I don't know how it was, but Pa didn't come to the funeral. Before it was time to leave, he just went into his studio and locked himself in and refused to come out. We just had to leave him there.

On the way back, as we approached our block, we could see things happening. Police cars were just about everywhere and cops blocked the way. Nearer to our place, we could see a fire truck and a whole lot of smoke going up. We asked a cop what the trouble was. Some shack had gone up in a backyard. We'd be free to go through before long. We pressed him for detail. It was our place so the cop let us through. The fire chief met us as we made our way along the sidewalk. "Guess, you're damned lucky," he said. "That shack was pretty close to the house. In another five minutes, it would have gone up."

We just stood there in the yard feeling pretty numb. The chief called off his men. Steam rose up from the charred timbers of Pa's studio. I moved like some guy in a dream towards the gap where the door had been. Someone called my name, but I kept on into the charred remains. I trod through the deep puddles left by the hoses. I could make out here and there the blackened stretchers with just a few fragments of canvas hanging. Pa's pictures had all gone. I caught sight of a strange, dark heap. I drew close to it – puzzled but somehow knowing what it was. It was a stiff, rigid thing. Something stuck out near the top. It was pinkish with the end split open like a starfish. Whatever it was gave off a sweet, sickly stench that made me feel like throwing up. Then it came to me, I was looking at Pa's burnt body. There was his head and his tongue sticking out. His beard and hair had all gone. His eye sockets empty spaces. But it was the tongue that sticks in my mind. It protruded from his mouth like some great, ugly obscene thing. The stench turned me up. It reminded me of that time I went into a goy home. It was around eating time. They had this great hunk of white meat they were slicing up. It had this sweet-sickly smell that made me want to vomit. That's how Pa's body smelt. I reckon I could have been in there for just about a few minutes, but it seemed just like an age. I took in all the details, and I guess it will stay with me for good.

I went out to face the men. Grandfather Traumann asked me what was wrong. I just pointed. He struggled through the debris to see for himself. The sound he made when he saw Pa's body still rings in my ears. It was like some demented creature. It just went on and on. Abe placed his hand on my shoulder. The others rushed into the wet, steaming timbers. They too joined in the howling. The racket got neighbours and cops rushing around. Before long, the whole of the yard was full of folk rushing around and shouting. But the Jewish men just kept up this howling. In time, one by one, they came out throwing dirt over themselves and tearing clothes. But I just stood there, cold and empty with Abe at my side. I thought of Ma in her wooden box. She didn't look like Ma. Her cheeks were drawn in and every bit of her skull showed through her tight skin. She was safe now six feet down in the cemetery or in Abraham's bosom. But Pa? Pa? There in the ruins of his studio looking like something out of some weird movie.

Things got confusing after that. I went off to live with my Traumann grandparents. Looking back, they were pretty good. The Grossmanns came into the picture, but I'm not too clear on that. Things slipped at school. I spent a whole lot of time getting up late and just mooning around. Then Abe Gronowski came around. I guess Grandpa fixed it. I just don't know. He suggested that I go off with him on a painting trip in a cabin way up on the lake. So I went off. The old guy didn't push me. He'd just set up his easel and got to painting. I'd go some way off and just sit on a log or a rock. Then I'd get curious about what Abe was doing. I'd stand and watch him for a while. He'd make remarks about what he was doing and why. His stuff looked dead simple. Just big, bold brush strokes in clear colour. But he made the landscape come alive. You could feel the wind passing lightly over the surface of the water and up into the trees. You could hear the waves touching the shore and the gulls in the sky mewing away.

After a day or so, I got to setting up the easel myself and get down to painting. I stayed pretty close to Abe. I didn't want to let him out of my sight. I had to keep him in view. If I looked up and he'd gone somewhere, my heart would start beating real fast. I'd get scared. I'd panic and have to call out. He'd come back. "Okay, Bennie, I'm just behind this rock making myself comfortable." When he'd finished, he'd just come over, put his hand on my shoulder and talk about my work. We were up there in the cabin for a whole week. I guess it did me the power of good. It started me getting human again. When we got back, I started my last term at high school, but I needed a cab to get me there and back.

I dreaded the night. I put off going up to my room. But somehow, my grandparents were mighty good at handling a kid like me going through a pretty bad time. I guess they were also feeling cut up by what had happened to their son. I remember Grandma urging me with, "Come on, Bennie. You're looking dog tired. Now just you get up between those sheets or you vill be good for not much." So I just dragged myself up to my room at the top of the house. The old problem didn't bother me too much. I guess I was just too tired going through a bad time. But dreaming caused me trouble. The dreams were vague and shadowy. They scared the pants off me. I was scared but couldn't see what of. Then there were eels. There were eels up along the lake. I had seen eels migrating across the land and going into the lake. They moved fast through the grass and over the beach, disappearing into the dark waters. So in my dream, I found myself down there with the eels. They slithered all around me. I felt shut in – stifled. I couldn't stop them or get away. I struggled and pushed. I couldn't get away. I'd start making this high-pitched wailing sound until I woke up – shaking and sweating. It was just hell.

The dream I hated most was the one I used to get when the problem was at its worst. I'd be standing as a young kid with Ma on the bridge feeding the fish. Up they'd come, and I'd laugh in a carefree way as young kids do. Then things turned real nasty. The fish would start leaping up. My pants had gone. The fish were making for my thing. It was pink, like a tongue with a mouth all round it with black, charred lips. I guess, by that time I was getting medication from the doctor. I started to dream less. But I got up feeling like a zombie on a bad day.

I suppose that Grandpa Traumann got the message – I just wasn't going to make it to the board of T & G. Maybe there was just a bit too much of Pa in me and not enough of Grandpa. Abe Gronowski and the old man got their heads together. Then on one of our painting trips, Abe sounded me out on enrolling at the Academy of Art. I'd passed the somewhat gloomy building with its pretty heavy architecture in Noble Square a good number of times. Abe, of course, had taught there God knows how many years. He was part of the place. It so happened that things got fixed, and I started that fall.

The academy was pretty traditional. They made sure you got your drawing right and got you drawing from these old classical statues. They just made you sit with these goddamned casts drawing them time and again until you were just sick of them.

Maybe I'd sit there feeling pretty pleased with what I had done. Then the teacher would come around, take a look at my stuff and comment, "Okay, Traumann, no so bad, but just a few things that we need to get right." With that, he'd start going over my work with a damned great thick pencil. "Now just note the eye you've drawn. Do you think that eye would roll around in its socket? You just have to see the eye as a ball that can move around and with eyelids that can blink. You have to get that across in your work." Then he'd draw something in the corner of my paper that'd leap right off the drawing board. So I'd have to go right back to the Michelangelo's head of David and try to get the thing right.

We had this guy in the class who just had no eye for proportion or anything. I just couldn't figure out how he got a place. Whatever he drew came out skewed. Heads were long and thin – you just couldn't see how the heck he could see things like that. Okay, they'd try to put him right, but somehow, he just didn't get it. Maybe he'd get the relation between the eyes right but then the rest would just go haywire with the nose and the chin just right out of proportion. He'd work in charcoal so at the end he'd end up with a smudgy mess. The others started guying him up and kidding him that his work was so well observed that he ought to think about staging an exhibition.

This guy was so dumb, or so we thought, that he went off and got his stuff mounted. I reckon his folk had plenty of dough so he got his work mounted in fancy frames. He brought one up to class. "That's a real nice frame," one wise guy commented.

"Pity what's in it is crap," came in some dame. At this, the guy got the message loud and clear.

"Okay, okay," he came back. "So my stuff's crap. Okay, you'll just wait and see. Your stuff stinks. It's got no feeling. No style. You just sit there doing what these jerks tell you to do. Okay. I'm quitting this lousy dump. But I'll tell you this, before next fall I'll be getting an exhibition in New York and raking in the dollars. You just wait!" You can just about guess the reaction. They laughed him out of the room.

That was the last we saw of Ron Gruber but not the last we heard of him. Next fall, there was a review of his work in the Herald Tribune, 'Young Chicago artist rocks the art world'. It was unbelievable. We just couldn't figure it out so we went back to our drawing boards trying to get our drawing right.

I guess the grandparents were tired of having me around the place. I disturbed their routine. I was coming in at all sorts of times. It just didn't suit them too well. That's when Abe suggested that I go live with him in his apartment in town. It was near the academy; it had plenty of space and a large studio. The arrangement suited everyone fine. By now, I was into the life and painting classes. I guess things were shaping up well. Abe looked at my stuff and made approving noises. He was one of those people who don't get to saying too much. He'd flip through my portfolio and make grunting noises. But I got the impression he liked what he saw. Now and again, he'd make a comment.

I guess the life class grabbed me. A darned sight better that drawing those damned plaster figures. But where the hell did they get some of the models? They were not all fancy dames. Boy, some of these old folk who were king-sized in the overweight stakes! Great folds of fat hung down from their bodies. Old dames with dags hanging right down to their knees. But it was great stuff to paint. I went to town on one model. They sat her in this old upright wooden chair. I was amazed that it took her weight. Her thighs were vast but her hands were just small and delicate. She sat with one hand resting on an ugly thigh. That made the picture. It gave me a thrill. It said something about this dame. Okay, she was big and ugly and was not easy on the eye, but there was just this touch of beauty in her hand. She had something and that's what I worked on. When Abe saw it, he gave me a great slap across the shoulder and commented, "Bennie, keep it up like this and you'll make a good artist. A good artist." That made me feel great.

There was one dame that grabbed me in a different way. I guess, she must have been just a few years older than most of us, but she had what it takes. I reckon I spent just a bit too much time letching after her so I didn't get too much down. By the time the pose was changed, I'd just got no more than a few lines sketched in. The model got to something of an obsession. She fed my fantasy life in a big way. I got to finding her name and where she pitched her tent. Jo Heffer lived some place downtown. Things started to get bad like when I was a kid. I'd just have to possess this dame or just go crazy. I got to producing some pretty hot drawings with me doing some interesting activities with Jo. I kept all this stuff in a special portfolio under my bed. It was just for my eyes. I got to a point where I just had to put those fantasies into action or go bust. I made a plan to follow her back to her place. At the end of a session, I got out quick and flagged down a cab. We waited until the dame came out and got into a cab. We followed close behind. The traffic was thick, but my cabbie kept glued on her tail.

Jo got out of her cab. I paid off the cab and made myself inconspicuous on the sidewalk. I just had time to note her slipping into an apartment block. I waited and then went in. There was a guy sitting in the office. He was well over six foot and broad. His nose was bent looking like it had been pushed in quite a number of times. The guy looked at me a long time. "Wadya wan', son?"

"Jo Heffer have a place here?" He chewed hard on his gum.

"Wadya wan' wiv Jo?"

"She left this at the academy." I held up a headscarf I'd lifted from the changing room. "I'd like to take it up."

The tough guy looked long before moving to his switchboard. He turned the handle. "Kid here, Jo. Got sumthin' yourn. Send him up? Okay." My heart was thumping damned hard. I wanted to turn around and get out. "Okay, son. Says you can go up. No monkeyin' aroun' – see." He showed me his great mitt. "Level thirteen – apartment six. Don' you go foolin' aroun' or you'll feel my mitt in your mush." I got the message.

I got into the elevator wishing that I'd just never thought up this crazy plan. I looked into a mirror. I looked just goddamned awful. My face was as red as an overripe tomato and sticky with sweat. I wiped myself with my handkerchief and ran my fingers through my hair. I reckoned I must have been plumb crazy to figure a dame like Jo could take a look at a guy like me. I pressed the elevator button hoping it might break down before level thirteen. It made it. I took some time before ringing at apartment six. Jo opened the door wearing a fantastic housecoat. I stood there with my stupid mouth hanging wide open.

She gave a real friendly smile. Her perfume sent my head reeling. "I guess you're one of the students." I held out her scarf. "I'm so stupid leaving things around. Thanks. Come right in." I just couldn't believe it. She was making it real easy, and I started feeling relaxed and confident. The apartment looked swell and the carpet was so thick my shoes sank right in. She sat me down on a large and ritzy sofa. "I'll get you a drink. Whisky sour?" I gulped.

"Sure, that's fine." I watched her as she slinked across the room to the drinks cabinet. I reckoned that it wouldn't be too long before I got that gown right off her. I reckon that I'd be the happiest guy in the whole of the city. She handed me the drink bending real low so I could see right down into her cleavage. My hand shook so I spilled the drink. Jo smiled.

"Don't you worry, honey; I guess that's not the first time a drink's been spilled here and a whole lot more!" I wondered why she found it so damned funny.

"So you're Bennie Traumann," she said after a time. I was getting real excited with Jo sitting right close. "I guess I've seen you looking real careful when I've been sitting." I told her that I liked it when she posed and that it made a hell of a change from the fat dames with dropped dags. I went on to say what a really swell figure she had. I looked at her in a certain way. "Have to keep it that way," she came back. "You get looking like a tramp and you're right out." I quizzed her about what else she did besides posing. She stretched herself back on the cushions. "Sure, I do. You don't think posing at the academy keeps me in a pad like this?" I took a pull at the whiskey sour as I got the message.

I felt somewhat stupid and getting desperate. If I was going to get Jo Heffer, I'd just have to get moving. I jumped right in. "Jo, I guess you're just about the most fantastic dame I've set my eyes on. Can't get you out of my head. Driving me wild. Just have to go back to my place and do these drawings. See how it is?" I passed on the drawings for her to see. She thumbed through them with a Mona Lisa look on her face.

"Sure do," she replied. "Seen you from the corner of my eye. You do a whole lot of looking but not much doing." She had a slight edge in her voice.

She moved over right close with one of my drawings in her hand. "Honey, you sure have a good imagination. You just seem to know just about every part of me – yes?" She pored over the drawing some more and gave me that real sulky, sexy look. I ached bad in the place where it hurts. "Bennie, have you ever had a woman?" she asked. I made some weird noises. I wasn't going to tell her I was still a virgin. "Honey, I guess you just haven't. I can see it in your stuff." I gulped and confessed that that's how it is.

Jo smiled in what I took to be an understanding manner. "So what? Most guys are virgins at some time. Had plenty of guys here needing an experienced dame to show them around. They soon get to learning, so don't you go worrying about that." My hopes rose and I started to feel just a touch easier. Then she stood up, raised herself up to her full height. She was tall for a dame. I guess she could easily give me an inch or two. Then she dropped honeyed tones. "Okay, buster, get up and drop your pants and let's see what you've got."

I shook quite a lot but did what she wanted. I got my pants down and just stood there with my thing hanging down. It felt like that dream I used to get as a kid on the bridge with fish leaping up at my groin. I stood there with my thing looking damned small and shrivelled up with fear. Things were going badly wrong. Slowly, she walked around me. I stood exposed and ashamed. She took her time.

"Jew boy," she spat. "You're a nasty, dirty, filthy, goddamned Yid with a bit missing from your dick." She raised her slipped foot and flicked up my thing. "What the hell do you call that? You think that'd do anything for a dame? Yid – just keep that for pissing." She just went on and on. I just felt dead numb. I wanted to get right out. It felt like some damned nightmare but for real.

"Just get this straight," she went on, "dames like me just don't fool around with Jew boys. I've just about had every kind of guy up here you could think of but no self-respecting girl's going to get between the sheets with dirty Yids with a bit missing from their dick. If I were right down to my last bit, I just wouldn't let a Jew boy get his way with me. No, sir! Do you get that?" I suppose I got it.

But she wasn't finished. "Now just you get this. When I'm posin' just you keep right out of the art room. I'm not goin' to have a guy like you runnin' his eyes all over me and thinkin' dirty thoughts. See – I've got those damned pictures of yours. I'm not goin' to put them in the trashcan yet. But if you come into the art room when I'm posing, I'll see this stuff goes to someone who matters. You know what'll happen? You'll get the bum's rush right out of the academy. You got it? So you just get that nasty arse of yours right out of this place. Big Louise will help you out. Maybe he'll call a cab; you'll be needing it."

Trembling, I pulled up my pants just about as fast as I've ever done. Jo pierced me through with those sharp eyes of hers. Then she picked up the fancy gold receiver and called down. "Louise, Mr Traumann is on his way down. Maybe he'll be wanting a cab. Okay?"

I made it out fast. I could see how things would make out. Louise with his great mitts would get to work on me. I'd get pretty mangled. I'd get the treatment for sure. I waited by the elevator in a panic. I just couldn't stay where I was. I had to get out but down there was big Louise waiting to sort me out. Then some pretty old dame came along. "Okay, son?" I told her I'd been fixed up by Jo Heffer. "Now you just stop your worry. I just don't have too much time for garbage like her. She just think she can run this place like God Almighty and the Mother of God all rolled into one. She's got what it takes, but she just ain't got everything a guy wants. She just don't have no heart – no heart. That's what guys want – a dame with a heart. They want a bit more than just a five-minute roll. No, sir! They want a nice, kind little ear to tell their troubles. That's what guys want, not some dame like Heffer who'll take a whole lot of dollars off them and give them not too much."

I guess I'll never forget Daisy and what she said. She made me feel a whole lot easier. "Now, son, I'll come along with you. We'll take the lift right down to basement and go out the back way. If that baboon tries to stop us at ground, I'll fix him." Daisy was right. Louise was waiting at ground. As the door opened, Louise's mitt stretched out to take my shoulder.

"Guess you're keepin' cab waitin'," he said in his deep, husky voice. He lifted me right off the ground and into the hall. Daisy stepped forward. She knew just how to handle Louis.

"Louis, that's real kind of you to get a cab for Mr Traumann. He's taking me around to his place to show me his paintings. Aren't you, Bennie?" She told him to put me down and made herself clear with a sharp kick.

"Whad'y do that for?" he came back.

"For a whole lot of reasons, you great dumb cluck." He put me down, and we got out quick to the sidewalk leaving Louis nursing his shin at the top of the steps.

Daisy bundled me into a cab and got in right after me. "Now what about going up to Vive La Difference! Up on the Lake? Pierre makes just about the best burgers in the county." That was fine by me, and I was beginning to enjoy Daisy's company. It took twenty minutes or so, but it was great when we got there. It was built over the water with the waves lapping right under the boards. The burgers were just what I needed after the session with Jo Heffer. They put new life into me.

Daisy was in a thoughtful mood. I just let her ramble on making a grunt here and there to show I was listening. It went something like this. "You know, I feel real sorry for the guys that come to me. Just ordinary guys way into middle age and some gettin' just a bit elderly. Respectable guys, bank clerks, insurance agents, that sort of thing. They come in looking nervous. They gets their pants off in a corner and then fumble around like the first time. Then they starts huffin' and puffin'. When they're down, I just put my arms right around them and give them a cuddle like they got from their mas when they were kids. Sometimes they pour out their hearts and I give them my ear. Maybe they come to me because their wives just don't have the necessary. Perhaps the edge has gone right off their hearts. Maybe I can give these guys something they just don't get between the sheets way back home. But they just don't get that from Jo Heffer."

Daisy took a big bite from her burger. The Lake was being touched by the setting sun. It made me want to set up my easel and get painting. I got to turning this sex thing over. I guess in the past it had given me hell. Now this business with Jo Heffer? Where had I read sometime about sex being a chimera? Perhaps that's why some guys in the past got to mutilating themselves. My eye moved to a poster of a dame posing against the Eiffel Tower in Paris. She was dead sexy with a mighty tight top. The urges surged up. Daisy must have picked up the vibes.

"Bennie, now don't you get to havin' fancy ideas about me," she warned. "I'm pretty old goods. Old enough to be your ma." I buried myself into a maple syrup crepe. I told her how desperate I felt at times. "Sure, it is," she agreed, "but it's just one of those things you just have to put up with. You just don't want to mess around with some old baggage like me. I figure the best thing is for you to find yourself some real nice girl. I guess there's plenty around. When you've found the girl for you, I guess you'll know, and then get yourself married. That's the best thing a guy can do. Darned sight better than banging around with some dame and handing over a whole lot of dollars. You know what? I get real green when I see married dames around with nice little kids. It churns me right up. I guess it didn't work out for me like that." I could see how Daisy felt. It made me feel a touch sad. In the cab back, Daisy put her fat arms right around me and held me real close. I guess she was dead right on this sex thing; I'd just have to live with it as best as I could.

I reckon that Daisy just about saved me from taking a jump from the top of one of the tallest skyscrapers in town. When I got back, Abe gave me a worried look. He never probed. He knew how to leave a guy to himself. He asked me if he wanted him to fix something. After the burgers, I just didn't feel too hungry so he just poured a beer and put it down at my side.

The next day, I got to the academy pretty early and went straight to that work of Chagall, *The White Crucifixion.* I rated the artist pretty high. He got right deep into how folk feel. I still felt mighty churned up with the time with Jo Heffer. So I let just about everything just flow right into that painting. I'd been hurt real bad. Okay, Daisy had done a whole lot for me but blood still flowed a hell of a lot. I guessed it'd take some time before I got over it. I'd just have to live with it for a time. That's how it had to be. I was a Jew, okay, so what, a guy had to be something. You just can't be nothing. So I was a Jew with a bit off the end of my dick and that's how it had to be. I picked up my portfolio and made off to the painting class.

I suppose, I didn't get too involved with the other students. They seemed to like my stuff. Some would gather around my easel and make approving sounds. There was this dame who got just a bit too persistent. She pressed me hard to go around to her place. So I gave in. I guess her folk were pretty well loaded. Her place wasn't too fancy. It was just full of art stuff – posters all over the walls, polished pine furniture and big cushions over the floor. She asked me if I liked it. I agreed. She fixed me a drink. I gulped down too much and nearly choked to death on the stuff. I'd brought around a portfolio of some of my stuff. We spread it around the place. She thought my stuff was great. "Reckon you're just wasting your time at our place. You need to get over to Europe – Paris, Florence maybe London."

She picked up a charcoal drawing of a nude. It so happened that it was Jo Heffer. "You've got a great feel for linc and form," she observed. "Reckon if I'd stay in the life class for just about ever, I'd never do anything like this." She looked at the sketch quite a while and then gave me a look. "She turned you on in a big way, you can see that."

Now this dame, Liz Smith, was okay. I guess sitting there in her arty pad and drinking pretty powerful hooch got me thinking that maybe we could get just a bit closer. Maybe something really interesting might happen. I felt the edge of her dress. Firmly, she removed my hand with 'Huh, huh'. She moved away somewhat. She then began to sing, "My heart belongs to Daddy, Dad, Dad, Dad, Da…" I asked her why she was singing that. She came back, "Because, little Jew boy, you just ain't gonner be my screw boy." She said this getting up and swinging her light skirt around and showing off her long legs right up to her pants. It was all I could do to stop myself taking her there and then.

"But I do have something very special for you, Bennie Traumann." I wondered what the hell that could be. Maybe something kinky. That's not what I was looking for. I wanted something dead straight. She made me close my eyes tight. "Don't you go peeking? Okay?" She came up real close, and I could feel my excitement rising. "Now just you keep those lovely eyes of yours shut tight and open those wonderful thick lips wide and put your tongue right out." My heart pounded. I opened my mouth, and she put something hard and sweet on my tongue. I opened my eyes. There on my tongue a dissolving sugar lump. I panicked as the sweet stuff went down. "Don't you worry, Jew boy. Come on. Just you hold me close as we're going on a nice long trip."

Within seconds, I was no longer in control of my body. I tried to push her away. I tried to get my fingers down my throat to vomit the stuff up. It was too late. Things started to look strange. The far side of the room got to looking like it was blocks away. I had to let myself back into the big cushion as the trip took me over. Violent colours cascaded down in front of my eyes like Niagara. They were hideous colours – crude and brittle that made me want to yell. I was trapped in some place I just didn't want to be. The colours were sucking me in – choking me. I tried to scream out but nothing came. Then the colours faded off into some strange vista with queer buildings. They were religious places – synagogues – churches – temples. They came up one after another like a great hellish procession. Then men – Jewish men in a long line. They wore their tefillin and tallits. They looked at me through thick, pebble lens that made their eyes appear thousands of miles away. Each one looked like the doppelganger of the rabbi who had prepared me for Bar Mitzvah. I couldn't tell if I was walking down the line or they were walking past me. But they just went on and on looking at me and making me feel real bad.

That all faded away, and I started to feel I was shrinking until I became like an infant. I was suspended over a shining bowl. I peered in not knowing what I would see and feeling a searing pain somewhere. The shining bowl went red. Everything went red. I tried to cry out with pain. Then lots of big fish with glassy eyes started to jump. They were jumping at me low down. Panic deepened. I wanted to hold myself low down to protect myself. But my arms wouldn't move.

All went dark and still. I could just feel my heart beating like it was going to burst. I just hoped it was ending. Out of the darkness, I could see a point of light. It grew until it became flames of fire. I was drawn in. A dark figure moving around. The face turned towards me. It was Pa – Pa. His eyes looked into mine looking for help. I was powerless. I watched the flames sweeping over him burning his beard and his hair. His clothes burnt. Then the flames got into his flesh. His arms shot up suddenly into the air and then he collapsed into a heap. Slowly, he was reduced to a great mass of burnt flesh. His eyeballs were consumed leaving just the dark, blank sockets. His mouth was forced open by the contracting sinews. His great tongue protruded grotesquely from between his teeth. The sweet smell like roasting pork sickened me.

Slowly, the blackened jaw eased wide open and the swollen tongue stretched out towards me. I was being drawn into the dark cavern on the mouth. Inside, the smell of the burnt flesh overwhelmed me. I heaved. Deeper and deeper I went. I was conscious of moving through the great, grey masses of the brain. Clusters of what appeared to be seaweed quivered. Tangles of threads stretched out from one mass to another. Pulses of energy flowed out leaping across into the threads. I looked, no longer scared but fascinated. The great pulsing movements continued as I wandered through the chasms of the brain; then on to an endless red tunnel lined with hairs. Down, down I went bathed in something of peace. I passed on to what I knew to be the great chamber of the heart. I could see it pulsating and thumping hard. Blood flowed strongly through. I now understood that I was not in Pa's charred remains. I was passing through but my own body. It was me in my own living body! This beating heart was my heart. From high up in the high chamber, something fluttered and rustled. I felt happy with anticipation. Something mighty good was going to happen. Everything was just okay.

Down into a warm and beautiful garden, a creature fluttered down. It flew into the flowers passing from one to another. My heart bounced with joy. I longed for the creature to come to me. It came. The colours of its wings moved me to tears. It was just beautiful – beautiful. Its beauty was almost painful. I was just so happy. I was carried up onto the creature's wings. I moved over the surface kicking up, like a young kid, great clouds of dust. I chuckled with delight. The colours rose up and made something like a rainbow around me. I was bathed in colour. I smothered myself in the dust chuckling away. I knew deep down that everything was sure to be okay. It just had to be. I kicked up my fat little legs chortling away. The creature's dust flew all around me. It covered my naked body making me laugh and laugh. I rolled over and over in the colour and warmth. It was fantastic. I was at home – really at home.

Then she reached down, the woman with the dark hair and smiling face. I just needn't be afraid anymore. I just didn't have to hide away or cover up. I could sing out – shout out, 'Hey, there, everyone, I'm Bennie Traumann. I'm a Jew. I'm getting to be a pretty good artist. I'm coming up to twenty-one and I'm still a virgin. Sure, I want a woman, but I guess I can wait. So if you don't like too much what you're seeing – well, that's just your problem. I'm okay.'

I suppose I started to come out of the trip. I got up out of the cushions. Okay, I was just a bit shaky, but somehow, I felt good and clean. My mind felt alert and sharp – all ready to go. Somehow, everything around me looked different. Liz was still under and screwed right up into her cushions. Her brow was screwed up tight and furrowed. She looked like having a bad trip. I felt moved and gave her a tender kiss hoping it might give her some easement. On the wall hung one of those Pirelli calendars with fancy dames. I turned over the pages. I did not letch after what I saw. They were just beautiful women with beautiful bodies. I took delight in their shapes. I took up the calendar and carried it with me. I picked up a small silver cup of strange design. I turned it over in my hand. The shape and form thrilled me. Over the surface were worked bunches of grapes hanging from the vine. It reminded me of the Kiddush cup at home. I placed it on the table with the calendar. Somehow, I felt that what I was doing had some very special significance. I took a bottle of wine from the counter. I found some bread. It wasn't like the challah bread that Rebecca used to make. It would have to do. On a high shelf, I spotted a branch candlestick. I found some napkins. I used one to cover the challah and another for my head. I was ready.

Liz began to stir and opened her eyes. "Hey what gives?" I told her that while it wasn't Shabbat and the stuff wasn't too kosher, we were going to have Kiddush. She seemed to be confused. I explained that this was something we Jews did on Shabbat. It was good and made you feel okay. She didn't seem to respond too well. I just told her that as a woman she had a part, and I'd see us through. She didn't get it. I pulled her up and dragged her to the table. "If you're going to do something religious," she protested, "'what the hell's that calendar doing?" I told her that the pictures were good, and I thanked the Almighty for beautiful women.

I got Liz to light the candles and then say, "Let there be light." I guess throughout this time I was still under acid.

I blessed the bread and wine, "Blessed are you, O Lord, King of all creation, we have this wine to offer, work of human hands…we have this bread to offer…" And so on. Liz thought it nice. I told her that it was what real Jews do at Shabbat. We have a nice meal and talk and sing. It was a great time. So we sat there keeping a sort of Shabbat Kiddush. We drank the wine and chewed our way through the heavy bread. It made my jaws ache. We just sat there touching hands, chewing bread and drinking the wine. It felt good.

"Glad you came?" she asked.

"Huh, huh." Then she reminded me that her heart belonged to her daddy. "Okay," I told her. "That's fine by me."

Soon after the acid trip, I went over to New York. [*circa* 1961] I needed to see an exhibition of Ed Hopper's stuff. He was a pretty old guy, but his work grabbed me in a big way. I liked his bold style and something about his painting that got me thinking. It took you to places that maybe you'd just never thought of. A lot of his stuff was about lonely people. Folk just sitting by themselves in bars or cafes looking just downright soulful. Folk wanting something really bad but not too sure of what they wanted. There was one that got me churned up at the Madison. A dame in a café just sitting there with a coffee getting cold. I wanted to get right into that picture, sit down beside her and just hold her hand. Maybe she'd been stood up or maybe she'd walked her feet off looking for a job. There were a whole lot of folk viewing Hopper's work. Most of them scooted around, chewing gum and not looking too carefully. I reckoned that was tough on Hopper. He'd spent a whole lot of time working on his stuff and these jerks would come in and hardly bother to take a proper look.

I'd like to tell the whole world about Hopper's work. I'd got to know most of his stuff through art books and that sort of thing. But the Madison exhibition plugged a few gaps. There was one I just hadn't encountered before. It was painted way back around 1939 when the movie world was making it big. Hopper just took part of this plushy cinema in New York. It was fantastic place, all reds and gold. You can just see part of the screen and the backs of a few heads. But the real subject is in the gangway. It's an usherette. She stands there just looking real lonesome. She's deadbeat and waiting for the curtain to come down so she can get back to her place. But what's a home like? What gives? That's how it is with Hopper. He likes to get you thinking around the folk in his work. What about this guy – this dame? What's their life really like? Are they eating their hearts out with loneliness? And so on.

I spent some time taking in New York Movie. A guy came and sat alongside me. He was taken in by the work. He turned towards me and spoke quietly. "I don't want to intrude. I'm something of a writer. Some of my poems have got printed in journals, and I hope to get a collection published sometime. I find Hopper moves me to verse." I nodded. He opened a notebook, thumbed through a few pages. "Would you like to read what I wrote on this work?" I nodded. The words stuck right in my mind. 'The flickering shadows feed a thousand fantasies, / But not for Josephine: / Her dreams were shattered by a guy called Jo, / Who took her for a sucker when she was too young to know, / With his slick talk, / And phoney rocks she took for real, / The swell apartment, / And ritzy automobile. / In furs and gown / She hit the good time big /

Broadway, Manhattan, bright lights, breakfast champagne / Her pictures in New Yorker magazine: / Vacations in the sun / With yachts and yachts and yachts, / The movies were hers for real / Until Joe showed himself a heel: / When Dolores walked in she stole the show / And Josephine was told to go / Back to the Bronx, / The sleazy blocks, / nThe bums, the blacks, / And rats and rats and rats, / With a room not big enough to swing the cat. /

Ma and the kids, / Pa boozed and on the dole, / Josephine was poor once more and big with Joe's kid. / Then she met a decent Yid / who made things right / And took her in, a Goy. / And when she had the boy / He made them his / With ring and name Traumann, / No dream this, but for real. / And when the lights go up / Josephine will go back home / To her Abe and the kid that looks like Joe.'

The words shook me. I looked at Hopper's work and then back to the guy's poem. And the name of the decent Yid – Traumann – 'Traumann'. I just couldn't believe it. The guy gave me an odd look as he took back his book. "You okay?"

"It grabs me. But look" – here I pointed to the name – "'that's my name – Traumann, and I'm a Jew." The guy opened wide his arms in amazement and we both sat there gobsmacked. What the hell could we say? The guy tore out the page from his notebook, handed it to me, squeezed my shoulder and went off. It was just one of those unforgettable moments that happen in life just now and again.

However, Hopper's work just grabbed me in a big way. Somehow it spoke to me I daresay because, okay, deep down in me there was this great empty space that needed to be filled up. It was like not eating for quite some time and the stomach just crying right out for something to give it satisfaction. I carried on through the Madison Exhibition and took in the work. Them I came upon a pretty elderly looking guy just sitting on the sidewalk by himself. The sun was shining down on the old fellow. He looked pretty cut up. I figure that things were not too good between himself and his woman. Maybe sex doesn't come right anymore. Maybe it never did. It looks like he's just thinking about taking a plunge in a river some place and just not coming out. I was just standing there puzzling it out when I get a great thump between the shoulder blades. I nearly took off heading right through Hopper's canvas. "Hey! Whad'y know?" came this voice. "If it just ain't Bennie Traumann! You still dream'n?" When I got over the shock, I turned round. It was that guy Ron Gruber who'd shook the dust of the

academy off his feet way back. I'd picked it up that he was making it big here in New York with that terrible stuff of his. Why the hell the art critics went wild over him just beat me.

As Abe commented, "It's all technique and no drawing." But that's just how it was.

"You gave me one hell of a shock. Guess I didn't expect to run into anyone I knew around here. Well, that's just how it is. Still at the old place and getting to be one hell of a good draughtsman? Guess Hopper's not too particular in that direction." I ignored that and told him that Pa, when he was alive, went for Hopper in a big way with his use of light and so on and Hopper saying that he just wanted to paint sunlight falling on to a white wall. Gruber didn't respond too enthusiastically making just a 'Huh, huh'.

I was just hoping that Gruber would mosey off and leave me to take in the Hoppers. "Art's just about making dough," he went on. "Don't go giving me art for art's sake boloney. What about us going off and getting a drink some place and chewing the rag?" That's about the last thing I wanted. So I found myself sitting in some fancy place not too far off with plenty of plate, glass and chrome tables in art deco style. Gruber drank some green stuff in a fancy glass, but I just stuck to beer. He raised his glass with, "Here's to us, there's none like us!" He took a long pull at his drink. "They know how to make a damned good cocktail here."

"I guess you're just itching to know how I made it big?" I shrugged my shoulders just a little. Then he got going. "Guess I got wise looking at your stuff and figuring it was not going any place I wanted to go. They didn't think too much of my work, those stuffed shirts who called themselves art teachers. So before I got the bum's rush, I pulled out. Put some of my stuff in fancy frames and got Pa to let me hang it around the apartment. It was the best thing I ever did. Pa was entertaining some business guy to fix up some deal. The guy saw my stuff and asked what I wanted for it. Pa taught me to think big so I came out with ten thousand bucks. This guy bought the lot and put them into his swell office here in New York. Folk started asking about them and I started getting commissions." I gave an inward groan and started fishing around for some excuse to get out. But he went on, "What they liked was not my stuff, that was crap but the frames. So I put on big price tags and I got to making big money. Then I got to thinking. Back at the academy, they said my stuff was crap, okay. So if my stuff's crap then why not paint in crap?"

I told him I thought he was kidding. "Nope. I reckoned they wanted crap so that's what I'd give them. I made an experiment with one of my stools and acrylic. It mixed well. The colour and texture was just fantastic. When it dried off, it gave a great surface texture and quality. I guess I'd hit on something pretty good." I commented that it sounded pretty unhygienic. "Nope, I just wear surgical gloves and a face mask. So I guess it looks like I'm carrying out some operation." I mentioned that I'd read in art magazines about his technique and that they must have asked questions. "They asked questions, alright. I just told them the truth that I mixed my paint with crap. They just thought I was kidding!

"The real breakthrough came after a press conference. I had fancy folk lining up at my studio wanting me to do their portraits. So they got their portraits painted in my crap! So if you paint crap with crap, then the dollars flow in and you make it in a big way. That's just about how it's going to stay with me and no way am I going to change the medium. So if I'd stayed at the academy trying to be a good draughtsman, I'd just about got nowhere fast." I drained my glass.

"So I get it. Most folk just don't see what's good or bad. You just dress it up with a fancy frame and work out some fancy technique and they'll break their necks to buy the stuff."

"You've got it," Gruber came back. "Whisky sour?"

I picked up the *Tribune* a few days afterwards. On the front page was a news item that hit me between the eyes. It read that a successful young artist had been knifed to death on the subway. I felt real sorry for the guy. What had he done with his life but paint phoney pictures and make a lot of dough? It was tough. Real bad.

When I got back to Chicago, I found my grandpa at Abe's apartment. They had been chewing me over. "Now, Bennie, my boy. Abe and I have been talking things. Time to get your future sorted. Nein? Remember you're Jewish. You never be forgetting that. You must get to thinking of making a life with some good Jewish girl. Ja? I don't want to see you like that poor son of mine. What did he make for himself?" I listened feeling a touch uncomfortable. I just didn't want the old man forcing me into some place I just didn't want to be, with some girl I didn't care for too much.

Abe chipped in, "Solly, my dear friend. Bennie's got it in him to be a good artist. Maybe a great artist. He'll get a distinction when he graduates from the academy soon. I could get him into teaching. He has it in him. He's getting to be a fine draughtsman. He has a creative flair. He'll be a good teacher and sell his paintings."

“Maybe, maybe, Abe. But if he’s going to start a real Jewish family, he will need something to get him security and respect from the community. You must not get me misunderstood, but an art teacher even at the academy will not get that.”

I sat through all this without being asked what I wanted. My grandpa carried on, “I’ve spoken to Jo Sterne. He is the head of the advertising agency Goldberge, Sterne and Goldberge. They have our account Traumann and Grossman Optics. Good business. Jo says he needs good artists in the studio. Mr Gronowski says you have taken the illustrating course – Ja?” I told him I had but that somehow advertising just wasn’t my scene and that maybe teaching would suit me better.

But the old man passed over my comment. “So I’ll be fixing an appointment, Bennie, with Jo Sterne, Ja?” I figure I just didn’t want to be forced into something I just didn’t want. I just wanted a studio where I could paint when I wanted to paint. Then it came to me that Ed Hopper worked for an advertising agency and spent a whole lot of his life doing commercial stuff but also getting to do the stuff he really wanted to do. Maybe I could work something out.

“Okay, Grandpa. I’ll go see him.”

So that’s how I came to be sitting in the art studio of Goldberge, Sterne and Goldberge feeling just about as bored as I could be. They gave me what they called a layout pad and got me pencilling adaptations from a basic advertisement layout. The adaptations were heading for some of the dullest media you could figure out. One sticks in my mind the ‘Contractor and Muckraker’. Hell. Only one thing could be said for the studio was that it had a great view right over the lake. If I had some glasses, I might be able to make out the point where Pa used to set up his easel when I was a kid.

A few days after starting the studio manager, a guy named Alan Wagstaffe, slapped down this damned awful ad on my board. It was something called the Comfy Boot and Shoe Company. They produced footwear for old folk whose feet were not so good. I had to draw up an adaptation from a double page spread. It was pretty tricky getting a big ad from the ‘Old Folk’s Friend’ down to an eight by two in the ‘Vermont Messenger’.

Vermont! Vermont! Was there ever such a place as Vermont? Not the sort of State that anyone with air in their lungs and something between their ears would want to live. I reckoned that no one under the age of sixty would want to set up their tents in Vermont. It was just a place for folk with bunions and hobbling about on sticks. Some time I read that Mark Twain, who just about had everyone falling about laughing at his stuff, did a presentation in Vermont. The hall was packed. He got up on the stage and gave his set piece. They sat there with straight faces. He came in with another dead funny piece. Not a face cracked. So he pulled out his sure-fire winner. No response. Not a smile or a titter. So he got through his stuff real quick and slipped out to the front of the hall and hid behind a bush. This little old couple came out first – both with real bad bunions and propped up with sticks. The old guy said to his little old lady, "Gee, Eliza, I guess that guy was so darned funny that I just had to stop myself laughin' righ' out!" I guess that's the sort of folk who read the 'Vermont Messenger' and get to purchasing their footwear from the Comfy Boot and Shoe Company. Somehow, I just didn't want to spend the rest of my life working on this damned awful account to get the buttoned-up folk over in Vermont to shell out dollars.

So I just had to get down to the undemanding task of producing a layout. It was made up of little boxes each with a shoe and copy so small that I wondered how the old folk could get to read it. Somehow, it just didn't tax my draughtsmanship. Wagstaffe okayed it and off it went to another department to send off to the 'Messenger'. I suppose that somehow I got used to scaling ads up and down. I could do it with my eyes shut. But it was tedious and boring stuff.

Then I got sent to what they called an account conference. It had to do with the family account Traumann and Grossman. The account executive, Fred Neuman, took charge. He called our company T & G. A campaign in trade journals throughout the States was being planned. It was dead dull stuff. It was just one of those meetings where you just sit back and let it flow over you. There was a girl, not too easy on the eye. She was the sort of girl who, if she got into the line of vision, might send you blind for a time. She was not just big; she was big – 'big'. She had great thighs that ought to be kept well covered. But dames like her seem to have a compulsion to show off as much as possible without being run in by the cops. She sat there with her great legs crossed. I just couldn't keep my eyes off. I tried to blot her out of my line of vision and think about the canvas I was working on in Abe's studio. But you know how it is, the more you try the more you damn well fail. Somehow, I found myself drawing those thighs on my pad. It proved a bad mistake. She caught me looking and gave me the look through her fancy glasses. The face went well with the legs. It was one of those impossible fat faces. I doubted if she was more than twenty, but I reckon she had three chins. She looked pretty myopic. The lenses of her specs were thick and set in fancy green frames with sidepieces that curled up and glittered with stones. I reckon they came from the T & G top of the range. She caught my eye and gave me a sickly smile. I was going to regret that look and that damned smile.

As a result of the conference, they got me to designing a new ad. This grabbed me more than just producing adaptations. The copy was written by the main agency copywriter, Gerry Hoey. Gerry could be a hell of a bore talking about his great grandfather who'd come over from Ireland. Anyway, I suppose he was good at writing copy for advertisements. His heading to the new series was, 'Guys date dames in T & G frames'. It went on about seeing profits rise real fast when you stock T & G frames. I did not have to push my imagination too far. They'd given me a selection of frames, among them the flashy green frames worn by the dame at the conference. That was it. I had made some quick sketches of the fat dame improving her face just a touch and cutting down on chins. I produced a number of variations with the head at different angles. Somehow, I felt quite pleased with my first effort at designing an ad. Steve Landau, the account executive, liked what he saw. In fact, he was really enthusiastic and gave me a mighty thump between the shoulder blades.

Landau shuffled through my sketches making approving noises. He reckoned that the sketches were so good they could almost be used as finished artwork. Then he stopped and gave a sketch a really close look. "You know, I guess this dame looks pretty familiar. Gosh – that's Jo's unbeautiful daughter Rosa. I caught you giving her the eye and sketching at the conference. Well, well." He went on to say that Jo was dead keen to get her off his hands and suggested that if I wanted a lot of dame for my money, I'd better get dating! I told him that he'd got to be kidding.

I went with Landau to take the layouts in their smart black folders to T & G's. I didn't know the Grossmanns too well although they were my ma's folk. I guess they were not too eager to get to know me. But they were friendly enough and so on. The layouts were passed around and agreeable sounds were made. Eventually, they hit on a version they wanted. That's when Grandpa Traumann came in and made remarks about leaving this sort of thing for the ones. The drinks came out, and I got into conversation with one or two of the guys who just happened to be my cousins.

Feeling ran pretty high when it got around the studio that I had been asked to carry out the finished artwork. I had picked it up sometime back that they somehow resented me. Maybe they could see my work was a touch or two above theirs. They could see that I was getting ahead just a bit too quickly. I just wasn't in the business for muscling in. I just did what I was asked and did it as best I knew how. The clients liked my stuff. That's how it was.

I worked up the head of Rosa Sterne flattering her as much as I could. The green of the frames was the only colour apart from the T & G logo. The illustration lived. It came right out from the art board. I hoped not too much would be lost in print. Some of the trade journals printed on paper that just knocked the life right out of illustrations.

Then she came in. Rosa in person. A few mocking whistles went around the studio. She just took them as a compliment. For Rosa, the whole world was her oyster, and she somehow thought that everyone thought of her as the bee's knees of a dame. Tough on Rosa. She came right over to me and leant over far too close. She reeked heavily of scent. It made my eyes run and got up my nose. She put on one of those soft, honeyed voices. "Mr Traumann, that looks real interesting. I just wonder who the girl might be? She looks real cute in those really swell frames." My fingers were getting sweaty so that I lost some control of the brush.

"Okay, I guess you've used me as a model. I caught you sketching at the meeting way back." Then she looked around at the amused faces of the guys in the studio. "Do you think that Mr Traumann has really done me justice?" The guys collapsed laughing. Then she went on when the laughter died down, "Last fall, I got that poor guy Ron Gruber to paint my portrait. You know he got knifed in the subway. It was a pretty good portrait, but it got to smelling not too good so we had to put it in the garage. Why do you think that could be Mr Traumann?" I smiled inwardly and shrugged my shoulders. A great bubble of laughter welled up inside me that suddenly burst into a great sneeze. “My goodness, I just hope you’re not getting a cold, Mr Traumann!”

“No, I guess there’s some things I’m just allergic to.” With that, she gave me a big wink and sailed out. I noted to watch out for Rosa Sterne. She was just a dame not to be trusted. The other guys pointed at me and slapped their thighs in a meaningful manner.

Rosa Sterne was determined to get her talons into me. She came around time and again into the studio. She pestered me for the illustration used in the T & G ads. “Come on, honey,” she’d coax. “Can’t you just get that picture for little old me?” I just had to point out that it wasn’t mine to give anyway. It was just right out of my hands. No way could I get the picture. The other guys got mighty sick of Rosa hanging around the studio.

It started as a joke and they’d get to mimicking her, “Come on, honey…” Then they’d started getting mad with me and got me to put her off. But what could I do? She was Jo Sterne’s daughter, not some chick from the typing bay.

I guess the agency liked my stuff pretty well. They got a new big fashion account Yomtov Gowns. It was headed by some fancy dame, Cherry Greenberg. Jo himself took me around to meet Cherry. She had some style. Tall – not far off six feet and slinky. She wore a black suit with a nipped-in waist and flared skirt. She wore her hair pulled right back like some swell dame from somewhere in South America. Her spectacles hit me. They were from T & G’s range with red stones set into the pink frames. Cherry was quite some dame if you like the style.

“So this is the kid you’ve been telling me about, Jo?” She gave me a sharp look that I didn’t like too much. My palms started getting sticky. Not a dame to get into a tangle with. Why the hell hadn’t Jo Sterne asked Wagstaffe to handle this side of things?

“Sure, Cherry,” Jo replied. “Bennie Traumann is just about the best in the studio. There’s nothing he can’t do. I’ve seen some of his stuff that he did at the academy.

“So I’m dead sure he can produce fashion plates that will send the readers of Harper’s crazy to buy Hayom Sports.” Cherry looked unconvinced.

“We’ll be seeing about that,” she replied with a touch of ice in her tones.

It looked like that Cherry wanted a really slinky presentation for her gowns. Jo produced some stuff that had appeared in the British fashion press some way back. There was this artist Francis Marshall who had done a lot of stuff in Vogue magazine. He made models look like being ten feet tall. His line and wash sketches were the goods. Jo asked me if I could produce something like them. I made it dead clear that okay it just wasn't my style, but I could come up with something that gave the same effect with these tall slinky dames leaping right out of the page. I needed some reference from which I could work. Cherry had a lot of ektachrome transparencies of this French-Tunisian dame with a fantastic figure modelling Yomtov Gowns' gowns. She handed them over with, "There's a hell of a lot of dollars tied up here – so…" I got the message.

I spent a whole lot of time working over the transparencies way into the evenings back in Abe's studio. I copied some of Marshall's stuff to get the feel of his technique. Then I made a whole lot of preliminary sketches in line and wash. Abe got really excited about what he saw and gave me a few tips here and there. I passed on the rough sketches to Jo Stein. He reckoned that Cherry would be tickled pink when she saw my work. He was dead right. She okayed my roughs and she was itching to see the finished artwork. I got to the agency studio real early. The early sun sparkled on the lake. I got to thinking about the hours I'd spent out there with Pa and Abe painting. Somehow I wished Pa were still around to see how things were shaping up with me. I got out my board and set things up to get going. I got a great tingle of excitement as I switched on the transparency viewer. I spread out the rough sketches of the gown I was to work on. Then I opened the draw where I'd put the ektachromes. I just couldn't believe it – the draw was empty. I pulled the draw right out. Maybe they'd slipped through somewhere? But that was just impossible. I went through every draw in the desk. Nothing. I looked under the desk and around the desk. Nothing. I searched all around the studio in desperation. Nothing. A cold sweat broke out. I went down to the washroom to relieve myself and try to calm down. I put my head under the cold faucet God – I clearly remember putting the folder with the transparencies into the drawer the night before. They just had to be there. How the hell could they have got out? Okay, Louisa the cleaner came in to clean up. Sure, but Louisa was the sort of lady you could trust. She was a great lady. If she found a fistful of dollar bills on a desk, you could be sure everyone would be there in the morning. Louisa just didn't have sticky fingers. But thirty ektachromes just couldn't disappear just like that – could they?

I stood there just looking out over the lake wishing that I were out there somewhere painting sunlight falling on to a white wall or whatever. I could see that dame Cherry Greenberg just about reducing me to very small pieces and feeding me to the creatures in the lake. The other guys started arriving. "Problem, Bennie? Fallen out with luscious Rosa?" I snapped back and they shut up. I wasn't in the mood for spilling beans. I got back to my place and tried to look like I was busy at something. My mind just wouldn't settle. My extension rang. It was Jo. He wanted to know how the Yomtov Gowns stuff was going. I gulped and told him I had a problem. I stood by Jo's desk shaking and sweating. He looked up at me and knotted his brow. He could see I had a big problem. "Okay, you'd better get it out, Bennie." I told him. He just sat there looking at me in disbelief. "Do I hear you right?" I assured him that they were in my draw last night and now they'd gone. I made it clear I'd just about searched everywhere, but they'd just disappeared. Jo got up slowly and came around to face me. "Listen, Traumann, it took me a whole lot of time, effort and dough to get Yomtov. If those transparencies don't get to coming back, Cherry Greenberg will wash her hands of us. And I just don't have to tell you how your future will shape up. Now you just get right onto the office manager and arrange to go through the agency – every drawer – every filing cabinet and right through the art store. So you'd better find them sharp and bring them straight to me. Okay? Okay?"

I went out shaking. My head was throbbing like one hell of a hangover. I came clean with Alan Wagstaffe, the studio manager. He was a pretty easy going guy. Nothing got him rattled. When accounts executives came in screaming for stuff that wasn't ready, he'd just smile his smile and told them to go and fix themselves a coffee or something. He drove folks pretty wild, but somehow, he got things through.

Wagstaffe, we called him Waggy, got the studio staff together and got them turning the whole place upside down. Somehow, they felt for me and were eager to turn up the transparencies. The office manager, a stiff sort of man named Blake, stood by making sure no corner or draw was missed. Waggy took me by the shoulder and made his usual suggestion to go get a coffee. Blake nodded. So I went out and made for the elevator.

I was just about to press the button to descend when who should come along? Rosa Stein. greeted me in an irritatingly cheerful manner. "Hey, what eating you? You just don't look too much over the moon. What's your problem? What about coming out for a coffee some place?" I felt trapped. I followed Rosa into a coffee bar watching with fascination her great buttocks working together. Those buttocks did nothing for me; they were downright repulsive. I guessed that Rubens would have gone to town on them. But somehow, the sheer grotesque proportions of her rear end drew my eye. Somehow, she must have caught my gaze. She half turned, patted her behind and winked. I coloured up and got confused. She then grabbed my hand and drew me into a chair right close beside her.

"Now Bennie," she whispered right into my ear, "don't go getting bashful with me. I don't mind how you look at me." I bit my lip. I sensed that my trouble was being compounded with another. I just wanted to get right out of town and find a rock to sit on right up the lake some place. Coffee was ordered and brought by this slim girl who was mighty easy on the eye. She knew how to carry herself, and she had a nice smile. She looked the sort of girl I could date. Rosa had ordered a great plate of cookies. I took the chance to take a closer look at the girl as she put the plate down. She had a head of fine, silky brown hair. Gosh, how I would just have liked to have run my fingers through them. She caught my look and lightly brushed the top of my hand with her long, thin fingers. My heart bounded somewhat. She smiled and moved away.

Rosa grabbed one of the cookies and started taking great bites out of it. Pieces of the sticky stuff stuck to the side of her thick lips. She stuffed her mouth with the stuff and muttered incoherent sounds as she pointed the plate of sticky things to me. I shook my head. But Rosa wasn't a dame who would take no for an answer. She picked out the yuckiest cookie and placed it in front of me. I told her that it just didn't look too kosher – not that that bothered me too much. "You, don't get to telling me that you're bothered by that sort of stuff? I don't get to seeing too many rabbis snooping around. Just you get stuck into that damned good cookie. Enjoy!"

I nibbled away at the edge of the sticky mess. It spoiled the taste of my coffee. I left Rosa working right through the pile on the plate. She gave me no more attention. I kept catching the eye of the waitress and exchanged smiles. It took my mind off the missing transparencies. Maybe Rosa would go and I could get on terms with the girl. I managed to break off a good half of my cookie and slip it under the table. She looked at the remains on my plate and saw I wasn't going to eat the stuff. She grabbed it and crammed it into her great loose mouth. I felt sick. "Better not have any more. Physician put me on diet. Better cut down," she said.

Rosa gave me a look through her fancy T & G frames glittering with stones. "Pa's pretty sore with you, Bennie." She reached out and touched my arm. I moved my gaze to folk outside on the sidewalk. "You don't think you'll be clearing your desk and going someplace else?" I shrugged. She moved her hand to my thigh. "Little old me will miss you a whole lot." She squeezed my flesh. "Maybe if you tell little Rosa what the trouble is, maybe I could help you out?" I swallowed hard and told her about the missing Yomtov transparencies. "That's real bad," she came back. "Pa worked real hard to get that account. Had that dame Cherry Greenberg around for a really swell meal. A tough cookie. You get to crossing a dame like that and wow, you are in the hottest water that's ever been. So I guess you've just got to get the stuff back."

I told her that Wagstaffe and Blake were going through the agency on a big search. She moved her creaking chair nearer mine and leant all over me. She reeked of some fancy perfume and did nothing for me. I felt like I was going to suffocate and throw up at the same time. The sweat just poured down just about everywhere. I felt like screaming out. "Now just you let Rosa make you feel better." She started stroking my thigh slowly getting higher. It was the last thing I wanted. I grabbed her hand and pushed it well away.

She got my hand in a tight grip and dug her red talons into my flesh. I winced. Then with surprising force, she forced my hand up into her thighs. I just managed to get my hand away, get up and tell her that I'd just got to be going back. She gave me a sharp look and firmly said, "No. You've just got to wait. Just you sit down. Maybe I could help you out of your problem." I sat down trembling. I figured that bringing this dame into things might lead to a whole lot more trouble.

"You did that swell portrait of me for that T & G ad. Well, I figure that if somehow a way could be found to getting it for me, well, you never know, maybe those transparencies might somehow get found. Who knows? What do you think, Ben? Hey?" I could see she was getting me over a barrel. She was just one of those dames that guys who know what's good for them just don't mess with. Here was I tangled right up with Rosa Stein. "Men date dames in T & G frames," quoted Rosa giving me her imitation of a Mona Lisa smile. "So why don't you just go right up to the studio library now and get that sketch for little old me? Okay? I'll stay right here." Somehow, I guess that's how it had to be.

I stood outside on the sidewalk for a bit. Maybe it'd be the best thing to write my letter of resignation and get right out of the agency. But that would just about wash me right up. Jo Stein would be so mad about the whole thing that he'd put it around. I guess Grandpa Traumann would be pretty sore too. I gritted my teeth and headed back to the agency.

I was buttonholed by a bright young kid from the typing pool. "Hey, Ben, Mr Wagstaffe and Mr Blake are just going nuts. They're just about taking everything apart. Mr Sterne's in a terrible rage. You'd better keep out of his way." I smiled and headed for the agency library and the artwork section. The librarian was just about the sourest old puss you could imagine. She'd been with the agency way back when it started and guarded the library stuff like crazy. She had a great system of booking in and booking out. I had a hunch that I had no way I was going to get that sketch without her knowing. The system was watertight. I had a portfolio with me, but she would be insisting on looking inside before I left.

"What do you want, Mr Traumann?" She asked curtly. I told her that I just wanted a little look into the Yomtov Gown section just in case the transparencies had somehow got there. That was not a clever remark. She came back with the business of everything being very carefully checked. She dressed me down like some old school marm hauling some young kid over the coals. "So what's missing?" I told her the Yomtov ektachromes. She gave me a penetrating look that scared the pants off me. She pulled down her reference book. "No more than just a few rough layouts. Nothing more." She snapped the binder shut and thrust it back on the shelf.

I pushed my luck. I told her that Mr Sterne was mighty angry and he'd be asking if I'd thoroughly checked the Yomtov section. She pursed her lips, drew in her breath and said in her best prim manner, "Very well then. Quite unnecessary but I suppose we'd better take a look." My heart sank somewhat. No hen ever guarded her chicks like Miss Smith guarded the stuff in the library. How could I snitch the artwork from the T & G section? She pulled out the large, flat Yomtov draw and pulled out the few pieces of my work. "There, what did I…" It was at that point the phone rang cutting her short. She responded to the ring of the phone like one of Pavlov's dogs. She did not salivate. But an eager glint came into her eyes and made a beeline for the receiver. Much speculation had gone around the place on the way she responded to the ring of the phone. It had been noted that somehow or other she would pick up the receiver and speak into in honeyed tones. It had been reckoned that way back she had a fantasy that some beau would ring to date her. So some joker rang to do just that. It seems that the result was electric. She spat something pretty vitriolic and slammed down the receiver! That call saved me. It gave me time to do what I had to do. I made straight for the T & G drawer, pull out the sketch of Rosa wearing the fancy frames and slip it straight into my portfolio. I got out mighty sharp while Miss Smith was still on the phone.

I cleared the building just about as fast as I could. A good tingle thrilled just about every cell in my body. I'd foiled the old dragon of the library and got what I wanted. I made straight for the Quick Snax bar to find Rosa eating her way through another plate of cookies. I caught the eye of the girl behind the counter, and we exchanged smiles. I figured she was the sort of girl I'd like to get around to painting sometime. An image sprang up in my mind of her in a flimsy dress, against a white wall in bright sunlight. My imaginings were brought to a sharp end by a sharp toe kicking my shin. I gasped.

"So did you get it?" she asked in sharp tones. I opened my case and took out some of the things I wanted. I handed the sketch over with the portfolio and advised her to keep it in the case. "You bet!" she came back and snatched the work from my hands. "Oh my god!" she exclaimed. "That's Me – Me – 'Me' – men date dames in T & G frames. Bennie, you'll date me, okay?" A number of folk half turned around to look and smirk. It was no good telling her to tone it down. She started to pull her diary out of her bag. "So when are we going to fix that date, honey?" I told her that I'd just have to ring her sometime. I guess I'd just have to humour her until I got the transparencies. I told her that I'd have to be getting back to the studio.

"Now what about those transparencies that you seem to know so much about?"

"Okay, you'll just have to wait and see what Rosa is going to fix for her Ben." She eased herself off her chair, giving me a wink and half singing,

"Men date dames in T & G frames." She waved the portfolio in the air, squeezed past the table and headed for the comfort station.

I gave a sigh of relief as she disappeared. The girl came out from behind the counter, placed her hand on my shoulder and asked if I could use some more coffee. I just needed to get out of the place and back to the studio. But I got out from her that her name was Jeanne, got her number and agreed to make a date.

I felt pretty drained that night and hit the sack early thinking about the date I was going to fix with Jeanne. She was like a breath of fresh air after that Rosa dame. I was just slipping off when I heard the phone ring. Abe called me. It was Joe Sterne. I staggered out of bed sweating with apprehension and fearing the worst. Joe's voice sounded surprisingly relaxed. I was not going to get bawled out. "Bennie, I'm just going to have to give you an apology." I couldn't believe what I was hearing. "You'll guess that I was really screwed up over the loss of those extachromes. I didn't feel too much like eating so after we'd finished, I decided there's only one thing I could do. Get down to some work. I went straight into my study planning to go over the new T & G campaign. The Grossmans were not too happy with some of the stuff. I open my case and there, I just couldn't believe it, there was the whole pack of the Yomtov transparencies. I was just over the moon with relief. Rosa and her ma came rushing in. That girl of mine just threw her darling arms right around me and gave me a great bear hug." I felt sorry for Joe that he'd been taken in by that daughter of his.

He went on to tell me that he'd rung Cherry Greenberg. He went on to say that he'd had to tell her that somehow the transparencies had got filed away in the wrong place in the artwork section of the library. She'd swallowed that but was still sore at what had happened and that a day's work had been lost. "Now," he continued, "how the hell those transparencies got into my case is a darned mystery, but I'd like you to get a cab now to my place, collect the stuff and burn some midnight oil in the studio. If I can get some finished work over to Cherry by noon, it may calm her down. Okay?" I guess it just had to be okay. But inside, I felt damned angry with that Rosa dame who had caused such a hell of a lot of trouble. How can you deal with a dame like that and how could she get to fooling her pa? Where the hell was her heart? Maybe it had got lost somewhere in that oversized stomach of hers. I was going to make real sure that this guy just wasn't going to date that dame in T & G frames. No way, no way or I'd just have to be downright crazy.

That night, right through to the dawn, I sweated my guts out in the studio. In those days, I was a pretty fast worker. I had a sure hand and a mighty keen eye. The finished sketches came right just about every time. By the time the light was breaking over the lake, I was just about on by fourth plate. I got up for a while and stretched my legs to get my circulation going. I stopped over by the window and looked right out over the great expanse of water touched by the early light. I could just make out some small craft moving over the surface. I'd have given a lot to have been on that boat at that moment.

It got me wondering what all the hell this was about, this business of advertising with folk screaming at each other for stuff to meet some damned deadline. What the heck did it all add up to? Maybe it got some swell dame going out and getting herself the latest gown from Yomtov. Okay, but for what, for what? Did any of these folk get to wondering what they were doing on this speck of cosmic dust of ours? What the hell was I doing? I figured my thinking was getting just a touch too dangerous. So I fixed myself a coffee from the machine and got back to producing the next plate of a hell of a fancy gown.

So Cherry Greenberg got her sketches of her fancy gowns, and in time, they got to being published on the advertising pages of the fashion press. Joe Sterne was maybe just a little too grateful to me over all this and fixed me a pretty good raise in salary. Miss Smith got mighty sore over the missing T & G sketch and got to quizzing me a bit too closely. She tried hard but no way could she pin it on me. Then she started getting really objectionable all around, lost her cool with a senior executive and got herself fired. Just about everyone breathed a great sigh of relief and no tears were shed when she'd disappeared from the scene. She went and the nice girl from the typing pool came in. She ran it just as well but without the hassle.

I started going around to the Kwick Snax Coffee Bar pretty often. I got really friendly with Jeanne, and we started dating, going out to a movie or two. She was one of those nice, simple, uncomplicated girls and real good to be with. It was easy and relaxing to be in her company. No, she wasn't dumb. I just couldn't have stuck around with a girl with just about nothing in her head. But you could talk to Jeanne just about anything and she'd come back with a bright remark. I got to thinking of how good it would be to take her up on the lake for a painting trip and paint her wearing her white dress against a white weather-boarded wall. It was early summer and the brilliant clear light was just about right.

So it was fixed. We took a cab out to the places where I used to paint with Pa and Abe. Jeanne was a natural model. She was patient and not a bit self-conscious. Some dames would fidget all the time, shift their pose and want to keep taking a peek. But not Jeanne. I got her supporting herself with her hand against a white boarded wall and looking right out at over the sparkling lake. She just kept the pose with her flimsy white dress billowing right out. I worked in gouache to get that bright, crisp feel to the whole scene. It came together like a dream. There it was, the tilt of the head and her shiny brown hair blowing around and her slim figure. Boy, she was just perfect. It just wasn't her looks but it was that simple good-natured character that came through. I told myself that I just wasn't going to rush things. Maybe the grandparents wouldn't be too encouraging with me dating a goy. But that's just how it was going to be. I was going to keep dating Jeanne and see if it got us under the canopy…? I carried out quite a number of sketches that day in a variety of mediums. Some were quick detailed notes in pencil, some I worked up in gouache. Jeanne looked at them all, smiled and said nothing. That's just how I wanted it. Some dames like Rosa would have been all over them making dumb remarks. But not Jeanne.

We took to going up on the lakeside pretty often. Sometimes I would paint Jeanne and sometime just the scenery. When it got dark, we'd go and eat some place just talking and just like being with each other. We got around to talking about our families and how things had gone with us over the years. I got to telling her about the family way back in Germany and how T & G optics grew. Her folk had come over from Ireland some way back. Her pa was a cop. Her ma had died having a child when she was getting on somewhat. Pa was mighty bitter about this and blamed the priests for the trouble they caused Catholic families. They just drove them on to getting about as many kids that came. Jeanne was the eldest of seven so she had to keep an eye on the rest. That was tough.

Jeanne didn't mind too much of going around with a Jew who wasn't too observant. Somehow, I fell into the way of going to Sunday mass with her. Okay, it was mighty strange at first, but somehow, I began to feel at home with flickering candles, clouds of incense and the mutter of Latin. Perhaps there was just a hint here and there of what went on in the synagogue and maybe the Shabbat meal. The priest was a lively young guy fresh from Dublin. He greeted me like a long-lost brother and introduced me to a few other folks who'd converted from Judaism. I wondered what Ma Rebecca would have thought about me converting. I guess she'd approve of Jeanne.

Jeanne got to taking me back home. She wasn't the sort that was going to rush things and putting pressure on a guy. Her Pa was friendly enough. But he seemed withdrawn and sad. I figured he missed his wife a whole lot. Her kid brothers and sisters pulled me apart and got me to drawing pictures for them. They lived in a real nice street, built a long way back with brownstone houses. Inside, it had solid doors with brass handles. It was great. The sort of place I could feel comfortable in. So I became part of the O'Dwyer scene, and it slowly became accepted that Jeanne and I were getting pretty serious in our dating.

But Rosa Sterne was not going to be shaken off too easily. After she got the sketch, she kept hanging around the studio. I got to make sure that all my important stuff got locked away firmly in my drawer. I just wasn't going to get a repeat of the Yomtov business. She kept leaning over me when I was working and making hints about eating out some place. I kept her off by saying I had to keep an eye on my sick grandmother. Joe Sterne got in on the act and hoped I'd come around for a meal sometime. I just hoped that the invitation would not be coming. Alan Wagstaffe got a touch impatient with Rosa hanging around the studio and made some pretty sharp suggestions that it held up production.

Jeanne and I were getting close, and I got to wanting her pretty badly. But Jeanne was not the sort of girl who would go down that road too quickly. She made it clear that you just had to wait to get married before you could go all the way. She didn't want to get pregnant and marched to the altar. I gently suggested that we could make love without her getting pregnant. She came back sharply in a manner that I'd never seen in her before. "Good Catholics just don't use those things, Ben, you must get that clear." So I just had to wait.

My reputation was growing in the agency and beyond. The Yomtov fashion plates established me as an artist. The Greenberg woman wouldn't hear of anyone else working on the account. I started getting invitations to lunch to talk over possibilities. One agency from New York offered to double my present salary. I just told them I'd think it over. Wagstaffe told me I was a fool not to take up this mighty good offer. I suspected his motive. Maybe I just felt at home here in Chicago where I first saw the light of day. There was Jeanne. Abe too, who'd been a sort of father. Yes, and the lake out there with sunlight falling on to a very white wall. New York just didn't have the pull. But maybe, looking back, I guess that taking that position with NSW, the leading agency in New York, would have got me out of a whole lot of trouble. Maybe. But, as they say, hindsight is a great thing if you can get it.

It was well into the fall that year. The parks and just about everywhere were ablaze with red gold. I had started experimenting with impressionism verging on to the abstract. I tried to get these great expanses of reds and golds on to my canvas. Somehow, what I was looking for just didn't come right. Abe would take a look, shrug his shoulders and move off without comment.

I was getting just a touch despairing. Abe would come back and say something like, "Struggle, Ben, just struggle. Art is a struggle. Life is a struggle. That's just how it's supposed to be. Remember our Father Jacob. What did he do? At the ford Jabbock, he struggled with the spirit of God. What happened? He won through and got that new name – Israel. You know what that means – God struggler. So just you keep at it, Ben, and you'll break through." I tried damned hard that fall to get those red golds down on the canvas, but somehow, I just didn't make it.

It came up to mid-November and my birthday. I kept dead quiet about this. Jeanne and I had planned to go to a nice quiet diner that evening. Rosa came into the studio around midmorning carrying a large, fancy envelope. She placed it on my desk with that sickly, smug look of hers. "For the birthday boy!" she said right out so the whole studio could hear. The guys kept dead quiet. They had got wise to her intentions. I had to open the envelope and take out a card dripping with glitter. I forced myself to thank her and mutter that I just had no idea how she found out the date. She then urged me to look inside. There was what looked like an automobile key. I shrugged my shoulders and raised an eyebrow. "Now you just come with Rosa down to the parking lot," she said dragging me to my feet. I groaned. She pulled me to the elevator and sent us down to the parking lot. I just couldn't believe what I saw. A fancy pink Cadillac convertible, shining and new. My heart sunk to somewhere where my boots should be.

Then she threw her arms around me exclaiming, "Ben, it's all yours from your Rosa." I froze. What the hell could I say? I was trapped. She let go. I just stood there looking with horror at the gleaming hunk of metal. Rosa stood there looking damned pleased with herself and not picking up my vibes. She blurted out, "Ben, I just knew you'd love it. Isn't she just a beaut? Now you can take me out to nice romantic places. Won't that just be great? Real Nice?" She made another move towards me. I just took a few steps back, but she didn't get the message.

I felt I was trapped. I just didn't know in those days how to respond. I guess that I ought to have put those keys right back into her hand and made my way straight back to the studio. God, that would have saved me a whole lot of trouble. It was like a nightmare. My mind had gone numb. I felt powerless. Somehow, I found myself sitting in the deep upholstery of the Caddy with Rosa purring away beside me. I switched on the ignition, let in the clutch and soon we were gliding through the city streets heading for the lake. I felt dead cold inside and wondered how I'd got caught up in this deadly trap. Was it one of those dreams in which one's worse fears were experienced? Soon I'd get to waking up. But no, this dream was for real. Rosa kept up her inane patter and now she'd booked a table for two at some swell place for that evening. It was no use telling her I was fixed up. Rosa was hooking me with this expensive gift and I was taking the bait like some goddamned fool.

Somehow, I drove out to the white clapboarded boathouse way up the lakeside. She grabbed my hand and urged me with her into the back. I felt just like jelly in her hands. Rosa was just about the last girl I'd want to get into the back of an auto with. Now Jeanne? But no way with Rosa. But here it was happening. She seemed to have a spell on me. She started removing items of clothing. It was all happening far too quickly. I sat there in a cold sweat. I just didn't want this girl and I just didn't feel aroused. She got her tentacles around me and started fumbling for my flies. I started sweating hard and tried to figure how I was going to get out of this.

She got the message that I was not responding. A sharp tone entered her voice. "Now come on, Ben. What's the problem? You're not one of those men…?" Here my imagination cracked in. I told her that when I got circumcised, the rabbi's blade must have been dirty and I picked up a bad infection that's never cleared up.

"So you see…? You wouldn't like me too much if I passed it on." She fell for it. I just hoped that it would put her right off my trail for good. She started getting her things back on while I wished that I had Jeanne in the back seat.

But Rosa got back on to my 'problem'. She suggested I get medical help. I told her that I had but nothing seemed to touch it. She carried on talking about a specialist and that her pa could fix something up and so on. I figured that I just wasn't going to get out of the trap that easily. I drove back to the parking lot in the basement of the officer block. Rosa had cooled off, and I felt a bit easier. "Like the Caddy?" she asked as I switched off. I told her I thought it was fine. Somehow, I lacked the courage to hand the keys back. She said she'd fix a cab for the diner that evening. I told her that the grandparents had asked me around and that you just couldn't let the old folk down. She pouted and made her way to the elevator. I looked at the pink Caddy and hoped that maybe someone would steal it and solve something of my problem.

Sometime after the turn of the year, Joe Sterne took me into a consultation on a new account. It was the Crackle, Snackle, Pop Company. It had its manufacturing complex up on the western side of the lake. It had its own quay where grain ships could unload into the silos. The set-up manufactured the most popular breakfast cereal in the States. Joe had to make sure that the first campaign we handled was a sure-fire winner. The company was looking for at least ten percent increase in sales. Joe had made pretty big claims that they could produce a campaign that would send Crackle, Snackle, Pop right through to heaven itself.

By now, my visualising skills had developed along with my ability to produce finished artwork. Ray Patterson was the company's ad manager. He was looking for a campaign that would 'sock it to them'. He wanted to use the whole of the media especially TV commercials. "What we need is the right sort of logo or image to get the brand across – BIG." He threw it out to the agency's team. Some guy suggested chipmunks. He thought that they were nice little fellows with plenty of public appeal. "You crazy?" Snarled Patterson. "That's used by Brecky-Wecky Foods. Not the sort of thing we want. Wrong image. Okay?" It was not a good start. Joe looked uncomfortable. It was not a good start. He put it around to the other guys, but they shuffled their feet and clammed up. Patterson was getting mighty impatient. "What the hell's wrong with you guys? Who was behind that hell of a good ad – Men date dames in T & G frames? That was a mighty good ad. It had punch. That's the sort of thing I'm looking for. I'm figuring that some of you guys have no more between the ears than a single senile chipmunk!"

It was at this point that Joe leant across to me. "You were behind that ad, Ben. Any ideas?" It so happened that I had my portfolio with some of the sketches of Jeanne up by the boathouse with her long brown hair blowing around. I took a deep breath and cleared my throat. The other guys looked at me hopefully. I laid out my portfolio and showed one of the best sketches.

"What about this? The Crackle, Snackle, Pop girl?" Patterson snatched the sketch out of my hand and struck it with the back of his sizeable fist.

"Wow! That's it. A bright, young, healthy girl who's got vitality without being too sexy. That's it! She'll look great just about everywhere, TV – packaging – magazines – news media – billboards – the lot. That's it!" That's how Jeanne became the Crackle, Snackle, Pop girl and was blazed right around the States and sent the company profits and shares right through the roof. But what did it do for me? I lost Jeanne.

The Crackle, Snackle, Pop girl went over great. The G.S.G. drew up the largest advertising budget ever and sent the agency right up to the top of the league. So many companies tried to get us to take them on. So Joe Sterne and the Goldbergs were having to turn down accounts and shedding others that did not deliver the goods. I was Joe's blue-eyed boy and well in line for becoming his son-in-law, not something I had in mind. So there was to be a hell of a lot of coverage just about everywhere and a catchy TV commercial was to go out over the channels. The guys somewhere or other turned my sketches into animated cartoons showing a girl who looked like Jeanne pouring milk into a bowl of cereal saying in honeyed tones, "Hello, just start your day like me with a bowl of Crackle, Snackle, Pop and get right off to your day with a ZING!" This was followed with her singing a jingle. Ray Patterson was over the moon and back again with it all. They fixed a launch day sending out just about everything through all the media at the same time. It was going to hit the States big – really BIG. So the day came. The agency was buzzing with excitement. Journals and papers from just about everywhere came in with features and ads marked for reference. Joe was tickled more than pink. Then the TV commercials were screened with the C.S.P. jingle. It was so catchy that kids started to sing it around the place. Somehow, I didn't think about how Jeanne might react. Maybe she didn't fancy herself as star of the show with her face going out from California right up to Alaska. But there she was beaming out with her radiant health from 'Cosmopolitan' to 'New Yorker' through to some publication in a one-horse town and from God knows how many TV screens. I just figured that Jeanne wouldn't see herself in all this stuff. I just got carried right away with it all. Joe Sterne kept socking me between the shoulder blades and telling me that I was just about the best thing that had ever walked into G.S & G's. I guess I was just in one great mother and father of a whirl. Whatever was happening, somehow had nothing much to do with me. Okay, I'd done some sketches of just about the nicest girl a guy could meet and I was itching to get a ring on her finger, but all this stuff had just about nothing to do with us.

I was mighty glad to get out of the place at the end of the day. But somehow, I just couldn't bring myself to switch on Abe's TV and see the commercial of C.S.P. I'd just had about enough of all the razzmatazz. I just wanted to switch right off. I fixed myself something in Abe's kitchen. He came in after teaching at the academy. He had a journal folded back at a full-page ad. "Looks like your stuff's making a big hit," he said in his thick Polish accent. I nodded without too much enthusiasm. He was quick to pick up my mood and suggested a trip up the lake to do some painting. Next day was Saturday and I was free. Abe was dead right; I needed to get right away from the advertising racket and get down to some real art.

The day broke dull and overcast and the wind smelt of rain. I set the convertible toward Milwaukee. Up along the waterfront in those parts were a whole lot of shacks looking the worse for wear. They had weathered in an interesting manner for those who have eyes to see. The weatherboarding had cracked and splintered and interesting lichen and fungus had sprouted up. For someone like me, it was an artist's paradise. It was a good subject for a dull day. I got out my roughest paper. I tingled with excitement. Quickly, I built up washes deepening the tones with inks. When the work was dry, I enhanced areas with pen and ink, conte crayons and swathes of charcoal. The sketches I was producing were a riot of materials, shapes and forms.

But then something started to bug me. Looking through the lichen and the broken weatherboard was a face. A familiar face. It was the face of Jeanne. She looked hurt – even angry. My stomach went cold inside. My concentration and inspiration started to go. Had I somehow loused it up between us? I just couldn't face things going wrong between us. Then I told myself that no way would she see herself in that cartoon image on TV singing that stupid jingle. No, she just wouldn't recognise herself in that. It just wouldn't connect. Why should it? I just had no reason to tell her that I'd been working on the account. I didn't talk too much with her about my work at the agency. So why should she see any connection between herself and the illustrations in the media? If she saw any likeness, she'd just write it off as a coincidence. That's how it would be. I felt convinced and relaxed. I put my fears to one side and got back to sketching.

Next day, Sunday, I headed with some eagerness toward the Irish section of the city. The bells were ringing out from the Church of The Holy Family. I'd always meet Jeanne on the steps leading up to the entrance. We'd squeeze hands, look into each other's eyes and go into mass. She was standing there as usual. My heart beat fast as always at the sight of her slim form and her long brown hair. What a damned lucky guy I was to date the girl from Quick Snax. I hailed her from the sidewalk. But she didn't wave back. She just stood there looking ahead. Maybe she just didn't hear me over the traffic? Maybe she just hadn't seen me?

I mounted the steps and called, "Hi, Jeanne." She turned and looked straight at me with that hurt, angry look that I'd imagined in the lichen up on the lake. This time, it was real. Her eyes burnt into mine and her lips were tightly drawn. Her words have stayed with me over the years. "Now get this straight, Ben Traumann. I'm through with you. You've used me. You've got your Crackle, Snackle, Pop girl, but you've lost Jeanne O'Dwyer." She turned suddenly on her heel and went into mass.

I stood on the sidewalk as crowds flowed past me into mass. I was shaken. Her sharp words buzzed around my head. Something went dead cold inside me. How could I have been so stupid? How? How? I felt like kneeling down and beating my head on the sidewalk. I moved away like a guy in a dream. I let my feet have their way as I passed block after block. I found myself back in the neighbourhood where I had been raised as a kid. Things looked bad around there now. Garbage littered the sidewalks. Windows were smashed. The whole place reeked of decay. A guy who didn't look too friendly told me to move my arse. I did. I wandered on. I came to the park where Rebecca used to take me as a kid. I thought about her and the way she would put her arms around me and hug me. And the stories she told me. Those stories. Yes. To have Rebecca around now. But. I owed a hell of a lot to her. My heart felt big and my eyes began to fill.

I got to the park. It just didn't seem the same. Strange people were around who gave me strange looks from the corners of their eyes. I didn't feel too safe. There was the lake. It looked pretty dirty. Stuff floated around the edge. Syringes floated around the garbage. I made my way over the rustic bridge. It looked in a bad way. It didn't feel too secure. It needed a whole lot of work. Bubbles came up. The fish? I had a hamburger in my pocket, but my appetite had gone. I broke it up and threw some down. A great yellow form came up. It was followed by another and then another until the water was boiling with fish. They came up time and again to gulp down the bread in their great maws. The dreams I had as a kid came back when the fish with their great eyes leapt up at my exposed penis. Even now, it brought back that terrible feeling of dread. The hamburger had gone. The fish were satisfied and disappeared back to the bottom. I felt hungry and wished I'd kept back some of the hamburger for myself.

I'd been so preoccupied with the fish that I just hadn't heard someone approaching. I started as a hand was laid on my shoulder. "Okay, Ben, not at mass?" said a familiar voice. It was Jeanne's pa on police duty. I told him what had happened on the church steps. He went on to say that Jeanne was mighty sore with me and that it was darn clear to just about everyone that she was the girl in the ads and in the TV cartoon. The Quick Snax bar was jammed full of folk coming to get a glimpse of the Crackle, Snackle, Pop girl. "My Jeanne just hated the whole business, Ben; you've got to see that. Why the hell didn't you get to talking it over with her?" But that just isn't how it happens in advertising, certainly not this time.

"Well Ben," said Sean O'Dwyer laying his hand on my shoulder, "I've been around a long time and things haven't always worked out too well. Life can be a mighty tricky customer, mighty tricky. You just can't get away from that. Things seem to be going real well and then something hits you right out of the blue. Your world gets turned right upside down. You get knocked right off your feet. You just don't figure out how you're going to get to standing up again. Somehow, you get around to it. But things just ain't quite the same and you just have to get on with it." I could see what he was getting at. He'd never quite got over his wife's death because the priest just didn't approve of precautions. It was tough. It was tricky.

He gave my shoulder a comforting squeeze and advised me not to hang around too long with some pretty bad guys around. I watched him disappear – the man who ought to have been my father-in-law. But now, it just wasn't going to happen. I felt damned stupid. I'd thrown away what I wanted most in life – Jeanne with the light brown hair. Stupid – 'stupid'.

Somehow, I continued going to mass at the Holy Family. It did something for me. But I'd arrive late and stand at the back. Just being with that great crowd of people somehow got through to me deep down. And the ceremony with candles, incense and chants remembering a Jew who had come to a sticky end nearly two thousand years back moved me. He found life pretty tricky too like just about all who have come out of Adam's loins. That's what's life's about. Facing the tricky and somehow not letting it grind you into the dust. I'd loused things up badly with Jeanne. That's something I'd never get over. But how did that song go? 'Pick yourself up and dust yourself down and start all over again.' Okay, easy to sing but somehow you go on making the same old mistakes in a damned tricky world.

While I kept well away from Jeanne at mass on Sundays, I noted that from a number of Sundays she just wasn't there. I grabbed hold of Dan, a convert, one Sunday and asked him about Jeanne – maybe she was ill? He had picked up some of the problem over the advertising campaign. All he knew is that she'd gone away for a spell. I stood there on the step for some while as the folk came in for mass. Then the big outer door was banged tight. I stood there feeling empty – unwanted. I was all washed up. Where the hell could I go? What could I do? I belonged to no place. I sat on the steps watching a cat licking its arse. I envied the cat.

After that, things got a touch hazy. Wagstaffe got concerned as my stuff was not quite what it had been. He took me out to a diner and tried to get me to spill the beans. But I guess, I was too clammed up and somehow Wagstaffe was not quite the guy I could talk to. He started coming out with his religious stuff. He was some sort of minister in his spare time and ran something of a church some place. He kept on about God seeing me through and the Lord Jesus was with me and so on. It just didn't gel. He was getting nowhere fast with me. Abe, back at the apartment, had the sense to keep quiet. It was good just to have him around. He set up a still life group in the studio with a flower or two and some interesting objects. He sat down to sketch himself, and before long, I joined him and set up my easel. That was okay.

I got to eating my heart out over Jeanne. I had loused it all up pretty badly. There was no sign of her at Quick Snax. I got to hanging around at her home. Some of the family came and went but not Jeanne. So something came to me. I got on well with her brother Chuck. He was nuts about baseball and collected a lot of stuff about Babe Ruth, the best ever. He spent a lot of time up at Wingley Field where he got to helping out and that sort of thing. He'd had a few trails and they were quite impressed. Maybe he'd get taken on when he'd finished at high school. Anyway, I drove up to Wingley and found him doing something in the dressing room.

Usually, Chuck would be all over me at sight. I held out a bunch of flowers I'd brought for Jeanne. He snatched it from my hand and flung it to the other side of the room. He was just about as red as anyone can get with fury. "What the hell…" he began but was so angry he could hardly get a word out. "She's gone to be a nun," he blurted out. "Enclosed." He went on about Jeanne bringing them up when Mom died. She kept Dad going. Getting to see her was mighty hard. A few minutes behind a grill. "What's the darned use of that! And who's to blame? You stupid Yid making her the Crackle, Snackle, Pop girl. You arsehole." With that, he grabbed me by the collar and swung a mighty right hook at my chin. I took off, flying right across the floor and landed on the flat of my back. I lay dazed for a while. Somehow, I felt I'd deserved that. I'd loused up my own life and the life of the O'Dwyers. One of the medical team came in, helped me up. I staggered to the auto park and slouched into the pink Cadillac.

Jeanne in a convent? Now way beyond my stupid reach. I felt, as Chuck said, an arsehole. But I just couldn't get Jeanne out of my mind. Jeanne with that wonderful long brown hair blowing in the breeze and her white dress shining in the sunlight. Oh my God! Oh my God! And 'now'? Like a strict Jewess, a nun with her hair shaved right off? Maybe. A white dress changed for some black habit? Her face – her face – with those bright, bright eyes and her wonderful, wonderful smile – covered up by a veil. No – no – no – it just couldn't be like that. It just couldn't be.

I just went crazy with longing. Whenever I saw a girl in a white dress, I got to calling out Jeanne. I got some strange looks. They thought I was getting fresh or something. Once, I got my face slapped hard. I welcomed that. Like Chuck's punch, I deserved it. I had to be punished hard for being a stupid damned arsehole. It was hell. Abe quietly suggested I might see the physician. I took myself to the surgery and ended up with some pills. Maybe they took the edge of things. Who knows?

Rosa may well have picked up what was happening. She was the sort of dame who just would not be letting an opportunity pass her by. She would grab it in a big way. So she got to hovering around and suggesting a nice trip up the lake in the pink Caddy. I guess I was trying to get Jeanne out of my mind. But somehow, I gave in to Rosa pushing me into those trips up the lake. She'd be happy enough for me to make a few quick sketches of her, but as soon as I got down to some serious work, she'd start bitching. Then she got to suggesting that she pose in the nude. Somehow, I agreed. Those great hunks of flesh did nothing for my sexual appetite. But it made for interesting art. I worked quickly on a rough paper with colour washes built up with some body colour. She looked a whole lot more interesting unclothed with her great buttocks, thighs and breasts that hung down to her navel.

It was some time before I caught sight of a figure watching us from a distance. I could just make out that it was Wagstaffe. He was just out of Rosa's line of vision. He waved and made off. I shrugged my shoulders and wondered. Rosa posed quite well. I suppose she was getting what she wanted – my full attention. She had brought a fancy lunch pack and stayed unclothed, as it was pretty warm. She said the stuff might not be too kosher. I was not bothered. Then out came a bottle of chilled champagne. She kept my glass topped up and my head started to spin.

How the hell it all happened? I just don't know. Rosa got me down on the rug from the Caddy and things started to happen. I guess I just don't want to get into details. I didn't fancy Rosa but just in my mid-twenties. So I lost my virginity to a girl I didn't want. That's how it was. But Rosa, being Rosa and me being me, I got firmly hooked. It got into a habit of going out to the lake, painting and making for what some might pass as making love. I didn't take precautions, and I guess that Rosa, being Rosa, had fixed that. As it happened, I decided that we'd find new territory. We went up the Kanakee River with some swell scenery. The fall had just started and the trees were on the turn. The wind had a touch of chill so Rosa kept covered. I got her to pose on a rock with the river in the background.

I stopped for coffee. “Honey,” she said in an unusually quiet and serious voice. “Honey, there’s something I’ve got to be telling you.” I nodded wondering what the hell it could be. “I’ve missed,” she came back looking straight at me through her lens. I wrinkled my brow and asked what she meant. What had she missed? I just didn’t get the drift. She then went on. “I’ve missed what women get to having each month.” What the heck could that be? I guess I was pretty dumb. She went on to say that whatever she’d missed had happened twice. It got me even more confused. Then she spelt it out that it had something to do with getting pregnant and having a baby. “Our baby! Our baby! Isn’t that just great Ben!” I didn’t feel too sure.

I looked down the river where it curved around a bend into the distance. I wished for a rowboat and to go that way and just get to never coming back again. The urge to go to the john gripped me. I slipped away to relieve myself. As the flow rustled down into last fall’s dried leaves, I wondered what would happen now. I got back. Rosa grasped my hand and looked a look into my eyes. “You know what that means, honey?” I looked bemused. She explained, “It means you’re going to have to buy me an engagement ring and book a quick wedding. Won’t that be just great?”

“Don’t look so worried, honey. We’re just going to be the happiest couple in the whole of Chicago. You just see.” I thought otherwise. She got her great arms around me and held me close to her great fat tits. Her perfume went right up my nostrils, and I gave an almighty great sneeze. She recoiled, and I got myself free.

Looking back, Rosa had set the stage and made sure I was going to play the part. I threw my gear into the back of the Caddy and headed back to Chicago where Rosa directed me to the fanciest jeweller in town. Rosa took over in a big way. Somehow, I think she’d fixed the assistant. She wanted a sapphire ring set in pearls. A tray came out, and there it was, sparkling at the centre. “That’s it!” she exclaimed. She put the ring on her finger and held it up for the whole store to see. A guy looked at me with a touch of pity. A dame smirked. I was dead worried. I was getting a good salary but not the sort of dough that would pay for the ring. Rosa gave me an unwelcome squeeze and told me that her pa ran an account at the place. So that would be okay.

With the ring firmly on her finger, put there by her and not me, we headed for the Stein homestead. Joe and his wife were hanging around looking casual. I guess Rosa had got the jewellery assistant to ring ahead of us. So she breezed in waving the ring. "Ma and Pa!" she cried out. "Don't you think this is the cutest little ring? Ben has asked me to be Mrs Benjamin Traumann. What do you think of that?" I felt like I'd been run over by a darned heavy truck and left flattened on the highway. Mrs Stein, who was a touch larger than her daughter, gave me a huge bear hug and a wet kiss on the lips. I nearly threw up into her sumptuous cleavage. Joe rescued me, shook me by the hand and clapped me on the shoulder.

Joe said something about being proud to be linked with the Traumanns. But Ma Stein dripped all over me saying what a good Jewish wife Rosa would make. It was all staged, but I didn't figure it out at the time. I will pass over the celebration dinner at some fancy place where the rabbis had not placed their kosher certificate in the window. My Traumann grandfather picked up something of the vibes but didn't say too much. Abe, as usual, didn't come out with good advice but managed to convey that somehow he wasn't too happy about the way things were going.

It was taken for granted that I would go along with the arrangements. The Steins, supporting Rosa, were all for the marriage taking place quickly. Long engagements were, in their view, not on the agenda. Somehow, I was just taken for a fall guy who was going to go right along with whatever arrangements they wanted. I guess I was just carried along with the tide. Joe Stein had found a place up as near to Forest Lake as a Jew could get. It was quite a fancy pad that was to be a wedding present. At least, it was near the lake and it presented quite a lot of opportunities for art. That was at least something.

A suite had been booked at the Waldorf. A place that made me want to run a mile or two. But that was it. An upmarket rabbi had been fixed to tie the knot. I figured that Joe was mighty pleased to get Rosa off his hands. Somehow, it may be that he had it on mind to get me on the board of G. S. and G. He dropped a few hints. If that happened, I just wouldn't be getting around to painting sunlight falling on a white wall.

No way. I wasn't in business to sit on boards as I'd made it clear to Grandpa Traumann. That's not how I wanted my cookie to crumble, but that's how it was shaping up. I felt trapped.

I found myself just letting my feet take over and take me around the city. Just anywhere. I needed to think. How could I get myself out of this? No way had I planned this. And why the hell had I let myself get into the back of the Caddy and get Rosa pregnant; I'd made a whole lot of stupid mistakes. Why the hell had I made those darned drawings of Rosa and then got her into the Traumann ads? 'Men date dames in Traumann frames!' Shit! But that's how it is – life deals you a hand from the pack. Sometimes you get a pretty good hand and then you get to playing it not too well. I guess I just hadn't figured out the play of the cards and now I was just having to pay for it pretty badly. Shit! So you play your cards badly and you just end up for the rest of your life paying. Shit!

As I got to wandering around the city, I found myself in the old neighbourhood. My feet took me to the synagogue where I made my bar mitzvah. I wondered if the old rabbi was still around and if he still told the boys not to touch themselves in the wrong way. I guessed he'd loused up quite a few kids over the years. I reckoned he'd have to pay for it before he got into Abraham's bosom or wherever. His house was still there. It looked the worse for wear, but his nameplate was right there by the door – Dr Lionel Mosewitch. I found myself ringing the bell and hoping he was not around. But he was. He stood there looking at me through those great thick lenses. His eyes looked thousands of miles away. He had aged quickly. His thick, black beard was getting pretty grey. He looked at me in that sour and unwelcoming way that I remembered some years back.

"Vell? Vat you vanting?" he asked in his thick Eastern European accent. I told him I just wanted to talk. "Vell – if you must." I followed him down the dark passage heavy with old furniture. Pictures hung everywhere with scenes and people from the dark past. He led me into the study lined with shelves of dreary looking volumes. The place was cluttered with Jewish stuff. What I was seeing gave me ideas for still life. The room smelt like it just hadn't been cleaned for one hell of a long time. He sat me in a chair that had been made for a guy somewhere around seven feet. I perched on the edge.

The rabbi sat in a swivel chair and looked at me like the time when he told me not to touch myself in the wrong way like that guy Onan. "So?" I spilled the beans about getting Rosa into trouble and that I just didn't want to get under the canopy with her. It would not be a love match. He stroked his beard and looked thoughtful. "How you know she's expecting a child? Are you knowing the child comes from you?" I said that she'd told me. He almost smiled. To my surprise, he burst into song, just a little off key. "Never, never trust a woman, you'll be sorry if you do or she'll just make a monkey out of you." I smiled. I asked him what I should do. The marriage was just a month ahead. He quizzed me about how I felt about Rosa. I told him. He pushed me about sexual relations. I told him that somehow I'd got trapped into it. He exploded. "Trapped? TRAPPED? You ver trapped? Vat sort of Jew are you? Jews don't get themselves trapped! Vat do you think God, blessed be He, did by freeing us from slavery? Do you think that he got us free to get trapped? Nein?"

He went on in this tone. Somehow, I got to thinking he was dead right. I'd got myself trapped when I needed to be free. I shuffled my feet much as I'd done years back as a bar mitzvah kid. He went on to say that if I'd got a woman pregnant, we were what he called one flesh. That meant a proper Jew had to get with the woman under the canopy and make things right. We sat silent for quite some time. Then he pointed to two mirrors on opposite walls, facing each other. He spoke. "See the mirrors? You know what Judah ha Nasi said? If a man find himself not knowing what to do – let him first make supplication to the Blessed One and then take two mirrors. He must place them apart and to face each other. Let him go to the mirror on the right and tell the man he sees there his trouble. Then let him go to the other mirror and tell the man he sees there the trouble. Then let the man sit between the two and see into both. He will then see himself stretching away into the courts of heaven and let the reflections speak to him." The rabbi said that is what he did when faced with a problem and invited me to do the same. I did.

So I sat there between the two mirrors. I reflected on the reflection of myself going on and on into infinity – into eternity. It hit me; I had the choice to be free or to be a slave. The rabbi, after a time, came back with 'So?'. I told him that I had to choose freedom or slavery. The rabbi went on, "So if you choose slavery, what will that do to you? Hey? Freedom? Vilderness! Slavery – safe. Vilderness – danger – uncertainty. Ve Jews, vat do we choose? Father Abraham, what did he choose? Moses and our people, what did they choose? My son, you must go and think."

At the door, Rabbi Mosewitch laid his hand on my shoulder. "The lady is Rosa Stein." I looked surprised. "Joseph Stein is a cousin. I am asked to take the marriage." He patted me on the back. He just knew that I just didn't have it in me to choose freedom. As I turned to go, he caught me by the sleeve. "Von more fing. Benjamin Traumann, in the heart is a little child that's vet his pants. You are no man until you love that child."

I made my way back to the park where I walked with Rebecca. I looked right down into the murky waters of the lake. No fish came up. I guessed I'd have to dredge up a whole lot of love for that little child in me if I was going to escape from Rosa Stein. I just didn't have too much time. In a month, Rosa Stein was going to make sure she was Rosa Traumann. A cold wave swept over my heart.

That month passed a damned sight too quickly. Somehow, a strange calm had come over me since the visit to the rabbi. I knew I was trapped and that I just lacked the guts to break out. Time was not on my side to change the scenario. I would just have to play the part. Maybe as I got to loving that little kid in me, I'd find a way to get out of the trap. Maybe.

The Fitzwilliam Hotel had the best facilities in town for a glitzy Jewish wedding. In spite of its name, it had been acquired by the Grossmans, my ma's family. By this time, my Traumann grandmother had died and my grandfather had got senile and was in some care place. The T & G business was now in the hands of my Grossmann cousins; they kept the optics side of things, but they had also diversified into property and were making it big. Anyway, the Fitzwilliam had become the fanciest place in town and had put the Waldorf in the shade.

Just about anyone who was anyone in the Jewish community was there on the day and quite a few goys. I dead calm had come over me. I was going to get under the canopy with Rosa Stein who just about revolted me. Abe Grosnevski helped me on with my tux. He was coming to support me.

So there was the cuppah set up in the grounds with the stars starting to peep out. A musical trio were playing whatever. The guests stood around looking mighty happy. I still felt dead calm, but deep down, it felt like a lump of ice was making itself felt. Well-meaning folk slapped my back, grasped my hand and wished me luck. Rosa's ma came up and gave me a great bear hug and got lipstick on my face. She got out a fancy handkerchief to wipe it off leaving a red smudge.

Rabbi Mosewitch entered wearing a big black gown. It looked like he'd had his beard trimmed. It gave me some assurance that he didn't despise me too much for not crossing the Red Sea. My eye wandered around the crowd of guests. An air of impatience moved around. The bride, her privilege, was late. Folk started looking at their watches. The rabbi was frowning just a little. My eye caught a familiar face. It was Wagstaffe. He raised his hand and wiggled his fingers. Somehow, I got the feeling that he was not a guy to be trusted. Okay, he was a goy and goys sometime took a little understanding. But somehow with Wagstaffe…?

So it was that five minutes became ten and then fifteen. Folk were getting really restive. A touch of hope welled up in me. Maybe she'd pulled out? Okay, it was not good for a woman to look too eager on her wedding day. You just didn't arrive dead on time. No. Rosa's ma was getting worked up. Her face was red, and she started mopping it with that lacy handkerchief. Her make-up was getting messed up. Then somewhere about twenty minutes after scheduled time, a signal came and the trio struck up.

Rosa was a big girl, but as she appeared on her pa's arm, she looked like Mount Washington after a very heavy snowfall. The great-hooped skirt was so wide that Joe had to lean over so she could take his arm. The puffed sleeves made her arms look mighty big. I wondered what Cherry Greenberg of Yomtov would have made of that! Then entered a great retinue of pageboys and bridesmaids. It was unbelievable. Photographers were letting off their flashguns just about everywhere. I felt that I was in some sort of Walter Mitty scenario. A crazy dream where I was being put in an impossible situation and folk falling about laughing at me. Then there she was right at my side under the cuppah. She got hold of my hand and gave it one hell of a squeeze and looked up at me through the fanciest T & G frames sparkling with sequins. It added to the mad surrealist setting. What would Dali have made of this?

So it was that the vows were made. We remembered somewhere along the line Abraham and Sarah. We shared the glass of wine. I smashed it on the ground, and they all cried out 'Mazel tov'. Somehow, I guessed I just wasn't going to get that. The reception? It happened with great tables loaded with food that I just didn't want to eat. There were the speeches. God, the speeches! Rosa nudged me to respond. I choked and gagged. Water was produced. I was let off the hook. God knows what I was expected to say. But whatever it was, it just didn't get said. Abe laid his hand on my shoulder, and the rabbi gave me a sympathetic glance. I made a lot of the choking fit and sat down while Rosa floated around. Out of my eye, I noted her spending quite some time with Wagstaffe. They were getting pretty close and intimate. Somehow, I got to wondering.

Joe Stein took me aside and sympathised over the choking fit. He presented me with an envelope with air tickets and hotel reservations for the honeymoon with a mighty big cheque. We were booked in for two days at the Fitzwilliam before taking the honeymoon flight. The marriage night was not exactly one of sexual ecstasy. So I'll pass right over that. When I got down to examining the honeymoon tickets, they proved to be for three weeks in where the hell? Israel. 'Israel!' Okay, that's where we all came from way back, so they say. But – but? I'm glad I'm a Jew – yes – but with Jews all over the place speaking God knows what. No, thanks! Rosa was mighty excited. It was, of course, her idea. "Just think of it, Ben, we're going to our very own homeland. Just think of that!" Somehow, I just couldn't share her enthusiasm.

In the pack of airline tickets, hotel reservations was a whole lot of introductions to God knows how many of the Stein tribe who had pitched their tents in Israel. So we found ourselves in an aircraft at LaGuardia waiting for take-off. Rosa was not quite her bouncy self. She was dead quiet and pretty uneasy. We were, of course, in the first-class section. This gave us room. Rosa hardly fitted into the seat. She looked white and nervous as she looked at me through her T & G frames. They were a deep red to match her outfit. She grasped my hand so hard it hurt. "Honey, I'm dead scared of flying. I hate it." I have to be frank; I'd made a number of inland flights for the agency but not a long haul like this. She went on, "What happens if we stall right up there? I just hate being shut right in and not being able to get off." What could I say? I tried to assure her that we were scheduled to stop off at Heathrow before the last leg to Tel Aviv. "Honey," she continued, "I'm scared – real scared." But no way was Rosa going to be assured.

I forced myself to take her hand. It was like holding a bunch of bananas dipped in treacle. She thrust her head into my chest and almost smothered me with her bulk. I could hardly breathe. Her fear got over to me, and I began to feel claustrophobic. The engines started to rev up and the aircraft started moving slowly towards the runway. The moment that I dreaded arrived. The engines revved up hard and the aircraft shook like it was going to fall to pieces. Outside it was dark. Then suddenly like an arrow, the aircraft shot off down the runway at speed. Rosa made noises I just couldn't make out. The airport lights blurred. Then the outside world heeled over and we were up. That was the moment when Rosa was badly sick over my suit. I had to live with that sweet-sour smell until I got a change in Jerusalem.

Those six hours crossing the pond was hell. Okay, the stewardess had helped us to clean up. She sprayed us with something that smelt worse than vomit. We were coming into Heathrow at a bit after midnight. I was somewhat interested in getting my first peek of Europe. Down below, the lights of the city sparkled. Traffic could just be seen moving along the roads. The lights flashed up overhead to instruct us to get our seatbelts fastened. I struggled with Rosa's.

I reckon that flying's just about the most uncomfortable way of getting around even first class. You get there in this long narrow tube. You struggle with a tray-full of food you don't really want to eat. To get down to the john, you have to lurch along the aisle. I guess flying's not the sort of thing you do unless you can help it. After that stop-off at Heathrow, we took off for the last leg to Ben Gurion Airport at Tel Aviv. Another five hours in the long narrow tube. Rosa slipped into sleep covered by a blanket brought by the stewardess. I drifted in and out of sleep.

I felt relieved when the pilot announced that we would be touching down at Ben Gurion in fifteen minutes. He gave out that the weather was cool and showery. I expressed my surprise to a guy on the other side. He told me that they were coming into winter and that up in Jerusalem they get snow. I just couldn't believe it. I gave Rosa a nudge to rouse her. The time was coming up to six o'clock. Together, we looked down into the sweep of the bay at Tel Aviv. Rosa began to liven up. "Looks just a bit like Florida," she remarked sleepily.

All that reminded me of Florida when we got out of the airport were a few palm trees. It was damn cold, wet and noisy with folk fighting to get cabs. God, why the hell hadn't Joe Stein booked us in at Florida? We had just about too much luggage for comfort. I like to travel light, but Rosa had to bring just about the whole of her wardrobe and a bit more! It was all I could do to get the stuff off the carousel and on to one trolley. Rosa was still pretty dazed and switched off.

We got outside and joined the crowds fighting for cabs. "Can you get one for just ourselves, honey?" But honey just couldn't. The cabs were crammed full of folk and their luggage going up to Jerusalem. I reckoned we'd have a mighty uncomfortable trip. I went up the rank waving a great fist full of dollars to a guy just pulling in. I caught the glint in his eye. I did some quick explaining about a lot of luggage and a sick wife. He seemed to understand English pretty well. I got Rosa and the trolley up to the cab fast and pushed Rosa in. Then a whole lot of guys in dark clothes and black hats tried to pile in. I guess I've heard a lot of screaming in my time. But this was like a whole lot of banshees having a bad day. The driver, in some language I couldn't figure, got them off. Soon we were off through the streets of Tel Aviv.

What I saw just didn't grab me. The streets sprawled just about everywhere with shops and dwellings not too easy on the eye. I figured if this was a place that Jewish folk raved about as the Promised Land, well, then I could think of better places. Now if Joe had picked Florida, Paris or even London. But this dump? We passed on through the outskirts and started going through citrus plantations. Rosa started to liven up and made her usual inane remarks.

I stole a look at the driver. He looked pretty dark and had fuzzy hair. He caught my look and asked, "American? First time here?" I told him. His accent was thick, and I asked him if he were Jewish. He gave out a great laugh and spat out of the window. I got the message. "So?" I asked him.

"Me? I tell you Allah is good. You think He make me, Ishmael, a Jew? If Ishmael choose to be pig or Jew – I choose pig!" He spat again out of the window. I asked him what he was. "Me Palestinian – Arab – that's me." I came back, surprised that there were Arabs in Israel. "But this is our land. You Americans know nothing. The Jews came from Europe and took our land. What do the Americans and the British say? Okay – the Bible says it's your land – okay take it. What happens to my people? They turn us off." Again, he spat.

We drove on up through rugged terrain with wooded slopes toward Jerusalem. He suddenly pulled in by what looked like a garbage tip. "You see that?" He pointed toward what looked like a rusty truck. He explained, "That truck is a Jewish armoured car going up to Jerusalem. Who shot it up? We did – Palestinians in 1947. I tell you, my friend, when this land was Palestine, we Arabs and Jews lived like brothers. The Turks ruled then. Then the British came." He said the word like a bad taste and spat again. "You know what? After the big war, the Jews come from Europe and make big trouble for the British so they get out fast." I asked him what then. "The United Nations take over and divide the land. Some for them and some for us akrabeirta!" he cursed in Arabic. "So the Jews come with their guns and push us off the land. We fight for Jerusalem. We have them trapped in the Holy City. So supplies come from Tel Aviv in convoy. So we shoot them up. So the Jews leave the trucks on this road. You understand, my friend?"

Rosa was getting impatient and gave me a big nudge and urged me to shut him up. But I wanted to hear him out. I wanted to know. "I tell you, my friend, the European Jews grab everything. They think Allah has made them a present of this land. They want to see us go away. But this is our home. My family came from Galilee – a beautiful place. You know what the Jews did? One night, they come with men in trucks. They get out their guns and force us to leave our homes and not come back. So all get out men, women and kids. Is that right?"

"I guess not," I had to say.

"You guess not! I tell you this, your United States, what do you do? You send plenty of dollars to the Jews to help them steal our land. Americans!" Ishmael spat again out of the cab window. I was feeling uncomfortable and in need of the john. Rosa banged me hard in the ribs. I didn't care for the cold mist coming down through the trees. I suggested we ought to move on. Ishmael had got the bit between his teeth. He swung right around and grabbed my shoulder hard and pulled me close. His words still ring in my ears. "You know what the filthy Jews want? They want us Arabs right out. What you Americans call the bum's rush. How do they do it? You see with guns, tanks, and bombs. How do they get these things? They get them from America. What do you call yourselves? Land of the free? Okay – fine for you but what of us Arabs?"

The guy was getting some of my sympathy. I got the feeling it was just about time we hit the road. Rosa was getting mighty impatient and getting ready to make herself felt. "Okay, okay. Just skip the rest. I'm getting damned cold. Let's get going." The driver gave her a sharp look from the corner of his eye, started up the engine and let in the clutch.

By the time we got to the Ha Tov hotel, Rosa's temper was getting in tune with the weather. The low mist and cloud had turned day into dusk. Automobiles had their headlamps full on. The sidewalks shone like glass. It was not too warm. Ishmael was not in a good mood. His body language was not very agreeable. He dumped the baggage on the sidewalk took a whole lot of dollar bills and sped off into the gloom. It was not a good start to a honeymoon of a lifetime.

Rosa started weighing into me about what sort of a husband was I who just couldn't handle a cab driver. Then she got going on about the sort of a dump her pa had booked us into. I must confess I agreed. The Ha Tov just didn't look too good. Our baggage was getting wet in the sidewalk. I went into the dimly lit foyer. Not too much glitz. It just looked like the place was deserted. I called out. A little old guy emerged from some back room. He looked at me, raised his hands and shrugged his shoulders. "You vant?" I showed him the reservation. He looked worried, thumbed through a register of some sort. Nodded. I pointed to the luggage outside. His body language indicated a problem. At that moment, some guy who looked like he had muscles came down on the creaky elevator. He picked up the problem. "Okay, I'll give you a hand." Together, we lugged the stuff up to our room.

In the meantime, Rosa started giving the old guy at the desk the works. I felt pretty sorry for him. There he was, a frail old fellow with just about the saddest face you can imagine. A few people had come into the foyer and listened at a safe distance. I took her arm and motioned her towards the elevator. She let out a final burst at the old guy. He gave a sad smile and replied, "My dear, this is Jerusalem. We have our problems."

So started just about the worst honeymoon that's ever been. It took some time to get our stuff sorted out in a room that was not particularly well appointed. Rosa's invective got aimed straight at me. I just sat in one of the threadbare chairs and let it all flow over me. Then she then decided to ring her folk back home. I'll spare you the account of her trying to get through. It didn't improve her temper. The hour in Chicago was not exactly social. Joe Stein was pretty put out by Rosa's whining. She was angling to come back pronto. Joe stalled her. She ended by banging down the receiver. "I hate this lousy dump," she protested taking herself off to the shower. Of course, the shower was not in good order. The water came through looking not too clear and on the cool side of tepid.

I got myself cleaned up and into a fresh suit. Rosa had got herself onto the bed and into a deep sleep. I felt damned hungry and decided to see if I could find a diner somewhere around. The little old guy in reception apologised that they could not provide meals and directed me to a diner. Okay, I guess I've eaten better, but when you're feeling famished, well then, you don't get to being too critical. The waiter asked in a thick accent if I'd enjoyed the meal. I told him it was fine and gave him quite a tip. His thanks was just a touch too embarrassing.

When I got back, the old guy invited me to his room at the back. I guess he was lonely. His room was full of too much stuff. Old Jewish things hung from the wall and littered just about everywhere. It was all far too heavy, oppressive and claustrophobic. He sat me in the one comfortable chair and perched himself on the edge of his bed. He invited me to indulge in a little something. He produced a bottle with a thick golden liquid. It had Hebrew characters on the label. He asked me if I could read it. I must confess that what Hebrew I had learnt had got just a bit rusty.

His fingers moved over the square characters as I spelt out 'Halleluiah'. I knew the word – 'God be praised!'

We sat in silence sipping the thick, sweet stuff. Maybe it wasn't too much to my taste, but it was soothing. It helped me to settle the tough, greasy meat I'd consumed in the diner. You know how it is, sometimes you get to eating something and wishing to hell you hadn't. That's how it was. The Halleluiah made me feel just a little better inside.

Max filled up my glass again. His accent was thick. But I was used to thick accents from some of the Jewish community back home. He told me his name, Max Steinberge. He invited me to use his first name. "Please call me Max. I have not too many friends, you see." He explained in Israel people say what they feel and think. No beating about bushes. You have to be direct. People who suffer cannot waste time wrapping things up. I understood.

"I think your wife is giving you some trouble?" I had to agree. "How you marry her? You don't marry a woman who makes your life a trouble. You know what it says in Proverbs? 'It is better to live on the housetop than in a broad room with a contentious woman.' I have to tell you, Ben, you have a woman like that." I nodded. "You had…?" At this, he waved his delicate hands, clucked his tongue moving his head from side to side. He sighed and told me that she was not a woman to be trusted.

"What do English say? Leading up garden path? She will do that." He went on to tell me that I had soul – I was sensitive – that Rosa would do me much harm. I would have to put a fence right around my heart. To keep her at a distance. I figured that would not be too easy. But I guess, he was dead right. I'd just have to keep my distance and watch out. Rosa was a pretty tricky dame. Pretty tricky.

Max moved over to the wall and took down the heavily carved and gilded frame that hung there. He sat for a while balancing it on his knee. He held it up for me to see. It was a faded photograph of a family group. I looked at the distinguished looking young man and then at Max. He nodded. He told me that he had a good life in front of him. His wife was very beautiful. He had three lovely children. He was going places in his profession. I could see that he had a lot that bugged him. "I can see that you can be trusted with a man's heart. My wife, Ruth, was all that a man could vant. She looked beautiful and she was beautiful inside." He went on to say that they could just sit in silence. Words were not needed. "You cannot be like that with your wife, Bennie."

He went on to one of the children. "Rueben was such a clever child. He asked many questions. He forgot nothing. He would have gone far." He pointed to another child, Sarah. "She was just like her mother. She was full of love and warmth. It is catching. How is it said? Infectious? She would have made a good Jewish wife." He then pointed to the baby. It was Moshe who had just been circumcised. "No basket for Moshe. No Pharaoh's daughter to take him in."

I asked him about himself. He sighed. "Here I was older than you, Ben, but young still. I had studied medicine. God, blessed be he, gave me a good brain. My university asked me back to teach. That suited me. Life was good and I had started a book on my subject – psychiatry. The inner life interested me. So all was well. I had this lovely wife with fine children. We lived in a fine house in a good quarter. We had many friends. Many were goys. So my book got published and sold well. I was in demand to lecture in Europe and the States. This was my promised land.

"I had to lecture in Leipzig. My host was Lothar Schmidt, one of my goy colleagues. He was a big blond man. Very German. But a good friend. We sat and talked after a good meal. A call came. Lothar returned looking worried. Stormtroopers had gone through my university. Jewish staff and students had been arrested. Women and children also. Of course, we could see storm clouds coming. But it was a long way off and what could I do? My cappel. Rebecca's work. See her stitches. Grapes, pomegranates, figs all over! Fine work – yes?"

Max went on, "I went mad with anxiety. I wanted to leave then. I struggled hard. Lothar grabbed me and gave me an injection. Lothar did not support the Nazis, and he had good contacts. He knew for me to return home would be the end for me. You know what? He drove me across Europe to Cherbourg, put me in charge of some Jewish doctors and got me on a boat to New York."

"You can guess how it was with me. I longed for my dear family. One of the Jewish doctors kept an eye on me and gave me sedation. Somehow, I cursed Lothar. I wanted my family and die with them. What of my life now? Hey? New York was like hell. Sirens going and crowds struggling. They put me in a wheelchair. They gave me much care. But what does that mean to a dead man? Nein? Lothar's contacts were waiting for me. I suppose it helped, as I was a name in the medical world. They got me into a Jewish clinic. A doctor came in to talk with me most days. He got on to my speciality, birth trauma. I had worked out that birth is something we do not get over. We spend much time in our mother's womb where we feel secure and then pushed out into a hostile world. We are rejected – separated. We yell. We are in the cold. Alone – alone. Who can get over that terrible time? Who?" Max's words were burnt into my memory. What he was saying rang bells.

Max went on, "So our lives are spent trying to get back to that sense of warmth – belonging. Yes, getting back to our Promised Land. Ja? Losing my Rebecca and children was like the birth trauma. My Promised Land had gone. Like the newborn I screamed and yelled. The past with its blessings had gone. Now I was where? In a foreign land. I was just a helpless infant. They did what they could at the clinic. Who paid? I never knew?

"It may be that in time I improved. Just a little? Then a familiar face appeared. It was Lothar with his mass of blond hair. I could not believe. He bent over me with much concern with tears filling his blue eyes. He put his great arms around me and hugged me to himself. What comfort. I shall never forget." I understood. I remembered those great hugs that Rebecca gave me as a child. How I longed to be wanted. To be valued after the bad time my mother gave me. Rebecca made me feel right. I was okay. That's just what Max wanted way back.

"Lothar must have stayed some time. He came every day and walked me around the grounds. The blood started to flow again. He talked about the good times we had when we were students together. Some of my strength came back. I asked him about my university and Ruth and the children. My house had been taken by a goy family. He had got a few things including the picture. My family had been taken away with other Jews. But he knew no more. Lothar helped me to get back to where?

"We Jews have the fortune to have the psalms. You know the line, 'Be strong and let your heart take courage, all who wait in hope for the Lord.' That helps me."

I asked him what happened to Lothar. Max told me that he had been arrested. He was involved in a plot against Hitler. He ended with others at the end of a length of piano wire. A cruel death for a good man. I thought of that painting by Chagall of the White Crucifixion. Max said Kaddish for his friend Lothar.

"Somehow," Max continued, "I got drawn into the work of the clinic. It was run by a Jewish charity. They had patients who had also escaped from Nazi Germany. Like me, they found the trauma too much. How could me, Max Steinberge, the expert on birth trauma not face my own trauma? But Max Steinberge is human! They found it hard to understand the patients in the clinic. I was allowed to prescribe drugs but counselling then was not possible for me. How could I lead others through pain and suffering while my own wounds were open? Could I, in spite of my theories, be of help to those who had gone through so much? Nein! Nein!

"The clinic was the place for me to be. I did routine medical work and just a little counselling. The war ended. The charity set up a clinic in Tel Aviv for the refugees who came flooding in. It was a busy time and helped to lift me up just a little. A patient recognised me. He had been one of my students. His face showed the marks of pain. On his arm was a number put there when in Auschwitz. He was able to tell me what happened to Ruth and our dear children. On the day they took all Jews in the university and many, including my student, arrived at Auschwitz. Women and children for the gas chamber and men to work. He was put to clearing the chambers. It was there that he saw my poor wife. It was an experience that haunted him. It brought him to the clinic." Max had to stop for a while.

"Professor Ruben Hirsch came from the medical faculty of the Hebrew University in Jerusalem. He wanted me on his staff to teach. He was kind. He understood. I was given a room looking down over the wild Judean wilderness on the eastern side of the campus. It was not pretty, but it suited my mood. They gave me much material. Copies of my books. I read and read. But what? They were written by another man at another time. Not me. Could I still go on to teach? What did the dynamics of the human psyche mean now in the face of the dark face of…? I prepared a few lectures for a foundation course. But what could I say? Really say?

"I stood at the rostrum. The eager students gave me what? Standing ovation? They knew my reputation. I gazed out at the eager young faces. To be lectured by, yes, Max Steinberg! It was high summer. The eager faces became glazed, heads nodded and notebooks put to one side. Max Steinberg had become a myth, a legend. I had to tell them I could not go on. That trauma was my special interest, but the trauma of my wife and children in a gas chamber had overcome me. I had died with them. As I stepped down, they stood in silence.

"Somehow a room was found for me here at the Ha Tov. I started to help. Why not? So I have to live with my trauma as best I can. I no longer belong to anyone. My home is nowhere. I lost so much. I have to live as many have to live with loss, with emptiness, with nothing."

Max Steinberg's words burnt deep. I got to wondering why the hell we human beings get to treating each other so badly. Wars, gas chambers and just downright plain folk tearing each other apart. Why the hell? What was that crazy thing that gets right into us and gets us tearing ourselves apart? I remembered that story Rebecca told me as a kid, of Eve taking whatever, giving some to Adam and something bad getting into them. And their sons get to fighting real bad so that bad guy, Cain, gets to killing his own brother, Abel. What does that explain? Maybe Max could throw some light on it. Maybe.

I got back to the room. Rosa was in bed looking pretty ill. "Okay?"

"The hell I'm not okay. King-sized two-ender." What could I say? Sorry? What the hell's the use of that? "Do something!" But what could I do? I walked around the dingy room with my hands in the air. I could paint pictures but fixing a two-ender? She treated me to the side of her tongue that was pretty rough, eased herself off the bed and headed for the john. No way was I going to get into the bed. So I fixed something up on the couch and found myself a blanket. It was cold and I shivered as I tried to make myself comfortable. It was a hell of a night. As I slipped off, Rosa got out to take herself to the john. I twisted and turned all night. Suddenly, I woke with the sun shining right into my eyes. I got out. Rosa was well away and making noises that were not too romantic.

The sun drew me out onto the balcony. The rain clouds were going. It was still chill. Below I could see the streets of Jerusalem now getting busy. I got out the map of the city given me by Max. I made out the old city with its wall and a dome of some place in the centre. It glittered with gold. [1964 restored] The air smelt good. I was getting excited and thinking about sketching. There was a hell of a lot here I could get to work on. A lot of what Rebecca told me as a kid came back. This was the city of King David. This is where his son, Solomon, got to building a great temple. It was here that King Herod built a really big temple that the Romans came and burnt and kicked us Jews out. I got pretty mad at that. We Jews kicked out of our city by a bunch of foreigners. Now we'd got our city back again, and it was damned well going to stay that way. My Jewish genes kicked in a big way!

Rosa slept on. I wrote a note and took myself off into the city. It pleases a foot-loose guy like me to wander through some new place just moseying around. I had a small sketchbook in my pocket. I took off from the Ha Tov in the Jaffa Road. There was a hell of a lot of activity around. Folk going about doing whatever the hell they had to do. There were buses packed to the doors going wherever. I hung around at one of the stops. I listened to whatever it was they were speaking. Some sounded just a little like the Yiddish my folk spoke when I was a kid. I picked up a word or so. When a bus came, it looked as if it had been around a hell of a long time, the folk pushed like mad things to get on. I moved away.

I struggled through the crowds on the sidewalk and off into the side roads. There was not too much glitter around the place. They were just about as run down as a place could be. There was garbage just about everywhere so I had to watch where I placed my feet. And the cats. It was a cat's paradise fighting over the garbage. Overhead strings of washing hung from one side to the other. It just didn't look too fancy.

As I passed through the streets, things started to take on a somewhat different look. There were guys in big homburg hats and some in fantastic round fur hats. They wore sidelocks and long black coats with faces to match if you could penetrate the beards. A banner stretched across the road in Hebrew and even English. It informed me that I was entering Mea Shearim. There was a poster on a wall. Some of it was in English. It looked like you had to be very careful how you got to conduct yourself in the neighbourhood.

A guy came up to me wearing one of these hats. In an accent I recognised, he asked me if I needed help. He was surprised that I couldn't figure out the notice. In a sharp tone, he told me that there were just too many Jews like me who just didn't know how to behave like a Jew. He asked me what I'd learnt about the Torah and if I'd made my bar mitzvah and so on. I shuffled my feet in just a little unease. He went on about our people getting free of Egypt and God, Blessed be He, giving us the Promised Land and the Holy City. He grabbed me by the shoulder and gave me a shake. "We are a free people – don't forget. We are free!" Somehow, he didn't look too free to me. He went on to say he was raised in Brooklyn. His folk came over from Poland, and they saw that he had a proper Jewish education. He knew what it meant to be a proper Jew and keep the traditions laid down by Moses.

He grabbed me by the shoulder and told me he was going to take me to a real Jewish home. I was going to have to see it if I wanted to or not. I guess I didn't! He dragged me along the sidewalk through some pretty dismal-looking passages and up into a cramped apartment in a broken-down block.

He noted my look as I eyed the 'real Jewish home'. The furniture looked like it had come off a dump some place. I didn't feel too comfortable in the chair he'd pushed me into. I got to wondering what sort of creatures might be living there. He went on to say the place before they took over was full of darned Arabs. "Palestinians – Philistines. So we gave them the bum's rush. So we took over. In time, we'll push these Arabs right into the sea." I asked about compensation. He gave a scornful laugh. "What did you learn at yeshivah? The Holy One made us free and gave us this present of the Promised Land and the holy city of Jerusalem. This is our land flowing with milk and honey. So we get to giving these people compensation? You've got to be kidding!"

A woman came out from a dark hole that passed for a door. Her head was covered in a kerchief. Like my mother and Rebecca, I reckoned she had a shaved head. I could never figure this out. Did Moses command this? If so, why didn't the Creator make women bald from birth? I started to get up but the guy looked sharp. She set a tray with two steaming cups of dark liquid and a few cookies on the table. "Moshe," he said, "let me tell you a man just doesn't look at another man's wife. It's not modest. Remember." I gulped down the hot liquid as best I could. I guessed the folk around here could not run to real coffee. Reuben Teshuvah took out an ancient pocket watch on a long chain, checked the time and snapped back the cover. He informed me that he had to get to the synagogue. Back on the sidewalk, he made his parting shot. "Just remember, Moshe, the Promised Land will make you a different person." I wasn't too sorry to see his back.

So I carried on through the narrow streets and passages. I had just no idea where I might be going. But that was fine. It suited me. There are far too many who get some idea into their heads as to what they want and where they want to be and end up lost. So why not just let life just come and get the most out of what it brings? I came to an area that looked like a demolition site. There was a bunch of young kids around. Teenagers. They yelled at me something I couldn't make out. Somehow, they didn't look too Jewish. "Hi, Yehudi!" they called. I explained I spoke English. "We speak English good," they explained. I must confess I didn't like their look. But I joined them sitting on a chunk of stone.

"Welcome," said one holding out his left hand and grabbed my right hand shaking it pretty warmly. The rest thought this one hell of a joke. I just couldn't figure that out. I was at a loss. But I played it their way and told them it was good to meet a bunch of such nice guys who could speak English. Another guy came up and shook my right hand with his left. Maybe it was just an Arab way of greeting?

I commented on how well they spoke English. They pointed to what looked like an English church tower a few blocks away. One explained that it was the English cathedral, and they had a school there where they learnt their lessons. "Good school. Best school," they told me. They started telling me about the lessons. I couldn't figure out how these Arabs got to going to a Christian School.

"You want to know?" came in one. "I tell you. Some of us are Christian some Moslem. It good school; we learn together. Good friends. You know something? St George was Arab and a Christian – you know that?"

One grabbed my sleeve. “Mr American Jew. See place? See stones? Home of my family.” The boy looked mighty sad. “Where do we live? We have nothing. The Jews take it all. What do I give my kids? Nothing.” The rest of them made sympathetic noises. They went on to say that the whole place was where Arabs lived. Now they came and played there.

“You know the trouble?” said one. “It’s the Jews who came from Europe. They make trouble. They take everything. Grab our land. Grab our homes. Kick us out. The land is ours. Palestinians here…” He looked around with his arms spread out. I guess he meant a hell of a long time. Then he gave me a sharp look. “You Yanks – what you do? You look another way. What about UN? Damn all. What do we do? Hearts bleed. Understand, mister?”

They went dead quiet. I shuffled my feet around. I felt for these boys not too much. “Sure,” I came in. “It’s damned tough, damned tough.” I went on to tell them about my folk way back in Germany how we’d lost a hell of a lot. And the Jews from Europe how they’d lost a heck of a lot and folk sent to the gas chambers. They nodded in some sympathy. “I just don’t figure how these people can’t just treat you Arabs right.” They agreed.

One came in, “You’re right, mister. Arabs and Jews, we are Abraham’s children. Our blood, their blood so why not be friends?” I got up to go. They shook me, this time, by the right hand. I figured that maybe it was an Arab custom to greet with the left hand and depart with the right.

“Mar salaam,” they said as I picked my way over the rumble that had been their homes.

I made my way towards what looked like an English church. I made to cross the narrow road. A taxi came at speed. I dodged back to the sidewalk then crossed over with a hell of a lot of care. I made my way into an arched courtyard. The winter sun lit up the flowerbeds. An oldish guy looked up from one of the beds where he was working. He smiled and greeted me in English. “You like to see the cathedral?” Why not? He took a large key from his pocket and explained that the door had to be kept locked.

I went in. I guess that I hadn’t been in too many churches except for the times I went to mass with Jeanne. This place looked a touch different. There were no statues or candles burning. There was a screen with what I reckoned might be an altar. It was pretty plain and simple. It hit me as okay. I asked him if this place was Protestant. He shrugged his shoulders. I asked him if he were Moslem. He laughed quietly and smiled. “My friend, my family are Christian. Christian from the time of Jesus. English people pray here and we Arab Christians pray here. This is the cathedral of St George. St George of England – St George for us Palestinians!”

I told him that it was a nice place. He nodded. I told him I was an American Jew. I asked his name. “Yitzack – Isaac.” I laughed and told him that was also my pa’s name – that it means a laugh. He knew. He went on to show me around the place. He knew just about everything. It was not every day he could give a guided tour. He got around to how the English Queen Victoria started up a mission or something in Jerusalem. It seemed to me pretty crazy that English Protestants should come here and convert Christian Arabs who had been here for God knows how long. Yitzack didn’t seem to get my point. The light was failing outside, and I reckoned it was time I got back to what passed for a hotel. I was getting pretty hungry and mighty tired walking about the place for most of the day. I hailed a taxi and was back at the Ha Tov almost before I’d got in the cab.

Max was nodding off behind the reception desk. He roused as I came in through the revolving doors. He greeted me with the customary ‘shalom’ and informed me that they had to send for the doctor for Rosa. It was just a bad stomach upset that visitors get in Jerusalem. I went up. Rosa was propped up in bed with a wrap around her. The room was mighty cold. The heating was barely on. She hardly looked up. “You’re back,” she commented in a weak flat voice. I got it out of her that the doctor had given her some tablets, and she’d be okay pretty soon. She went on to say that all the vomiting and so on had brought on a miscarriage, and she’d lost the baby. I went over to her and tried to drag up some feelings of affection. I reckoned that no woman could look more damned unattractive on honeymoon than Rosa. I wondered just how the hell I’d managed to get sucked into all this. I’d been taken for a sucker. Had she been carrying a baby? Had she bamboozled me just as she had tricked me over the T & G artwork? God knows. I sat on the edge of the bed.

I told her, “I’m sorry, honey – real sorry.” Somehow, reading back over this stuff, she’d taken me for a sucker. I reckoned I was just about the dumbest cluck that had ever clucked.

Rosa gave me a glazed look through her myopic eyes. The fancy T & G frames lay on the side-table. She asked me if I really meant that I was sorry.

I gulped and told her I really did and was sorry she'd lost our baby. She flung her fat arms right around me in a bear hug and burst right out great sobs. She rubbed her plump wet cheeks against mine and massaged my shoulder blades with the tips of her fingers. She even suggested that if it hadn't been for the problem, we could have made love. I told her that I could wait.

Rosa got me to sleep in the big double bed. As it happened, I would have preferred the divan and shivered somewhat. She turned around on me and got her arms around getting my head wedged into her breasts. I could hardly breathe. I tried to get out, but the more I squirmed, the more she tightened her hold. I kept as still as I could drifting in and out of some sort of sleep. She began to snore. It was one of those short, snorting snores. First, she started to breathe hard then followed by snorting. It was hell. Then the snorts stopped, and I slipped into some sort of sleep.

Then suddenly, I was jerked right back into being wide-awake. Some hellish wailing sound came from somewhere outside. God, it was just about enough to wake up the dead. It sounded like some diabolical creature twisting and turning in agony. I tried to ease Rosa away so I could sit up and try to figure out this sound. But her arms tightened and pulled me back into her breast. I had to open my mouth to draw in what breath I could. The hellish sound stopped. Rosa loosened her grip. I got my nose out of her breast and got some air into my lungs.

At last, sleep came in great soothing draughts. I guess it was impossible to tell how long it lasted. Maybe an hour or so or even just a few minutes. Then my bladder started sending out urgent signals. I was wide-awake again. My bladder felt mighty uncomfortable. It was a mistake to drink so many cups of what passed for coffee at the diner. I struggled to get out of Rosa's arms. Somehow, I managed to slide out and down. Her arms enclosed my head. I was nearly through. Then her fingers got hold of my hair. I was damn glad I'd kept my hair short. I was through. I rolled over slowly taking myself over the edge of the bed until I lay on the floor. I pulled myself up and headed for the John. I emptied my aching bladder and held on to the wall feeling weak but relieved.

The early morning light was breaking. Then that wailing started up again. My heart pounded fast. I pulled down the toilet seat, stood on it and pushed open a small window. I could just look out if I stood on my toes. The sound came from just about everywhere. A teasing sound like I'd never heard before. The nearest it came to was on those occasions when Lake Michigan was full of fog and shipping sounded off their horns. It was strange, eerie and queer. It stopped suddenly. The eastern light blushed with the sunrise. Tops of hills outside the City turned pink. My fingers itched for brushes and paint. I regretted not packing even a sketchpad. Maybe I could get something here? Sure, they'd be artists around the place. Who was that English guy? David Roberts? He got around these parts sketching and painting before all this modern stuff got built. I'd have to get around to looking out some place that sold art stuff.

I came out of the john. Rosa was awake. I asked her how she'd slept. "Not so good," she came back. I scratched my head and raised my eyebrows. She made it clear that I would not be welcome hanging around all day and suggested I take myself off and see the place. That suited me fine. I looked at my watch. It was just coming up to a quarter to eight.

Max was sitting at the reception desk. I asked him about the hell of a racket I heard in the small hours. He smiled a little and said, "You have to get used to that around here. It's the muezzin calling the faithful to prayer – it's better to pray than to sleep." I came back that it was not too easy on the ear. I added that on Sundays you get the Christians ringing their bells.

"But what do we Jews do? We just don't make a racket on Shabbat – no we just turn up quietly at the synagogue." Max nodded and smiled his quiet smile.

After getting a bite in a nearby café, I turned myself loose on the sidewalk. I found myself following much the same route as the day before. The early sun had a touch of warmth, but the air was cool. I walked fast weaving through the Jaffa Road into the orthodox neighbourhood of Mea Shearim and through into the lot where my young Arab friends had lived. I looked at the heaps of broken rubble and broken furniture that once meant home to these folk. This was the place where their kids were born, grew up, married and died. Something moved deep inside me. This place had meant just about everything to the people who lived here. What did they have now? I got to thinking how it would be that folk could get to taking the homesteads of other folk. What the hell? Conversations came back to me that I'd heard as a kid. Conversations in the home of my grandparents. They talk about being driven out of their homes leaving all their stuff behind. It had torn their hearts. I guess that's how it'd been for these Arab folk.

My mind went back to picking up a picture magazine lying around at my grandparents' place. I couldn't make out the German words. But it showed pictures of Jewish people. They were being marched through the streets – men, women, children carrying whatever in bundles – alongside were soldiers in helmets and guns at the ready. I wondered at the time of how those kids felt leaving their nice homes and their playthings. One picture stuck in my mind. Three young naked women standing shivering by a deep pit. A young soldier had a gun trained on them. The women didn't look scared or angry. They just looked resigned waiting for the soldier to get on with it. As a kid, I felt real sorry for those women and maybe a touch sorry for the soldier too.

I got through the Mandlebaum Gate without too much trouble. I showed my American passport in front of a guy, and he waved me through. On the other side was an Arab guy selling bread and eggs from a cart. He held out what looked like a brown ring covered with some sort of seeds. I gave him a few coins. I guess I'd given him too much so he tried to pass on another bread ring. I waved it away and started to bite into the bread. He smiled and showed me that you had to break bits off. I then got a piece into my mouth and started to chew. It was pretty good.

I passed through a few narrow streets. Just over to my left, I could just make out the tower of St George's. What a hell of a place Jerusalem is with all these religious things going on from way back to who knows when? I passed quite a block with a YMCA sign. What do you know? How that organisation gets around on the face of the globe! Maybe I'd get a chance to have a look-see inside? Then I got sight of a finger post pointing to something called Garden Tomb. Now that sounded pretty interesting. I followed the narrow road and came to what looked like something of a bookshop. I looked in. The shop was full of books and religious stuff. A stiff English dame greeted me and squeezed out what she took for a smile. She told me I'd better get going if I wanted to see the tomb. A tour was just starting. So I went through.

A number of folks were sitting around on benches. It didn't take too long to figure out that they came from back home. A bright young woman with 'Jesus loves ME!' on her sweater grinned and pointed to a place beside her.

She asked me if I were a real Christian. I played dumb and pretended I didn't understand. She turned to a dame next to her and asked if she thought I might be an Arab. She gave me a funny look and said she didn't like the look of me too much. The girl next to me pulled away and said she figured Arabs were not too hygienic. That suited me fine.

The English guy started up with the tour. He had one of those thick, educated English accents that you just don't follow too well. I had to concentrate hard to follow his drift. He was saying that this is the place where Jesus was crucified, buried and rose from the dead. Sounds of amazement went up all around. He pointed to a rock way up and said that it was just like a skull and that's why it's called Golgotha, the place of the skull. I couldn't figure that out. It didn't look too much like a skull to me. The folk around me got pretty excited and started singing something about Jesus dying for sinners. I figured it was pretty strange how Christians majored on sin and Jesus dying. Then it came back to me. At the academy, we had that painting I just could not figure out. It was by the Jewish artist Chagall called *White Crucifixion*. It showed Christ on the cross with bad things happening to our people all around. Why the hell did he bring in this Christian thing? A mighty strange religion about God sending a son to die like that. They started praying. Prayers were going on just about everywhere like firecrackers. The English guy didn't look too easy with these folk from the States letting fly. He started adjusting his tie. At last, he cleared his throat and held up his hand to get silence. He told them to keep prayers for the end of the tour – it was better that way. [256]

The group was on the large size, maybe thirty or thereabouts. Then I caught sight of a face that looked just a bit familiar. You know how it is when you see someone that looks somewhat like someone you know. You find yourself approaching them and then finding they're not the guy you thought they were. But somehow, I kept this guy in view. Just about everything I could see in this guy was just like…he was the doppelganger of, yes – hell, Alan Wagstaffe. Just about everything about him had the cut of Wagstaffe. But how the hell could it be him? I got myself closer. Then this guy who was the wrong side of being badly overweight waddled up alongside me. He looked at me through eyes that just about needed a pair of T & G glasses. He beamed. "Don't you think this is just great? This is the place where the Lord died for you and me." So he went on. I made some weird noises that might have passed for Arabic. Then this bright girl came up, tapped the guy on the shoulder and advised him not to get too close and that I might dip into his pockets. He moved away feeling around to make sure his dollars were in the right place.

Then the others started giving me the wide berth. I was somewhat amused. I sidled up to one or two to get their reaction. One dame complained to her husband that she was pretty sure that I'd been trying to dip her bag and suggested I should be given the bum's rush. Elmer was one of those guys to whom somehow don't want to be making yourself too conspicuous. He suggested I might go off some place. So I got close and said in a thick accent, "American?" He nodded and looked away. I just couldn't resist keeping on. "Yankee good. America good," I commented looking around the group. They shushed me. The English guy was starting up again at a place looking down to the rock face. He started telling them that down there was the very tomb that Jesus was laid after being taken from the cross.

They all started muttering in low tones, "Fancy that?" Elmer's wife started sobbing. It looked like she'd forgotten that I might dip her bag!

Then the guy who looked strangely familiar broke out, "Alleluia!" Then they all started singing out with their alleluias. That's when it hit me I really did know that guy. It just had to be Alan Wagstaffe, the studio manager from the agency. I rubbed my eyes hard, shook myself and gave myself a real hard pinch. But there he was Wagstaffe in person of that there could be no doubt.

I guess that it was time I got out quick. I tried to make myself inconspicuous and edged myself towards the back of the crowd. But they kept edging away from me. What was I to do? Come clean and make it clear I was not an Arab. Pass it off as a joke. But with some folk, they might get pretty nasty. You just can't tell. So I wormed my way back hoping that Wagstaffe didn't get his eyes on me. The English guy was still going on about the tomb. I caught that there was a place in the Old City that Catholics and Orthodox thought was the place. They were wrong. The Bible said the tomb of Jesus was in a garden like here, not in a building full of statues and superstition. I caught one guy saying that superstitious people like Catholics needed to be rubbed right off the face of the earth. Somehow, I guess that I felt glad to be a Jew. Okay, we were not perfect but these folk who think they're so damned good – what the hell can you say?

I made my way slowly on to a side path to make my way back to the exit. I didn't want to make it look too obvious or they might think I'd been dipping a pocket or two. Then came a voice I knew. I was hoping to get out without making contact. It was, of course, Wagstaffe. "Hey, there! Hey – Bennie Traumann!" I turned and there he was striding out towards me. He came right up and slapped me hard on the shoulder. "Bennie, you're just about the last person I'd get to be seeing right here in the Garden Tomb!" I stood, somewhat dazed and asked him what he was doing here in Jerusalem. He came back with this business of leading a group from his church back home.

"Church?" I queried. He then went on to explain that he wasn't just an art director at the agency but minister of some church or other. I raised my eyebrows and shrugged my shoulders. He went on about bringing a group to walk where Jesus walked and so on.

"So I guess you're right here with that little peach Rosa on honeymoon and having a wonderful time." He asked why she wasn't around. I had to tell her she was not too well. The group started moving. A guy came up and congratulated me on speaking Arabic. He looked puzzled. Then it all came out. Wagstaffe spilled the beans about who I was and I was no more an Arab than the president. Wagstaffe's folk were not amused. One guy called out I was dead nuts. I made it clear that I was a US citizen like them and was also a dirty Jew. Somehow, I just didn't like the way these people looked at other folk. I guess I was pretty angry. They started shuffling around and looking uncomfortable. Wagstaffe tried to cool things down and suggested they went into the shop and get themselves some stuff to take back home.

He started pawing my shoulder. I didn't like that too much. He suggested looking us up at the hotel. Somehow, that didn't please me too much. Then he was off clapping his hands and calling the group together. It looked like they were off to Bethlehem or some such place. I waited for the folk to clear and made my exit.

I pushed my way back into the crowded street and made towards an intersection. On the other side ran some pretty old-looking walls. Maybe the walls of the old city? My map told me that I was right opposite what was called the Damascus Gate. On the corner, a newsvendor had his papers displayed. I ran my eye over the titles. He seemed to have just about everything from everywhere. I caught sight of, I couldn't believe it, *The*

Herald Tribune. I bought it and shuffled through the pages. There was a whole lot of stuff that didn't get my attention. Then it hit me hard. It leapt right out of the page – 'Rosa Stein weds Crackle, Snackle, Pop man.' Right under the heading was a picture of me kissing Rosa under the wedding canopy. The write-up went on for a hell of a lot of columns making it to be the great romance of the year. I folded up the paper and dropped it in a bin and made a quick dash through the traffic to the other side. Hell, hell, hell! How the heck did I get caught up with Rosa Stein. I guess somehow I was plum crazy or something? I gave the bin a hell of a kick and made a dash across the heavy traffic.

I stood a while looking at the walls of the old city and down to quite a large entrance. Folk of all sorts were pouring down the steps and through the gate. My map told me it was the Damascus Gate. The wind was a touch chill so I joined the stream of Arabs rushing down the steps. I joined in the flow and was soon carried through the gate into an area of shops. A guy came but on a donkey dragging a truck full of stuff. Another came up the other way with what looked like a green coffin on his back. I stood still taking in the scene. Something went through me. A kind of shiver went through my spine. It lifted me up and hit me hard and shook me somewhere deep down. It came to me that somehow or other we human beings are, we just had to be, linked up through our genes with each other right through Abraham, maybe, to Adam. That's just how it had to be. My eyes filled up and tears trickled down my cheeks.

The passing folk jostled me all around. But I just stood there shaken my whatever it was. It came on me that we human beings whoever we are darned amazing. My heart warmed and tears flowed. I turned to Rosa and somehow a great flood of burning love for her swept over me. Poor little Rosa just locked right on in herself. Then the crowd swept me up and carried me right down through a narrow intersection up on to the other side. Here the way was roofed over and the shops spilled over on to the sidewalk. I wedged myself into a corner and watched the river of humanity flowing past. Some of the men wore pretty shabby suits with some sort of large handkerchiefs over their heads. The women wore long dresses right down to their feet. Some carried stuff balanced on their heads. A guide passed with a few westerners.

So this was the holy city of Jerusalem that we Jews make so much of. What would David make of his city today? The city of peace? I got to feeling real sad. Why the hell couldn't we humans get to living at peace? How is it that we Jews and Arabs here in the city of peace don't just get on with the business of living? How was it that the Nazis gave us Jews such a hell of a time? Why way back couldn't Redskins and settlers hit it off? Why can't Negroes and whites tread the sidewalk together? My heart burst with that longing for peace for just about everyone everywhere. It shook me. Maybe sometimes I'd get to painting something. Something like Chagall's *White Crucifixion* back at the academy. I filed that away somewhere deep down.

I caught sight of an old guy wearing one of these Arab headdresses. He sat at a table smoking something linked up to a bottle. He was sipping coffee. He smiled. He looked a pretty kind sort of a guy. He motioned me to sit beside him. I could see he was a wise, dignified man. He invited me to drink coffee. A tray arrived with just about the smallest cups I'd ever seen. The coffee was black. I sipped. It was strong and sweet. Not like the stuff I drank back home at Quick Snax. We sat for a while in silence. That was okay. He was a relaxed, homely sort of a guy. He was a guy at peace with himself and no doubt just about everyone else.

He looked at me after a while. He took the mouthpiece from his lips and asked, "American? Jewish?" I told him. He went back to what I took to be his pipe. Smoke bubbled up through the water. My fingers itched for a sketchpad. I reckoned I'd have to look around for something. I just didn't want opportunities to pass. "I had some good Jewish friends many years ago," he said in good English. [p.266] He went on about the problems in the land. Jerusalem was not a city of too much peace. He figured the trouble was with the Jews from Europe. They just didn't get the hang of the way folk lived in the east. The old guy reckoned that Jews and Arabs were sort of cousins. They came right out of the loins of Abraham and so on.

He drew on his pipe, and I drained my coffee. I choked on the thick grains at the bottom. He motioned me towards a glass of water. "You married? Children?" he asked. I told him.

"Yourself?" I asked. He smiled in a contented manner.

"Allah has been very good. My wife knows how to ease my heart. She has given me seven very good sons." I asked if they lived in Jerusalem. "One only. He's not good in the head. He helps me with the shop." He moved over close to me and went on to tell me of the others. They were all clever and brought him honour. They had gone to university and become professionals.

"Do they works here in Jerusalem?"

He continued, "No – Germany, States, England, Australia – every place." He took a long draw from his pipe. "You know why they leave?" He continued, "It is not easy for Arab boys to get work here in Jerusalem. So they have to leave. That makes me sad. You know these Jews from Europe, they are sharp here." He patted his elbows. "I ask myself why is it with you Jewish people all over the world you come here and force us from our land?" I guess he has a point. I felt real sorry for him.

The old guy, Ibrahim, went into a long silence. He drew deeply on his pipe. I got the feeling it was just about time I disappeared into the crowds. I made to get up. He placed a restraining hand on my sleeve. "Let me tell you, my friend, of a thing that happened in 1948. My wife, Samira, she had a Christian friend. She lived up in the Galilee in a town called Birim. It was a good place. Then the Haganah came – the Jewish fighters. What do they do? They throw the people out. Then men? They never seen again. They smash the church and everything. That's what they do. They say the land is theirs – these new people from Europe. They treat us like…?" He let go of my sleeve and went back to his pipe.

I got up slowly and moved off into the dark, crowded souk with its shops selling just about everything you could want and a lot more. [268] The narrow way was packed with folk going just about everywhere. I elbowed my way through not knowing where the hell I was heading. I forked off down right. Great smells came up of spices, vegetables, fish, meat and just plain human sweat. I let myself be carried along with the stream going uphill. Three religious-looking guys came down wearing heavy beards, flowing black robes and strange, strange hats. Who and what the hell were they? My fingers itched to get them down on paper. They were soon gone.

I stopped by a shop with postcards and pictures on display and other stuff. Maybe they could fix me up with something I could sketch with? I went in feeling somewhat uneasy. Inside were a lot of stuff for kids. A young Arab got the hang of me pretty quick. "You want?" I explained. He scrabbled around at the back of the shop. I noted a pretty ancient-looking column supporting the roof. The guy came back with some kids' drawing books and a whole lot of pencils. "Okay?" I bought a few books and a few pencils.

"You artist?" I told him. He asked me to make a picture of him. I made one or two quick sketches and passed them over. His eyes lit up and he gave a great smile. "Mister, wait," he said as he disappeared into the back somewhere. He came back with three young kids. They looked at me with great wondering eyes. He sat them on the counter. "Picture?" So I got down to producing a whole lot of sketches. While I was at it the guy went out and came back with a tray of tea.

Then a whole lot of folks started crowding in. I could see I was going to be making portraits of the whole neighbourhood. I quickly finished the drawings of the kids, gulped my tea and got out quick as he called after me, "Mister!"

I made my way back along the dark, narrow, street elbowing my way through the crowds. I kept my eyes open for a place where I could sit and do some sketching. I went on up and came to a place where some steps went up to the right. I climbed up and looked down on the congested walkway. I looked down onto the street and got down to sketching. I looked through the pencils and found one marked 4B. That was lucky. It gave me the good deep tones I needed to get into the areas of dense shade. On the far side was a butcher's shop with great hunks of meat hung up. It did not look too kosher but maybe Arabs were not too fussy. A guy looked up at me with a cleaver in his hand. He didn't look too friendly. He eyed me and tapped the chopper on his hand. I felt somewhat nervous. Suddenly, he spat on the sidewalk and disappeared.

I guess that I ought to move on. I came on a shop that looked like a candy store. But the candies on display looked like nothing I'd seen back home. The colours just hit you right in the eye. I just couldn't believe what I was looking at. I started sketching but lead pencil gave no indication of the colours of the candies. So I just had to make notes on the page like bright pink – lurid yellow and so on. The guy inside gave me a welcoming look. He said something I couldn't figure out and then tried English – "You like?" Now these candies were pretty big, the sort that you chewed bits off. He handed over this candy. I tried a bit. It was so damned sweet I reckon it was over one hundred percent sugar. I handed a buck to the guy and got out and dumped the candy pretty soon. Not the sort of stuff I could get hooked on.

I carried right on up through the masses going just where my feet took me. I got to a fairly open space with a church of some size with a mighty high tower. Nearby was a fountain. It was just what I needed to get some of the sticky candy off my hands. Small clouds drifted over a blue sky, but the air was a touch chill. I figured that in Chicago right now, it was mighty cold with a hell of a lot of snow around. I sketched this wide street with the church in the background. Shopkeepers would come up and invite me to their shops. One guy came out holding a sheepskin coat telling me that it would be a good present for my wife.

As I sat and sketched, that feeling came over me that touched me on going through the Damascus Gate. This time it went a whole lot deeper. How the heck can I describe this feeling? Maybe it was like relaxing in a great bath of warm, scented water after being out in the cold. It was like being surrounded by what we Jews call hesed – loving kindness. It was like going right back to the point of creation and looking into the heart of God. It was like getting caught up and being part of everything that has ever been or will be. Whatever it was touched every cell in my body and each thread on my DNA. I felt part of Adam, the man of dust. I felt part of, yes, everyone who has walked the face of this earth. My life was everyone's life and everyone's life my life. It bowled me over. My heart welled up. I wanted to rush over and give that Arab guy a great hug. I wanted to embrace the whole world in just one huge hug. Tears welled up in my eyes and trickled down on to my sketchpad. I buried my face in my hands and sobbed tears of peace and joy. I guess that if I'd only lived for this moment, then my life would have been okay.

Had I flipped? No way. I felt as sane as any guy could be. How long did this last? Seconds, minutes and hour? No way of telling. I stood outside time. The earth stopped spinning. Time had no meaning. It was an experience that…? Okay, let's leave it at that.

I looked up. The Arab guy was looking at me from his shop front. Maybe he couldn't figure out what the heck I was doing. I closed my tear-stained book and made off down through the arcade. I called out to the guy, "Hi! Great day! Life's great!" He drew his headscarf around his face and moved back into the shop.

Warmed and glowing inside in a way I'd never felt before, I carried on through an archway into a large courtyard. What looked like a church of some sort filled one side. I made my way over and entered into the dim interior. In spite of the dark, the place had a homely feel. A flight of steps to my right drew me up. It took me to a higher level. Lamps and candles glittered. I was intrigued. A few folks moved around, some looked like they were praying. I guess the place had to be Christian. A pretty big cross hung over an altar. An ancient figure covered in black sat by a stand with candles. She gazed at me with sharp eyes and a hint of a smile. I felt the need to communicate. Was it okay to speak in a holy place? I moved over. The old woman took a candle, placed it in my hand and pointed to a box for offerings. I put in a few coins. She got me to light the candle and place it on the stand with the others and pointed to the seat next to her.

Our talk went something like this: "My friend, you have been blessed," she said in a heavy accent. "I could feel you coming up the stairs. Yes, I could feel the warmth coming, coming, coming."

"You could," I said with some amazement.

"Oh yes," she went on, "I can feel, I can feel. Oh yes, I can feel." She chuckled quietly, and I could feel a touch of her humour. Somehow, I could figure how she sensed me coming up the stairway. "You know this place?" I shook my head. She went on to tell me that this is the place where Jesus died. It puzzled me. How could Jesus die in two places at the Garden Tomb and here? How come? She went on to say that the whole of this place was a great rock quarry and just here was a rock on which Jesus was put on the cross. I couldn't figure this, but somehow, it didn't matter too much.

I asked her what the place was called. "The Latins, the Roman Catholics, call it the Holy Sepulchre, but we of the east call it the Church of the Resurrection." We sat for quite some time in silence and a few people came around and burnt candles. After some time, she said that somehow she felt I might be Jewish. I agreed but told her that I wasn't too observant. She smiled. "But your heart is good. God cannot bless a heart that will not take it." I listened. "Many years I struggle with my heart like Jacob. You know how he struggled at Jabbok? Yes? Like him, we have to struggle hard. That's how God can bless when we overcome the bad heart." She went on to say I had to fight the bad in me. The bad, she told me, is like iron; it must be broken. "I will keep you in my prayers at Golgotha, Moshe."

I was startled that she knew my Jewish name. She rose and looked down on me. Her lined and wizened face glowed in the candlelight with fantastic beauty. She half turned to go into a dark passage. “Moshe, I will pray for you in your struggle,” she said as she disappeared.

I sat for quite some time. Stunned. Too much had happened too fast. The words and the face of the holy old woman burnt deeply inside me. I guess I’d never forget her face or what she said. Somehow, I got the urge to get her down in the sketchbook. But it just didn’t come right. Her face was somehow sacred. No way was I going to get it down. Her face and words would remain somewhere inside that brain of mine. So why get her down on paper? I would keep her with me in my struggle and do whatever to keep my blessing fresh and alive.

Slowly, I walked down another set of stairs. Underneath the rock was bare, just covered by protective sheets of glass. There was rock right in front of me and going right up to where I had been. Maybe this was the place where Christ was supposed to have died. Maybe. It came back to me, those days when I went to mass with Jeanne. The mass when it seems the Christians remembered how Jesus died and so on. I wondered about Jeanne. Jeanne now a nun. Jeanne who might have been my wife. What a hell of a dumb fool I’d been getting those sketches I’d made of her and making her the ‘Crackle, Snackle, Pop’ girl. Why? Why? Why had I been so dumb? Here at the place of the skull, I cursed myself for losing a blessing. Words drifted up from somewhere inside my skull, words where God urges men to choose life and not death, to choose a blessing and not a curse. Through that fool act of mine, I got myself a curse and lost the blessing of Jeanne. The ground under my feet seemed to shudder – to rise and fall. I tiptoed carefully out of the place of death out into the wintry sunshine of Jerusalem.

I felt dazed, confused, muddled as I stood there in the courtyard. I guessed I’d just experience too much too quickly. My footsteps led me along a path going up. I passed passages, mighty strange looking buildings and whatever. I came to another gateway. A sign told me it was the Jaffa Gate. I figured that the Jaffa Road was not far off. I went on through and down to the roadway. A cab slowed down looking for a fare. I got in and soon we drove in at the Har Tov. I paid the guy off giving him just a few bucks too many. He looked pretty pleased. Max was at reception. He looked up. It was hard to figure how a guy with his background could sit around all day just letting folk in and out.

"Good day?" he asked. I told him it had been great. Max went back to his paper, and I carried up to the room. Rosa was sitting out in her dressing gown. She looked mighty cheerful and beamed as I came in.

"Good time?" she asked. I felt an unusual warmth towards her.

"Feeling better?"

"Sure. Sorry I lost our kid, honey." I told her that it was just this bug and not to feel too sore and that we could try again. She gave me a great toothy grin. I bent down and kissed her. "Hey, honey, don't you get any ideas – I'm just not ready yet." She gave me a great bear hug and the diamante on her T & G frames glittered.

She then went on to say she'd had a visitor. "Honey, this is going to bowl you right over." She took my hands in hers and turned herself around towards me. "You're never going to guess. Just couldn't believe it. Guy came through with just about the best bouquet ever. My favourite red roses. The guy? Just hold your breath – Alan Wagstaffe!" I then had to tell her that I'd already seen him with his group in this Christian place. She looked a touch disappointed.

"Don't you think it's a hell of a coincidence he's here at the same time as us?" I started getting a bit uneasy about Wagstaffe. How the hell did he know we were at the Ha Tov?

"Guess it was real nice of him to come and visit poor, sick little me. You know he runs some sort of Christian church back home. Guess he's not our faith, but he's a real nice guy. He's real sweet. His wife's a cow. Gives him a real bad time. Doesn't like him running this church. She treats him real bad. Won't cook or fix his clothes. She's just about the worst sort of cow you can get." Something started clicking right at the back of my brain. How the heck did she know all this. Something just didn't add up too well. Rosa went on, "You can be sure, honey, I'm not going to be treating you like that. I'll cook you such meals, and I'll make sure every shirt button is right where it needs to be. I'll make you a real little Jewish wife and put you right at the dead centre." [p282]

I gave Rosa a real, loving kiss. Somehow, I got to wondering how I got to being so damn negative about her. Okay, she wasn't a beauty. Her figure wasn't the sort that a girl would want to show off on the beach. But she was okay. She had a lot to give. What was it that the rabbi said when we were under the canopy? Something like the Almighty, blessed be He, calling

Jewish men and women to be one flesh and getting to draw out the best in each other. Something like that. So that's what Rosa and I had to do.

Rosa went on about Wagstaffe had told her about the Garden Tomb. He'd filled in the background of how these English folk had got to finding just where Jesus had died and the tomb where Jesus had risen. She reckoned it was pretty fantastic. I pointed out that we Jews believe Christians just got it wrong. "But the way Alan put it over made it sound pretty convincing," she came back. "How can we be so sure they've got it wrong and we're right?" I shuffled my feet and shrugged my shoulders. This was the first time I'd had anything approaching an intelligent conversation with Rosa. It got her right off her usual slant – herself.

That night, we made love for the first time as man and wife. It did something for me. Maybe the wind of change had passed over us. Okay, I had got myself snarled up with the unlovely and demanding Rosa. I had got myself sucked into making some fearsome promises and putting a ring on her finger. I thought myself a sucker for getting into this situation. But somehow, something had changed. Here I was feeling real warm to Rosa. That was good. Maybe it had to do with whatever it was I experienced at the fountain up in the Old City? What was it that the rabbi talked about at my bar mitzvah? Teshuvah? Turning around, facing another and better way. Maybe that's what had happened. I smiled to myself in the dark; I held the body of Rosa close and a tear or two trickled down my cheeks.

The next day, the sun burst through turning Jerusalem golden. The sun had just a touch of warmth. Rosa was up good and early and pretty lively. She looked almost radiant. Maybe she was overweight and her features not too classical. But her complexion was pretty good and her hair crisp and glossy. "Now honey," she came in, "you've been getting around while poor old me has been lying here. So you're going to get me to see places." I agreed.

I took Rosa through the way I had followed before. Down the busy Jaffa Road, cutting through the side streets leading to Mea Shearim. She exclaimed on the things she was seeing and how mighty good I was at getting around. We held hands and exchanged a squeeze or two. That was good. As we approached the Orthodox Quarter, I advised her to put a scarf around her head. She protested pretty strongly but gave in after I pointed out the notices. She thought it plumb crazy. When we got to the Mandlebaum

Gate, she got a touch anxious. I made it clear that no way were we going to get to the Garden Tomb unless we went through. We cut through into the Nabulus Road following the signs to the Tomb.

The garden was full of folks from the States – Southerners. They were big and showy people, the sort that would flatten you to the ground if you got in the way. The English guy was trying to protest but without effect. His voice was just not getting through. The leader, who was something like eight foot tall and pretty wide, started his spiel. He went on something like this, "This little ol' place is just where the Saviour rose right out of the dead!" The group responded with quiet whistles of amazement. The Big Guy let it sink in. He made to go on. The English guy took him by the collar and reminded him that he did the guiding. The big fellow pushed him away and started, "Okay, folks. We've got him out of the way. So let's just get fixed on this place and what it means to us believers," or something like that. He went on, "Let's be sure, this is 'the' place where Jesus was buried when they took him down from the cross." He extended his arms and looked around. "Now you, folks, are goin' to tell me why he died on that cross?"

It came back all around. "To save us from sin," they chanted like first grade kids.

"Why did he rise from the dead?"

It came straight back. "To give us eternal life."

Rosa gripped my arm hard. She was switched on in a big way. She had that keen, eager look in her eyes that I didn't like too much. I got to wishing that I had taken her some place else. Big guy went on, "I tell you this you just ain't truly born again until you come into the tomb, lay down like dead and let the Lord raise you up in his loving arms. Will you let him do that for you?" The folk started to shuffle. He started to urge them to come on in and what he called be born again. He expected them to rush in but just no one moved. It was then that Rosa let go of my arm, pushed her way through. The Big Guy called out, "Here's a little lady who wants to be born again. So you just tell us about yourself."

I guess that Rosa was one of those kids who pushed herself to the front at parties to do her act. She went on something like this, "Well, everyone, I'm Rosa Sterne – sorry Traumann. I'm from Chicago and reared as a Jewess. I'm right here on honeymoon with husband Ben right over there." They turned and gaped at me and started to clap. I noted the English guy in the corner fingering his necktie. Big guy put up his hand for silence. "Okay, so you're Jewish. That's fine, so was the Lord Jesus."

"But I'm not too kosher," Rosa added. "Guess the Lord wasn't too kosher either – that got him into real trouble with those Pharisees!"

"Now, Rosa, I have to ask you some questions. Are you real sorry for your sins?"

"You bet I am!" she came back.

"Do you really believe Jesus died on the cross to take those sins right away?"

"I sure do!"

"Now, Rosa, do you want to rise with Jesus and be born again in him?"

"I really do – I really do!" At that, Big Guy and Rosa disappeared into the tomb. Time dragged. I got just a touch fidgety. The Englishman was getting mighty twitchy. Big Guy had gone somewhat too far. Folk started getting anxious and looking at their watches. They'd been in there for at least twenty minutes. It was getting near the time for a break for lunch. Mutterings all around.

Then it happened. Big Guy came out with his arms around Rosa. Tears streamed down her cheeks. Big Guy looked mighty pleased. "It's happened! It's happened!" he cried out in a croaky, emotional voice. Rosa was speechless. She just pursed her lips and shook her head up and down. "It's happened! Jesus has given birth to a Christian! Halleluiah!" This triggered off and explosion of halleluiahs and praise the Lords. The English guy looked mighty uncomfortable. When the racket had died down, Big Guy suggested that some of the sisters might take Rosa aside. Two or three shot forward and carried Rosa off someplace. I stood not knowing what to do.

"Okay, you all," shouted Big Guy, "who wants to follow Rosa and be born again in Jesus?" The crowd rushed forward like a stampeding herd of steer pushing their way to the tomb. But no one spotted the Englishman sneaking around the wall leading to the tomb. Before the crowd got there, he had clanged the Iron Gate closed and got a padlock on. The tomb was secure.

A great cry went up. Big Guy made a fist and swung it towards the Englishman who ducked. Big Guy skinned his knuckles badly on the iron bars guarding the tomb. Big Guy came out with some pretty strong Southern curses and moved off with his mighty sore party. Resentment smouldered on the chill Jerusalem air. "Limey arsehole," hissed Big Guy. One pretty old dame with a blue rinse moaned about coming here to be born again and the English guy who had slammed the doors of the kingdom in her face. Big Guy joined in the tirade calling the English guy worse than the Pharisees and quoting from scripture.

"Amen!" Came from all around.

A skinny guy came in with, "I'd just like to put my heel into that Limey's mush and grind it right down into the dust." Big Guy gave out a great amen to that.

Somehow, I felt uneasy about getting caught up with this bunch. I wanted to get right away. But what about Rosa? I could just slip off. No problem. I just hoped that Rosa was some place where I could get her out. I fancied it was not going to be too easy. I was swept along by the group through the garden, into the souvenir shop and right out into the narrow street. A coach was waiting at the end to take the group on board. Rosa was there, on the sidewalk, looking too radiant for her own good. "Hi, honey," she greeted me, "you'll never guess! These good folk just want us to join their tour. Isn't that just great?" I went cold inside but found myself agreeing that it was just swell. Big Guy came up and gave me one hell of a bang between the shoulders that nearly knocked me right off my feet. He put his arms around Rosa and said what a hell of an honour it would be to have us honeymooners in the party. I guess I didn't see it that way.

The scheme shaped up something like this – the coach would take us back to the Ha Tov to collect our baggage. Then on down to the Dead Sea going right up north along the Jordan Valley to Galilee. Rosa drooled away at all this. She turned to Big Guy and said, "We're sure indebted to you, Freddy!" I thought not. Why the hell had this lot been around to louse things up?

Within the hour, we had booked out and were heading east out of Jerusalem. Max looked pretty morose as we left and pushed a parcel into my hand. I looked back as I passed through the exit. Max was looking back looking mighty sad. I guess we both needed to get to know each other better. But it just wasn't going to happen that way.

The guide kept up a ceaseless patter over the intercom as we made our way down to the Dead Sea. I wished to hell he'd just shut up. There was a Bedouin encampment with folk living just as in the time of Jesus. So what?

Then a stop by a place called the Inn of the Good Samaritan. They all poured out itching with excitement. It seemed like that this is some place where Jesus had stayed. So what? Big Guy Freddy got the folk all around telling them that this is the place where Jesus came and helped a man who had been beaten up. Rosa squeezed my hand and looked up with more than a glint of excitement in her eyes. Prayers sparked off all over the place more sprinkled with alleluias. I was relieved when we started getting back on board.

So off we went on down. A stop at the sea level sign and another spiel from the guide. Another thousand feet to go down. Who cares? I was getting a touch irritable. I felt hemmed in – trapped. I wanted to scream right out and start tearing into Big Guy. Rosa turned around and asked if I happened to be okay? I gave her an unconvincing nod.

On we went down through the brown sand hills. They were touched by green where the rain had got things going. The guide droned on about the flowers that would soon be coming out and so on. I managed to switch off and slip into an uneasy doze that hit one on coach trips. Confused images flitted across my soggy mind. Those great carp from the lake in my knee pants days floated up. They gazed at me with those huge sinister eyes. Their eyes began to change. First, they looked like the eyes of Max back at the Ha Tov. Then they changed to look like the eyes of Rosa looking at me through her thick lens. I tried to turn my head away, but they had me fixed. The fish faded back into the watery depths. Then I got to being in a long dark passage or a room. I felt shut in, confined, constricted. I just had to get right out. A terrible pain shot right through my left ear. I panicked. I started to run towards what looked light. I felt a touch hopeful. I ran hard to get out. I was just about to burst out when bars suddenly clanged down. I was shut in, trapped. I tried to scream out, but nothing came out. Then I wandered through a hot, sandy place. I was real scared. I was lost. How the heck did I get to this place? I had no idea where I had come from or where I was heading. A dark tent came to view. It gave good vibes. It was, yes, where I wanted to be. A beautiful girl stood in front of the tent. She smiled and held out her arms. It was Jeanne. A great weight fell from me. I was wanted. I ran laughing. Jeanne was wearing that white cotton dress. It billowed all around just as I had painted her way back. I was just about to embrace her. She had turned her back and was now draped from head to foot in black. The pain in my ear became unbearable. Something shook me hard. I woke. It was Freddy Big Guy.

When I saw him grinning down, I hated him. I just wanted to push his mush right in – gouge out his eyes and grind them into the dust – to hear him scream out in pain. I hated his stupid guts. He bellowed out that we were right at the Dead Sea. The Southerners fought like a lot of first grade kids in their hurry to get out. Here they were just a lot of kids on their first trip to the coast. I must confess that the sight of the Dead Sea didn't do too much for me. Compared with Lake Michigan back home, it was just a muddy little pond. I was just not impressed.

A chill wind came down from somewhere. The surface was whipped up somewhat. On the far side, the mountains, if you can call them that, came right down to the edge of the water. They were tinged with pink and purple. Somewhere they rang a bell. But where? My mind was teased. Rosa grabbed my hand excitedly and urged me to come on in. Some of them had stripped of and were ready to take the plunge. "Come on," they urged. "It's a great experience." I made my excuses that I was not a good swimmer. They came back saying it was so salty you just couldn't sink. Rosa had packed our things in a shoulder bag. I tried to put her off mentioning the recent trouble. But she got her way.

I guess the Dead Sea experience is one that I could have passed over. Not quite the thing that anyone in their right mind would undertake. The pebbles just about crippled the feet. The water was not too warm. The racket the group made was just about enough to get the dead out of their tombs. I got right out as soon as I could, trying to clean off the oily stuff. It was just about impossible. I figured I needed a few showers to get the salt right off my skin. I wished to heck that I'd kept right out.

I sat with the chill wind blowing down my neck and driving fine sand into my eyes. Rosa was still wallowing around with the crowd. I got to taking in the scene some more. The pink-purple mountains – the sea. I knew I'd seen it somewhere. But where? My mind was teased. The sound of falling rocks came somewhere up behind me. I looked back to see dust rising from the gully. Then it came again – a clashing sound echoing down from up there somewhere. I crossed the highway and made my way over rough ground towards something of a valley. Then I saw them. Two creatures with great curved horns locked in combat. They came at each other time and again. It grabbed me. To get them down in my sketchbook. But the action was too rapid. I edged closer. They ignored me. I figured that this was a whole lot better than watching a crazy crowd behaving like kids in the water. The animals rushed at each other time and again sending the sound of their clashing horns right down the valley. All else was still. It looked like these creatures were doing their best to tear themselves apart. So the head wrestling went on for quite some time. First one was driven up the slope and then the other. They looked pretty well matched. Maybe it was some sort of game they were playing. Then suddenly, they both turned and looked at me with their strange goat-like eyes. Were they going to turn on me? Then they twitched their tails and trotted off at an unhurried pace up into the hill.

Back at the lake, the bathers had dried off and were settling down for lunch. Packets of sandwiches were being passed around. Rosa pulled me down and handed me a packet. I guess the contents were not too kosher, but so what? Big Guy Freddy bellowed out for silence and began a long and complicated grace telling the Almighty things he already knew – 'Lord as though knowest…' The group then got into the serious business of consuming the sandwiches in more or less silence. As I looked over the sea towards the mountains the other side, it came back to me in a flash. I was pretty certain that they reminded me of something. It was the painting by that English guy Holman Hunt, *The Scapegoat.* That was it. The mountains and those goats I'd seen back there. It seems the artist came right down here to paint the picture. It was in the study of the rabbi who'd got me ready for the bar mitzvah. He got to telling us that way back in the time of the temple come the Day of Atonement, the priest took two goats. One he offered up to the Almighty and over the other he confessed the sins of the people and sent it into the wilderness. So Holman Hunt gets the creature into the sea where it breathes its last. As a kid, I figured that as mighty strange. I still do.

The journey up north along the Jordan Valley was not too exciting. It was just mile after mile of sandy hills with not too much to see. The guide kept up his corny patter pointing out whatever. We came to the Arab town of Jericho. The coach came to a stop and the guide pulled his punches. He got to pointing out how green the place was with palm trees and that sort of thing all over the place. But all around just dry desert. How come? Blank looks all around. He went on to unpack something about the high rainfall up there in Jerusalem and how it got through to spring of water all around this place. Quite a few wows went around the coach. He went on to unpack early man getting down to getting farming going around here instead to wearing himself out with hunting. The group were busy getting it down in their notebooks.

One old scrawny guy came in about the walls that came tumbling down. That's what the group were really interested in. He went on something like this, "When the ancient people got to farming the land, they got to needing good places to live and to get together. So they started to make bricks and build themselves a town. That great heap over there is where they started Jericho." More wows. The scrawny guy really wanted to know about the walls falling down. "You know when Joshua came across Jordan with the people of Israel?" Heads shook. He told them, "Around 1200 BC. But first Jericho, 7000 BC!" More wows. "So the first Jericho was a ruin long before the Israelites arrived on the scene."

"So you're just itching to know about those walls?"

"Sure are!" Came from just about everywhere.

"I have to tell you," he went on, "we've had some fine archaeologists working here and some from the Hebrew University. So I'm going to have to disappoint you, the site of the Biblical Jericho just hasn't been found." A great wave of shock and horror swept the coach.

Freddy Big Guy boomed out, "You means those sons-of-bitches have not found it. Why the hell not?" The guide pointed out that archaeology takes patience and time. That's just how it had to be. He motioned the driver to go on.

The green of Jericho was soon left behind to be replaced with great stretches of arid desert. Rosa soon slipped into sleep and her head rested on my shoulder. I then remembered the parcel Max had pressed into my hand when we left the Ha Tov. I pulled it out of my bag and took off the wrapping. It was the picture of the young Max and his family. It was his greatest treasure. Why had he passed it to me? I was dead puzzled. I felt uncomfortable and pushed it well down into the bag.

The motion of the coach on the long, narrow, winding road soon lulled me into a deep doze. This time, I didn't get to dreaming. Every so often, the coach would lurch and bring me back to the conscious world for a few seconds. Then back again into sleep. Didn't that Shakespeare guy say about sleep knitting something together?

The coach came to a halt in a parking lot under some mighty large trees. The guide came back on the crackling intercom. The place was Yardenit. This was where the Jordan flowed out of the southern end of Galilee, down the valley and into the Dead Sea. We followed Big Guy down through the trees and to the water's edge. The light was failing and the air was chill. Big Guy came in with, "This is the great moment for Rosa, our newborn Christian. She's going to be baptised right here in the holy river Jordan." Rosa let go of my arm and moved to the water. I wondered what the hell was going to happen. Big Guy put some questions to her like, 'You give yourself to the Lord Jesus – you're real sorry for your sins – you want baptism' and so on. Then some women took her off some place. The crowd burst into some song or other about the Lord washing away sin. I thought about that poor damn goat kicking its heels around in the desert until it dropped dead.

I just didn't want to get too involved in this business. It looked like they had got Rosa tuned in to all this. I felt damn mad. I wanted to go right up to Big Guy and let him have it straight – that as Rosa's husband I needed to be consulted. Something welled right up in me. I wanted to get my fingers right around his throat and strangle the life right out of him. I'd kill the bastard and stamp right on his ugly mush. I shook and pulled myself back into a dark corner.

Out of the corner of my eye, I glimpsed Rosa with a white gown down to her knees. Big Guy wore bathing briefs. He got Rosa down into deeper water. What he said or did, I was in no mood to note. Anger still shook me right deep down. I really wanted to kill that bastard. I heard a splash and saw Rosa's white form go right under. Alleluias broke out all around and singing about the risen Lord leading us to heaven, or something. Then I heard Freddy Big Guy calling me to come and get baptised like Rosa. Two big guys made towards me and started dragging me down to the water. Well, I guess I'm not too tough, but somehow, I got a foot under one guy who went sprawling back into the water with an almighty great splash. The other guy had an arm in a pretty strong grip, but somehow, I swung around and brought my fist on to the point of his chin. He went right back and lay like a dead man by the waters of Jordan. Cries of protest went up all around. I took to my heels and made it right back to the coach.

The Jewish guide let me in. I was still shaking with anger. The guide noted that something was badly wrong. I managed to get it out. He went on to tell me that Rosa had been lining it up to get me baptised. That made me even more mad. I kept repeating, "That damned bitch!" The guide, Joshua, made sympathetic sounds. He went on to say he'd been raised in the States, served with the Marines in the war. Then he came to Israel and took citizenship. He'd reckon as a guide, Bible Christians from the south were dead tricky. He'd seen it happen before. They'd get hold of some Jew, put the screws on and try to get them baptised. I'd had a mighty narrow escape. I asked him for the use of the mike when the group got back.

By now, it was dark – really dark. The group started to return. They were strangely quiet and ignored me as they climbed aboard. Rosa gave me a funny look as she hauled herself up. "Asshole," hissed Big Guy Freddy. I followed the guide in. He switched on the mike and announced that I would like to say a word. The coach went dead still. I took the mike and took a deep breath. I was dead angry but well in control as forty sets of eyes looked straight at me.

I started, "I am a Jew. My folk got out of Nazi Germany. They came to the States to live free. They knew that in the States you could be real free. They would be treated right as real human beings. They came to live among people who believed in democracy. No matter where the hell you came from or what you believed, you could live free. You get it? What happened down there just doesn't fit in with what we value in the States. You just don't take a guy and try to make him do something he just doesn't want to do. That's just not democratic. I guess I just don't know too much about Christianity, but I know Jesus was a Jew like me. Somehow, I guess he wouldn't be too happy about a guy getting forced into baptism. Okay, my wife wanted to take that step. Okay. Fine. I'm sorry if I hurt anyone, but there comes time when you just have to use force against injustice. I'm not a good Jew, but I stand by my right to be Jewish. No one – just no one is going to take that right away."

The folk sat dead quiet. I just didn't get a round of applause. I handed the mike back to the guide who squeezed my arm. I went back to my seat next to Rosa. She leaned across, gave my cheek a peck and whispered that it was great. I sat just about as still as any rock and thought some dark thoughts and the coach made off alongside the lake heading for some place way ahead.

The kibbutz was right down by the lake on the far side. They put us in these cute little cabins. Lights glittered all around and up on the hills above.

But I was in no mood to appreciate the atmosphere. Rosa figured it would not be too good to eat with the others in the dining place. She suggested she get a tray. I was feeling pretty hungry so I agreed. She returned with a tray with steak and salad. We sat in silence as we chewed our way through tough and overdone meat.

After the meal, we wandered outside. I still felt pretty sore. Rosa snuggled up, gave me a peck and said something like, "Real sorry. Upset you real bad. Dead wrong of me. Forgive?" I told her okay and just hoped she'd got the message but didn't feel too confident of that. But I said okay. We went right down to the water's edge. The air was full of bugs chirping away and frogs croaking. Night birds whistled and called somewhere across the water. The far side was lit up from a place the guide called Tiberias, named after some Roman guy way back.

Voices carried over the water from what looked like a small boat some way out. A light flickered and oars splashed. Maybe they were fishing. Maybe. Rosa shivered and suggested we get back to the cabin. She rummaged deep in her bag and produced an expensive looking book bound in red leather. Its gold-blocked edging glittered. The cover was secured by a locking brass clasp. She looked at me with a twinkle and held it up. I commented that it looked a pretty swell book. She held it out so I could smell the leather. I agreed it smelt real good. She went on to tell me that it was her journal. Her pa had bought her first journal at seven, and she'd got one from him ever since. She patted the book and told me it's all in here. Everything. Everything. She had on a sort of deep, secretive look that made me feel a touch uneasy. She pointed to the locking clasp. "See that? That means I'm just about the only one who's going to peek inside!" I took note.

Rosa settled down to write up her journal. I scratched around for something to do. Rosa's heavy form spread over the edge of the chair. I got out my sketchpad and flipped through some of the sketches I'd made in Jerusalem. There were the Arab kids and some old guy wearing some mighty strange scarf over his head. I got some of the orthodox Jews down by the Western Wall. I had to be mighty quick before I was spotted. I got a group forming a minyan around the Torah. They were Hassidim wearing black kaftans, dark hats and these fantastic forelocks. I guess I didn't know too much about the Hassidim. Maybe they were just a bit too enthusiastic for my taste. But I could see that I could work up the sketches into something interesting. Yup, possible.

I turned to a new page making sketches of Rosa's anatomy. There was the great curve of her buttock hanging right over the side of the chair. Great masses of thigh disappeared under the table. The slope of her heavy head and that substantial shoulder and the plump flesh cushioning her elbow. I filled page after page. I got lost in my sketching as Rosa was lost in her journal.

Suddenly, she looked up, gave a Mona Lisa smile and wondered how the Crackle, Snackle, Pop girl might be doing. I knew of course but shrugged shoulders and wrinkled my brow. She reminded me that she was the girl at Quick Snax. I raised my hands and shook my head pretty firmly. Rosa smiled her smile and went back to her journal. I had a hunch that she might be writing something about Jeanne and how Rosa had got her way over the T & G artwork. It hit me that Rosa somehow had figured that it was Jeanne who was the model for the Crackle, Snackle, Pop ads. But how? How?

We slept late. I looked out. The clouds were low and a fine drizzle was falling. The lake surface was being whipped up by a mighty stiff breeze. A cold wind forced its way into the cabin. I switched a heater on and let the warm airflow over my body. Rosa sat up and rubbed her dim eyes. Without her T & G frames, she looked at me in an unseeing way. I told her what the weather was like and told her that I just didn't fancy too much going around with Freddy's crowd. I still felt pretty sore about what had happened and that Rosa had fixed it. I just wanted to get right out of the place. Somehow, she agreed. Maybe she felt that what had happened yesterday would not make us too welcome. She went on to say that she hated this lousy joint and felt like going right back home. I told her that it would suit me fine and somehow I'd get it fixed.

I did. Fortune smiled on me just a touch. I tracked down a guy in the kibbutz who just happened to be driving over to Tel Aviv on business. The kibbutz was into manufacturing electrical components, and he was trying to fix a deal. He would take the route over the Galilean hills and along the coast road to Tel Aviv and Ben Gurion airport. We packed fast and soon were heading towards the coast. We climbed a steep hill. At the top was the coach. Big Guy was giving his spiel. They spotted our auto and turned to watch us go by. Not a smile or a wave. They just stood there and stared. Levi, who was driving us, turned and commented that the group would not be seeing too much of Mount Hermon on a day like this. He burst into a great gale of laughter, gave a great blast on his horn and burst into a gutsy song in Hebrew.

We managed to fix a flight going out later that day to New York from Ben Gurion. I guess I felt mighty relieved to be heading back. And boy – when we eventually hit Chicago, the city was covered in thick snow and the sun shone out of a blue sky. Everything looked clean and crisp. I was sure glad to have got out of what they call the Holy Land. If there's a Holy Land any place, I guess it was right here under my feet, and it was going to stay that way.

The cabbie drove us out to our residence on Lake Michigan near Lake Forest. This was Joe Stein's wedding gift. It was a pretty swell place to start married life. It was set well back from the highway with an avenue of maples leading right up the drive to what I recognised as a classical portico. It looked great with the covering of snow. Lights were on. As we drove up, the door was opened by an English-style butler. He welcomed us calling us 'sir' and 'madam'. I felt I was treading on air as a gust of warmth from the house swept around me driving out the chill. In the hall stood just about the largest bouquet I've ever seen and a mighty large box of chocolates.

Rosa made straight for the chocolates and read the label. She let out a squeal of delight. "Isn't that real sweet of Alan. What a dear, good, lovely man! Alan!" I went to pay off the cabbie. But a great big question mark buzzed around somewhere inside. It looked like the English-style butler was just hired for a few days to see us settled but a dame from somewhere or other would come to be a sort of housekeeper cook. I guess that Rosa did not have it in mind to be a good Jewish housewife. Anyway, she had converted, hadn't she? But I felt mighty certain that, like most things in her life, Rosa had got things fixed her way, just how she liked it. So where was I going to fit in? What of the years ahead? I guess I just wasn't going to feel about Rosa as I felt about Jeanne. Would there be kids? Somehow, I couldn't cast myself as a good Jewish dad. But who knows? Whatever I'd just have to see how the cookie would crumble living in this fancy pad right alongside Michigan not too far from Lake Forest.

I found my status at the agency had been jerked up a few notches together with my salary. That was okay. Joe Stein, now my father-in-law, told me he had it in mind to get me on the board as soon as he could fix it. I must admit that what he had in mind and the style of living that was taking me over was not what I had in mind. My personal agenda was something of a different order. Just something nice and simple like painting sunlight falling on to that white wall. That's what I wanted. Just to paint sunlight on a really white wall.

It so happened in time I found myself getting increasingly involved with the agency's key accounts. It brought me into contact with my family's business, G & T Optics. My Grossmann cousins were making it big and somehow treated me at their level. Frankly, I was not too comfortable with that. It was not my style. I just wanted to get in the auto and take myself to paint way up on the lakeside and paint. But no, I just had to attend these top line meetings, churn out my ideas – okay; I had them and get others to carry them out. Wagstaffe was not too easy about all this. He was the studio boss and here was I briefing him! My fingers itched for the drawing board and carry out what I'd been trained to do.

This led me to the idea of setting up a studio back at the house. I got this fine, timber-clad place put up with a great sloping window fitted with an electrically controlled blind. It was a dream. I figured that times would come when I needed to stay at night. So it had a sleeping area and a place where I could fix something to eat. Rosa thought it was just fine. She suggested that married folk needed some personal privacy. So I found myself at weekends spending more and more time there in the studio. Rosa seemed mighty keen to encourage me in that direction.

Rosa was still right into this Christian thing. Joe Stein and the family were mighty sore about it. They got this rabbi to come around and talk with her. The poor Guy got just nowhere. At the door, he came back that as her husband I'd just have to bring her around. But he just didn't know Rosa. It would be easier to hurl the Catskill Mountains into the Atlantic. Joe Stein also leant on me somewhat to bring Rosa around. He was getting pretty tired on her going over the experience at the Garden Tomb and getting baptised in the Jordan. The Steins were not too observant. They'd make some show of keeping Pesach, but I guess they were easy about eating stuff that was not too kosher when dining with goys. I stalled Joe as best I could.

It was soon after what passed for a honeymoon that Wagstaffe started hanging around. Somehow, he's got Rosa linked up with this church he ran in town. Parties of his folk started coming around and having a ball of a time. Their prayer meetings or whatever seemed mighty wild. So I took myself well out of the way in my studio. At time, the din got so much I just had to stuff cotton wool right into my ears, but the racket still got through.

Wagstaffe cornered me in the studio. He started putting over the Christian sales talk. How was it that I just didn't come to the prayer meetings at my place – it would mean a whole lot to Rosa – they'd give me a great welcome and so on. I tried to get it over that it just didn't grab me. It just wasn't my scene. I needed to me to reflect and paint. Somehow, he didn't get my drift. He fixed me with that look and said they'd pray for me that I'd come right around. Somehow, I got the feeling that he thought I had some sort of blind spot that would get taken right away by their prayers. What then? Wow – I'd get the message and I'd come right over. I'd see the light – whatever the hell that might be! I got real mad inside. I nearly gave Wagstaffe's tight ass a kick as he made off. I felt like giving my phylactery and prayer shawl a dusting.

Weeks past. I came to spending a hell of a lot of time in the studio and not too much time with Rosa in the house. Joe Stein started putting pressure on me. He wanted me to get to entertaining clients back at my place. Maybe to start with my own family the Traumanns and the Grossmanns. Rosa would make a good hostess and so on. He went on to get me taking up golf, fishing and maybe hunting. You got to meet the right sort of people and get new clients. He wanted me on the board, but the other directors would not be too enthusiastic unless I got around to getting new accounts.

I managed to stall Joe somewhat. But somehow, 'Lakeside', as the place got named, was developing into an almost non-stop prayer venue. Wagstaffe practically lived at the place and got around to staying over. Rosa got a room set aside just for him. I must confess this didn't bother me too much. I had the studio and my work was developing. I passed through perhaps the stage of producing carefully observed stuff with dead right draughtsmanship into something that was gutsy. I started to lay on the paint with great flakes of colour. It was vibrant and exciting. Light and dark collided with each other. Great sparks of light shot out that almost hurt the eyes. Subjects came leaping out deep from inside me. There was fire – lots of fire. Deep in the fire were heads screaming out in terror. My stuff put Munch's 'Scream' in the shade. Panic yelled out from the canvas. Panic – panic – panic. Flames –

flames – flames. Eyes – eyes – eyes. Heads bound with phylacteries. Prayer shawls aflame. Terror. Shattered columns. Sidewalks littered with glass. Bodies like living skeletons – cadavers. I just had to paint this stuff. It was a compulsion. I painted until I was exhausted. I painted until the brush dropped from my fingers and I dropped to the floor and slept.

Forms and shapes moved and changed. I painted in blood. Great drops of blood flowed down over rocks into pools. The pools of blood turned from red into sparkling water. Water flowed out from dark, dark places out into where all was dry and arid. Desert became green and lush. Life burst out. The Garden of Eden was right there in my canvas. I came to fixing on Eden and the tree of life. What was the tree? It had deep, deep roots stretching right down into the earth's crust. My brush moved right down to where the magna glowed. And the branches, the branches reached just about as high as could be. They pierced right through into whatever was beyond. Fruits of many sorts hung down – luscious fruits. Fruits of blessing all ready to be plucked and eaten. Up there in the branches danced a man. The man? He looked liberated – free. He sort of welcomed whoever to come up and join him. I gazed long at the finished canvas. Bitter gall came up in my craw. I shook with anger. I cried out with a great cry. I took hold of the pallet knife and hacked and hacked at the canvas until it hung in shreds. I took up the stretcher and smashed it time and again on the floor until it was reduced to matchwood. I sobbed and screamed until my throat was as hoarse and threw my shattered self on to the bed in the corner and slept an uneasy sleep.

It took me a heck of a long time to figure out what had happened that night. Was I going crazy – getting deranged or something? What was going on deep down inside my cranium? Ought I be going to see a shrink or what? Did it matter anyway? Or what?

I guess it must have been somewhere around five months or so after getting back from what passed for a honeymoon. Rosa came up to me in a somewhat coy manner. She came up with something to do with missing. I played dumb and suggested she might get around to finding whatever. She laughed and slapped my shoulder with her plumb little hand. Then she came right out that she was pregnant. I figured that I'd get to playing it her way and put on a happy face and told her it was just great. But something deep down sounded a note of caution. Somehow, I just didn't fancy Rosa too much. We had made love a few times – if you can call it that. I got through it by my imagining it was Jeanne and not Rosa. But we hadn't shared the same bed too often and my sleeping time was spent in the studio. So – okay it may be that what Rosa was carrying could be…or could it be?

Wagstaffe was more or less living at Lakeside. How he squared this with his wife I just don't know. But there he was most nights running his prayer meetings and sleeping in the room Rosa had fixed. I spent my time in the studio trying to figure out why I had hacked the tree of life painting to pieces. I had a creative blockage. Nothing would come. I went back to some basic drawing with classical heads. Elementary stuff. I set up some still life arrangements. Nothing demanding with just a few interesting objects. It was a time of marking time. That's how it had to be. Something was working away deep down in whatever part of my cranium dealt with producing creative ideas. It needed time. I would just have to wait until it worked out.

Rosa unpregnant was pretty big but Rosa pregnant was massive. Getting around was not too easy. A nurse was in Wagstaffe's congregation. She came around pretty often to check Rosa out. Rosa started getting pretty bitchy with me. I got to feeling that my presence was not exactly wanted. So I took to living in the studio. I had just about everything I needed there so that was okay. I kept well out of the way.

Wagstaffe was making himself really at home. He got his feet right under the table at Lakeside. Prayer groups went on. Parking had to be extended to take in the autos. Of course, I was not consulted. I just came back from the agency one day just to find that a great section of the lawn had gone and replaced with hard surfacing. Things just happened. I brought back some word of Joe's who tried to get over to me that I should just show his daughter who was going to wear the pants. Somehow, things just didn't get to work out that way and – did it matter anyway? I figured not.

That weekend, I was working away at some still life and getting into it. There was something in getting together a few interesting pieces and getting them down on a canvas. Some of those old Dutch guys were pretty good at that. Then I got to hearing shooting. I was pretty close. I went out. I made my way through the grounds. At the end near the lake was a large patch of trees. Wagstaffe was there firing at a target. As I approached, he turned, gave me that syrupy smile of his like the cat who's just got into the cream. His automatic was pointing somewhere towards my solar plexus. I felt somewhat uneasy. He said he was darned sorry for disturbing me, but he just had to get some practice in. There happened to be some strange characters around his church, and he needed to be able to put in a slug where it counted. I nodded but got to wondering where trusting in the Lord fitted in to packing an automatic. But that was his problem.

One evening, I sneaked up to the window when a prayer meeting was in full flight. The folk were squatting around just about everywhere. The music group was in the groove. Someone got up and conducted some sort of dance routine. Folk clapped their hands, sang and waved their hands around with a few eyes getting poked out.

Somehow, it rang bells. Years back, Grandfather Traumann took me to the bar mitzvah of a client's son. I guess they were Hassidic. I was just a kid. It scared the pants right off me with their kaftans and side-locks. They looked like freaks. They all went crazy like Wagstaffe's folk. They danced and clapped and made one hell of a racket with their singing. They went right over the top. I shrunk right into myself and started to weep somewhat. Grandpa put his arms around me and told me not to worry and that this was how these Jews showed their praise for God. I found myself shrinking back into myself at the sight of these Christians letting rip. It was scary – real scary. Shivers went up and down my spine. I wanted to get back to the safety of the studio. I was rooted to the spot. It was hell – real hell.

The racket stopped and Wagstaffe started haranguing the folk about those who had faith would be okay with the Lord. The Lord would just stick right by you and never let you go. All would be just about as fine as it could ever be. Isn't that great? A great roar of agreement went up and a whole lot of alleluias. He went on about folk who had real faith danced with rattlers or poured poison down their throats. The Lord saw they were okay just because they trusted in him. I got to wonder why the hell anyone would want to go fooling around with a rattler of pouring poison down their throats! He went on about a time when he was driving some place off the highway. It was not more than a track. He took a curve when an automobile came at speed on the offside and hit his car head on. It was then that he felt the Lord's arms go right around him and hold him real tight. He got out. His Oldsmobile did not have as much as a scratch. A miracle! The other auto? Smashed right up. The driver? He waved his hand to indicate the worst. He shouted out, "The Lord saved me because I had real faith!" Alleluias again all around. Somehow, it didn't quite square with Wagstaffe going around with a pistol in his glove box. Why the hell would he want this if the Lord looked after him? It just didn't stack up.

Rosa had a pretty bad pregnancy, not that I was not too involved. I just stood on the touchline. She went off to this fancy maternity clinic. Joe, of course, was picking up the tab. That's how it had always been with Rosa. Joe always lavished more than enough dough on his daughter. He always saw she had just what she wanted and in the style she was used to. Okay, he paid me a pretty good salary but not the sort of dough that could keep up with living at Lake Forest and the standard that Rosa expected. No way.

Rosa's time was pretty close. They took her to the Hanna Rubenstein's Memorial Clinic. I hung around the plushy reception lounge. I just couldn't figure things out. Somehow, what was going on just had nothing too much to do with me. Joe and his wife dropped in, and we just sat talking about nothing too much. Wagstaffe put in an appearance. The nurses seemed to expect him and came to him to report progress. I made a mild protest. He just shrugged it off. I began to feel pretty mad. I suggested that maybe he ought to be back home looking after his wife and kids and not hanging about the clinic. He gave me an odd look and said that as Rosa's minister he had a duty to be here! What the hell could I say? But something real hot was boiling up inside me. I was getting damned angry. I was getting pushed aside by damned Wagstaffe. I was right in the way.

Joe Stein also seemed to cool off. I was getting sidelined at the agency. Joe passed on certain commissions to other guys including Wagstaffe. I wasn't getting into accounts planning meetings or getting probed for idea. I slipped back into being something of a studio hack. Wagstaffe gave me pretty basic stuff to churn out. I just got on with whatever. It was well below what I could do. My Crackle, Snackle, Pop days were over. Rosa was a hell of a long time in labour. The baby was born after at least three days' struggle. It seems it was a boy not far short of ten pounds in weight. The nurse called. Wagstaffe, who was hanging around, went for it like he'd got the ball and making it right through to goal. In his arms, he had this great bouquet. There he was drooling over Rosa and telling her what a brave girl she'd been and so on. I tried to get in on the act, but he elbowed me right out of the way. He told me he had a ministry or whatever to perform and went into a long and complicated prayer. Rosa lay there either in prayer or sleep. I guess it was sleep. The kid started wailing. I could see nothing there that looked like the fruit of my loins. The nurse came back looking somewhat anxious. She whispered in Wagstaffe's ear that his wife was pretty tired and maybe he should leave. She jerked her head towards me and motioned me to the door. I shook inside. What the hell had been going on? What?

In the corridor, I grabbed Wagstaffe by the lapels and pushed my face into his. He gave a sickly smile and tried to push me off. But I held him. I yelled at him something about muscling in. A nurse came out and protested. I told her to shut up. I nearly ripped off Wagstaffe's lapel. Two orderlies came out. Beefy guys. They looked like bouncers. They grabbed me from behind and lifted me from my feet, struggling and yelling. They threw me out at some side door and told me to beat it or they'd send for the cops. Outside, I screamed with rage and wept with humiliation. I made for the parking lot. Wagstaffe's black Oldsmobile was there. I kicked a pretty good dent into a door. I waited. He came out laughing and walking tall. The blood bubbled right up inside. I sprang out and socked him hard beneath the belt. He doubled up and met my left hook. He jerked back, rose from the ground and landed flat on his back. He was knocked out dead cold. I guess I didn't want the guy run over. I dragged him over to the side of his auto and left him. This time, I guess it was me who was doing the laughing.

I got back to Lake View. Wagstaffe had a full set of keys, Rosa had seen to that. So just in case he had any thoughts about coming back, I applied the security bolts just about everywhere. In time, I heard the sound of his auto. I heard him trying the key in the lock. He then went around the place trying windows and so on. He knocked and called my name. I had turned off the lights and could see his shadow moving around. I laughed and told myself that I would finish him so that even the Lord would be pretty helpless. Where Wagstaffe went just didn't bother me. He'd loused things up for me so why the hell should I bother?

Rosa came back after around a week or so. The kid had to be left at the clinic. It seemed there was something not quite right. I guess Rosa had picked up something about the trouble with Wagstaffe. She was pretty cool and made it clear she didn't want to see me around too much. That suited me fine. I pitched my tent in the studio for keeps.

I quizzed Rosa about the kid when I got over to the house. She didn't give too much, just an okay or so. I brought up the matter of registration and name and so on. She shrugged her shoulders. I got onto the fact that her pa has brought up the question of circumcision. Seven days had now passed. So? She put her foot down mighty firm. She made it dead clear he was going to be brought up as a real Christian and her pa had better get that dead straight. She went on that he was going to be named Christopher and Wagstaffe was going to dedicate him to the Lord or some such thing. So we'd better forget all the Jewish stuff.

Wagstaffe soon came back into residence after this. I kept well away and lived and worked in the studio. That suited me fine. It looked like the kid was having to be kept on at the clinic for quite some time. Rosa stopped communicating and I had to rely on Joe Stein dropping a crumb or two when I saw him at the agency. He was pretty cut up over the whole business. He had been looking forward to the kid being brought up as a proper Jew. That just was not going to happen. He hinted that he would like to see the back of Wagstaffe and maybe get me to fill his shoes. But somehow, that didn't grab me too much. He made it pretty clear that Rosa, who'd been the sweetest little apple in his eye, had been a mighty big disappointment. She'd left a hell of a gap. As for her ma? Well, she just couldn't stop moping around and the physician had got her on pills. As for the kid? It seems like there was something badly wrong with a whole lot of complications. It looked like being some mighty delicate operations needed.

Then came '*the night*'. The cookie crumbled like this. It so happened that I'd been working on a canvas. My creative drive had been coming back real strong. Abe, back at the Academy of Art, had been planning an exhibition of my stuff. He reckoned that this would set me up as an artist and get me out of the world of advertising. I liked the idea. It got to a point where I was mighty hungry and needed to fix myself a cheeseburger. I looked into my refrigerator and found I'd run right out of cheese. It was something past midnight. I could see a light burning in Rosa's bedroom. I crept into a side door and made my way through to the kitchen. I snitched a hunk of cheese and started to make my way back.

Something, God knows what, drew me into the lounge. It was pretty big with a lot of showy furniture that did not do too much for me. It had an unfamiliar feel. It had been some time since I had been in the house. I switched on the light and looked around. On the floor by Rosa's big plushy chair lay her red leather journal. I picked it up, smelt the leather and took in the gold-blocked leaves. I examined the crafted gold-plated clasp. It was unlocked. I hesitated. Maybe I should have put it down then. But somehow, curiosity got hold of me. I opened it and flicked through the pages of Rosa's crabbed writing.

I settled myself into a chair and started to read the stuff. I found the pages where I first met Rosa back at the agency. She wrote about her pa taking me on and that I was from the family that ran T & G Optics that made her fantastic butterfly frames. She noted me looking at her at the accounts meeting and that she was going to get ME! The next entry brought in Wagstaffe and that his wife wasn't too helpful in his religious stuff. He wants me to go to his church sometime. Maybe? They drove out to some motel and booked in. Then, my eyes nearly went right out of my head, the details of what happened in bed. She ended, 'Alan's a great lover. GREAT! He really brings me on and gives me such orgasms. Wow!'

I laid the book down and combed my fingers through my hair. I couldn't figure out why the hell I just hadn't figured what had been going on. Was I dumb? Plumb stupid? A hell of a dumb cluck. Or what? I just hadn't seen that Rosa and Wagstaffe had been lovers and sure were still lovers. Were they up there in bed together right now? What of the kid? Was it Wagstaffe's? I reckon it was looking that way.

I leafed through a few more pages. Then it came to her wanting that original sketch of her wearing the T & G butterfly frame. She wanted it damned badly. She reckoned she looked real cute with that slogan, 'Men date dames in T & G frames.' She was determined to get that original. So she planned this scheme to get me over a barrel. It was that bastard Wagstaffe who made the suggestion that she snitched the Hayom Ektachromes from my desk. So that's what happened. She went into a whole lot of detail about Alan making a damn great search throughout the agency. It worked like a dream and so on. What a bitch! She got down that her pa went crazy. Cherry Greenberg of Hayom threatened to take the account away and so on. She listened in on Joe bawling me out and threatening to give me a king-sized bum's rush.

She then got down how Wagstaffe suggested she took me out to coffee to Kwick Snax. She reckoned she'd train me up so she could become Mrs Rosa Traumann and keep on with Wagstaffe. She referred to me as 'Gooky Boy'. Gooky Boy? What the hell? It made me real mad. God, I'd like to show her what Gooky Boy could do, and it wasn't the sort of thing she would like too much.

She went on about how she's got her hands on the original. She took it back home where she gave it a hell of a kiss up in her room and smudged it with lipstick. She'd tried to clean it up and just about made one heck of a mess of it. She went on to tell of her pa's terrible mood over the lost Ektachromes. So what does the bitch do? She goes into his study and slips the transparencies into his briefcase. She was damn please that I wouldn't be getting the bum's rush. The next thing she gets down is getting me under the canopy! What the hell? What the hell?

I shook with God knows what. I was well beyond anger. I could yell. Smash up the damned place. Smash her fat, ugly face right in. Hell – hell – hell. I went on to read up other parts of Rosa's story. There was the business about my birthday. She got it over to Joe that she was nuts about me and that her pa said it was okay. I was a good Jewish boy and had talent. I was sure to go places and so on. So that damn awful pink Caddy was fixed, and she got down that me – Gooky Boy – had fallen right into it.

Then Rosa got wind of Jeanne and that I got to giving her the eye over at Kwick Snax. She saw me taking Jeanne out in the Caddy so she follows in a cab. She was going to get me whatever. She wonders what sort of lover I'd get to be. I'd have to be damn good to get up to Alan's level. So Rosa homes in on the Crackle, Snackle, Pop campaign. So what does she get around to doing? She gets a note around to Jeanne suggesting she tunes into a commercial channel and sees herself smiling out at God knows how many folks. She wrote that I was just a heel who had used her and suggests she gets shot of me pretty damn quickly. Does she sign it? You can be pretty damn sure she doesn't. So she just ends, 'A well-wisher!' I guess without that note Jeanne would never have guessed I had used those sketches of her. No way. Rosa had loused my life right up.

I sat for some time letting the steam out of my ears. I read on. She wrote about getting that dame right off the scene. Then going on to a trip in the pink Caddy up the lake. She got me into making for what passes as love. She reckoned I was not too expert but hoped I'd get to improve. But she reckoned she'd always have her number one lover Allan to fall back on. Bitch! She reckoned his technique was pretty terrific. He knew how to bring her on and deliver real satisfaction.

Then she gets on to the time we went up along Kanakee River in the fall. She puts the next part of her plan into action and gets to telling me that she'd missed. I guessed at first I just didn't get her drift, and she'd reckoned I was just plain dumb. She then got through that she was pregnant. I bought it big! What a hell of a sucker to take it in! I was like dough in her hands and got me along to the fanciest jewellers in town. It looks like she'd already had it fixed. She'd already bought the ring on her pa's account. She then took me back to the family place and a surprise little celebration with Joe being mighty pleased. There was plenty about me being a dead easy fish to hook and so on.

She had the wedding fixed while the iron was mighty hot and reckoned that she'd be having her good times with Alan and me – she called me the gook – just didn't get to figuring it out. All this had been worked out with Wagstaffe. They'd got it all neatly tied up. My blood boiled and my heart throbbed mighty fast. Dark thoughts flashed up. God, I'd like them to pay a whole lot for this. I read on with a pounding heart. She reckoned that she'd got her pa twisted right around her little finger. She reckoned she'd got pretty good at it. She reckoned she'd get him to fix a really swell wedding at the Fitzwilliam and book the best rabbi to do the necessary. Joe wasn't too keen on the idea of a honeymoon in Jerusalem. There was always trouble around there. He suggested the Bahamas. She had fixed this with Wagstaffe who was planning a trip to Jerusalem himself with his church. Joe had fallen for Rosa's scheming. So I was not just the only sucker around.

I flipped through the pages. She was not too happy about the honeymoon in Jerusalem. The hotel a hell of a dump and so on. I had to agree there. She felt pretty lousy with what she called the two-ender. She then got around to fooling me that the two-ender had led to a miscarriage and she had lost the kid and so on. She reckoned I was just far too stupid to getting to ask too much. She reckoned I was like a dead hungry catfish taking a fat worm and she'd have those years ahead getting fooled by her. She'd got me hooked. My body shook like a volcano just about to go up.

The more I read, the more that damned great volcano boiled up inside. Any moment I'd be sending out rocks, flames and God knows what. I'd get my fingers around that thick throat of hers and have her scream out. Treat me like a gook? I'd make her pay. I'd make her pay for lousing up my life and treating me like a guy who just didn't know his mouth from his ass. I'd make her pay, and Wagstaffe?

So what happened when Wagstaffe came on the Jerusalem scene? She wrote, 'Phone rang. Gloomy guy on reception. A Mr Wagstaffe to see me. Alan! Alan! Gorgeous lover boy Alan! Quick shower – perfume – negligee. Alan came in. Fell into his arms. Swooned – swooned – swooned. No word. What could we say? Bed. Stupendous love making. Like million – million dollars. Then champagne – champagne the best medicine – heaven wonderful heaven. Got to talking about Gooky Boy. That's what Alan and the others back at the agency call him – Gooky Boy. He doesn't go down too well. His work is pretty good, but he blinks and stutters and, well, he just doesn't come across. He's shut in. But that's why I've taken him on. He's gooky and you can fool him any time. I get marriage, and I get to having my own good time. That's just how I want it, and I've got it. Who wants a husband who is too damn cute and pushing you around places you just don't want to be? Alan reckoned my telling Gooky about the two-ender and the miscarriage was mighty good. Alan knows all about miscarriages – that lousy wife of his has had plenty. Made love again. Heaven – heaven – heaven!'

The more I read, the more the volcano inside me boiled up. I wanted a long sharp knife. I'd get it to her throat and have her yell for mercy. I'd get her right down on her knees sobbing – terrified. I'd make her pay a whole of a lot. I'd tear the pages right out of the diary and make her eat her words. I'd prod her naked flesh with the knife – gently then harder and harder until the blood ran. I'd run the blade deeper and deeper over her flesh – slowly – slowly until…

So maybe you can figure how I was feeling reading all this stuff. They'd all got it damn wrong about me. Figuring I was just plain dumb – the sort of guy that folk could walk right over. Gooky Boy? Gooky Boy? I'd just like to shit right into their dull, stupid faces and then make them lick my ass. God, I'd make them pay. I could see the whole bunch of them back at the studio. Not one was any real good as an artist. Daubers – scribblers – the whole lot of them. I could see them sneaking glances at me and whispering – giving sneaky grins and mouthing God knows what. They were just damn jealous that I was a real artist and could put it over. I was the one that illustrated the T & G ads, Ha Yom and the Crackle, Snackle, Pop accounts. I got known and featured in 'Advertising Today' and so on. They had it stacked up on me right from the start. Yes, I'd shit right into their stupid mugs.

And Rosa? Rosa? Nothing was good enough to make her pay. I'd have her squirming right at my feet. She'd regret landing me with that damn pink Caddy. Carve you up, honey? No. That would be just a touch far too nice. What about shutting you into a dark cupboard and just leave you there to rot? Just about nothing would be enough to pay you out – bitch. Thumbscrews, racks, water treatment. I'd make you pay – really pay.

I turned back to the diary. 'Real nice to Gooky. Told him about Alan calling and the miscarriage. He bought it! Said he'd seen Alan at some garden place. Let him make love. Not much good. Next day got Gooky to take me to Garden Tomb place. Bunch of folks from southern states. Great. Real Christians. Led by a big guy with hairs on his chest. Fancied him in a big way. Sorry, Alan. I 'really' fancied him in a big way – you know what? I got him! I got him! Well, there was this tomb place in the garden where they reckon Jesus was buried. They said lots of prayers and stuff. Big guy asked folk to get into the tomb and get reborn. No stampede. So I got right down there and laid right out on the slab. Big Guy shut the gate and came right up. I knew what I wanted, and he knew what he wanted. So we both got what we wanted and how! Great! Great! Great! Was I just born again? You bet. Sorry, Alan, you're pretty good, but this guy from the south, he knew how to deliver the goods!

'Outside, I got to telling the folk what a great experience it was being born again. They bought it big! The alleluias and 'praise the Lord' rang out. Big guy looked at me and I looked at him, and we smiled. The Southern jerks thought I'd been through some sort of religious experience. Okay, maybe I had! It just depends on what you mean by a religious experience! I guess folk are pretty easy to fool if you know how to play your cards right.'

I bang the journal hard. The shit! The shit! Louse just didn't get to crawl so damn low. I felt real sorry for those folk from the South. Maybe I didn't go too much on their angle, but I felt real sorry for them to be taken in by a shit like Rosa. I'd like to take her right down the South and read this out to those folk. Maybe they were the sort of folk who fooled around with rattlers and hoped the Lord would keep them from getting bitten. Maybe they'd put her in a roomful of rattlers and lock the door on her. That'd get her sorted in a big way.

I turned back to the journal. 'Went along with the folk from the South. Big Guy Freddy thought it would be swell. Suggested I went through some sort of baptism in Jordan way up in the Galilee. Why not? Could be 'very' interesting. Hinted we could get Gook in the water too. Freddy said he would fix. Had some guys with muscles! Got up to the Galilee end of Jordan. Said some words and got into this white gown. Into water. Real cold! Freddy standing right over me. Mighty big. A hell of a lot of hair on his body. Wow! Alongside Freddy. His hand strayed all over me. Wonderful. Heart beating real fast. Then right under the water. Help! Was I born again? I just guess that Freddy had given me a hell of a lift. He gave me what I want. So don't take the religious stuff too much. The physical counts. That's it. The physical! That's what counts with a feisty girl like me!'

I read on from what happened in some tomb. She carried in, "Stayed at a kibbutz by Galilee. Fine in summer but damn cold now. Slipped out and met Freddy. Dark. What arms! Just about to find a cosy place where we could get what we had before. This dame came rushing out. She slapped me real hard in the face and then turned on Freddy. Guess it had to be his wife. Freddy beat it fast like a kid in trouble with his ma. The dame got on to me. She reckoned that if I knew what was good for me, I'd better get to disappearing real fast."

God, I was right beside myself. I boiled right up inside. I was darned mad with myself. How the hell could I have got tangled up with this dame? How – how – how? Had some damned dybbuk gotten hold of me? How could I have got myself caught right up in her sticky web? How she lured folk and sucked them dry. How the hell did she do it and how the hell did I get trapped? God – Eve just took a real small bite out of the apple – but this dame took in the whole tree and a heck of a lot more. I got back to the damned journal with its fancy leather binding but with a hell of what inside? I got to reading the stuff. I just had to get through it.

"Showed Gook journal. Gook just isn't ever going to see inside. It would eat him right up! He's not going to get one little peek. This is just mine – mine! All I've got to do is unclick the lock and wow – it's all there. Just about how I got just about everyone from when I was a kid in pigtails right round my dear little finger. Gook's sketching me right now. Says he likes the great curves of my flesh. Says it reminds him of some guy called Rubens. Maybe he's one of the teachers at the academy. Who knows? Got Gooky worked up. Asked him about that Crackle, Snackle, Pop Girl and how she was just a little bit like the dame at Quick Snax. Guess he just didn't like that too much. But if he knew! I got just about a whole lot of satisfaction in breaking up that nice cosy little affair. Wonder if she still dreams back at the convent of her lover-boy, Ben. Kidded Gook I'd had enough of Israel. Promised Land is a hell of a dump. But with Freddy's dame likely to spill the beans, guess we'd better beat it."

I carried on flipping through the pages. I picked up a bit here and something there. The anger boiled right up inside. It then hit me hard, "Gook has a swell idea – build a studio away from the house. Great. Suite me fine. Sold it to Pa who put up the dough. So, Gook got his studio that makes him happy and keeps him right away from treading on my toes. What do I get? Lover-boy Alan gets a clear field. He brings folk from his church. We have a prayer meeting. I just go along with it and do the right things. It's just a whole load of hooey. Alan thinks I've taken it on board! I guess you're as easy to kid as the Gook! So, Alan moves in and I fix a room for him. Gook takes it in. But where does Alan sleep? So, I get what I want and Gooky gets what he wants in his studio out there and keeps tight out of the way."

"Reckon Gook's a pretty queer fish. Pa let it out that Gook's Pa was mighty strange. Something turned his mind way back in Germany. Got caught up in a fire or something. No good at business. Just spent his time like Gook, painting. Went plumb crazy and burnt himself up in his studio. Guess Gook's a mighty queer fish too. Anyway, he suits my purpose fine. But reckon I'll have to keep an eye on him. Might do something real crazy. Told him we're having a baby. Not too interested. But Gooky boy whose baby? You can bet your bottom dollar not yours. Lover boy Allan's? Nope! No way. Sorry, Alan, the kid ain't yours either. It just has to be that lover of lovers, big Freddy, from the South. There we were just into the garden tomb in Jerusalem. Freddy worked the magic – and HOW! Okay Alan, maybe you'll get your chance next time? Gooky – I'll keep you right out of my bed, that's for sure."

I guess I didn't care too much about the kid. The rage cooled down. Something like a great lump of ice moved right down in the pit of my stomach. Somehow, I'd get even. I read on a bit.

"Alan worried about Gook. He's going around talking to himself at the agency. Picks quarrels. Says folk talk behind his back and so on. Started shouting around the place. Says they're gunning for him. Alan keeps his gun to hand when he stays over just in case Gook goes crazy. Poor Alan thinks the kid's his. He's just never going to know!"

So, the swabs at the agency don't like me spilling out the truth? Okay – what the hell did they think? What the hell did they take me for? They got to sneering and saying goddamned awful things about me. They're just downright sore that I'm a darned sight better artist than the whole lot put together. I'd shit on the whole lot of them. I'm just a darned sight too good. Could they beat my stuff? Crackle, Snackle, Pop and the Traumann dame wearing the T & G frames? Those rave reviews in the press? No way. Do they feature Wagstaffe stuff? No – it's me, Ben Traumann who gets a whole lot of column inches. No sir, Wagstaffe nor any of the others just don't get a mention. Their stuff's just a load of crap not worth a second glance."

I took in another page of the diary.

"Went into Hanna Rubenstein's Memorial Clinic. The best around. Told them Alan was the father. Slipped a few bucks around so Gook gets the bum's rush if he shows up. Alan went along with this. Bad time. Hell – HELL – **HELL**. I'm damned well not going through this again. Alan great. Terrible row when he left. Nurse said something about a drunk getting in. Gook? Baby Christopher twisted gut. Needs surgery later. Looks just like Freddy – blue eyes and a whole lot of ginger hair. Nurse says Alan's had a punch up with some rough outside."

I skipped some pages.

"Back home. Jumpy. Heart racing like mad. Faces at window. Gook? Not too easy. Ma and Pa not too pleased Christopher will be a Christian. They're a whole lot worried about what the rest of the Stein family will think. Why should they worry? Okay – they're not too observant. Feel flat. Legs just won't bear me up. Can't do anything. Can't read – watch TV. Nurse comes to stay. Alan back. Why did he stay way? Alan clammed up. Dead inside. Cold. Feel nothing – not even for Alan. Shaky. Trembly. Alan brought salmon, strawberries, and champagne. Not interested. No appetite. Alan watches me writing journal. Hell of an effort. MUST write. Alan twitchy. Plays with gun. Keeps walking around. God's sake sit. Key of journal on floor. Can't reach. Bed."

I knew what I had to do. I was dead cool. I'd fix that dame with the T & G frames. I took the stairs slowly with the journal firmly in my hand. Beans were going to be spilled. I turned into the long dark passage at the top of the stairs. I paused with my hand on the door handle. I was dead calm. The truth was going to get out – and how. These two had had me jerking about like some damned puppet on a string. Now I had control of the strings. I was right in control. Not gooky boy. I was Bennie Traumann, a guy to be reckoned with. They were going to find out who really counted around the place.

I eased down the handle and inched open the door. Inside it was dark. Heavy breathing. Grunts from Rosa. I took my time. Why hurry? I'd get them both squealing. I'd have them pleading for mercy. I reached for the switch. Soft lights came slowly on. Confused sounds came from the bed. Suddenly Wagstaffe sat up and looked straight at me. I asked him what the hell was he doing in bed with my wife. He came back saying Rosa was not too good and that we'd sort things out in the morning, okay? But it was not okay.

I held up the open journal. I told Wagstaffe that there were just a few passages that he ought to hear. Rosa started to stir. Wagstaffe tried to draw the bedclothes back round her. But she was getting her eyes open and pulling herself up. She saw me and gave something of a scream. She saw the open journal in my hand. I told her that it made mighty interesting reading and that I was just going to read some nice little bits. Wagstaffe made to get out. I held out my hand and told him firmly just to relax and listen. He made some dumb comment about it wasn't fair – the journal, was mighty private. So, I told him straight that he thought Rosa's kid was his but he'd got it wrong. So, I read out the section of what happened in the Garden Tomb with Freddy Big Boy. That he was one hell of a good lover and so on. How she had fooled Wagstaffe that the kid was his. At this, Wagstaffe went crazy. He shook Rosa real hard. She started to blub and say she was sorry and that sort of thing. He was the only one she could really love and so on.

You can guess that Wagstaffe wasn't having any. He leapt out of the bed and started beating her around the head. He was yelling and screaming and calling her all sorts of a whore. He threw on his things and grabbed the gun out of my hand. He fired a slug into Rosa and threw the gun toward me. I caught it as he disappeared into the dark passage. "So long," he called back, "don't forget you pulled the trigger," and he gave a hoarse laugh. He disappeared into the dark passage. Then came the starting up of his car. Wagstaffe was off the campus mighty fast.

I stood there for some time fingering the gun and looking at Rosa's body. A trickle of blood flowed across her forehead. I felt numb. Somehow, something like that feeling I got way back in the old city of Jerusalem. A strange, warm feeling. I felt a great wave of sorrow flow over me. A sorrow for Rosa. Okay, she was a schemer. She used people to toe her line. But ….? Now there she was, dead. Finished by Wagstaffe. **Wagstaffe**. I made my way over to her side. Took up her lifeless, plump hand and put it to my lips. I picked up her fancy T & G frames and put them into my pocket with the gun. I turned back the sheets over her dead face and made my way slowly down the stairs wondering where the heck I was going.

I made for the studio. This was my place. It had suited me fine. There was my easel with a part-finished canvas with what was going to be something real great. I had been trying to get through to what was really real. Going through what you could see to what gave it shape – what made it real. There was a hell of a long way to go. It was not like some of the stuff in the studio. The illustration of some dame with an empty face – a guy with a fancy automobile. What I had up there on the easel was art. This is what grabbed me. I guess Abe would approve.

Then it came to me. I just had to hoof it to someplace a way off. Catskills? That's it. A bunch of us used to go camping out there way back. But I figured that I just was having to leave the studio with all my stuff. I got out my old rucksack and stuffed it with a whole lot of things I reckoned I was going to need, including a wad of dollar bills. I looked out a can of gas and spread it around. At the door, I threw in a flame. The place went right up. I started up the pink Caddy. That would get me some way. But it just had to go. I let in the clutch and headed fast for the highway. I looked back. I made out the flames eating into my studio. That was it. A real nice slice of my life was on the way out.

I kept going up to the highway. God knows what the time was but trucks roared by. What of the Caddy? It had to go. I turned off some place. It was pretty wooded. I noted a track going down through the trees. I drove along. I came to a slope. It looked like it led down to a pit or something. I got out and looked. Just the place? I got the rucksack out. Put the Caddy in gear, released the handbrake and got out fast as it started to roll. It went straight down into the pit and crashed way below. I was damned glad to see it go. Where the hell had that Caddy got me?

I made it back to the highway. Where to head? Just about anywhere. Trucks and a few automobiles thundered by. Day was on the break. Soon, it would be sun up. A truck slowed down and stopped ahead.

"Can you use a lift, buddy?" the guy up in the cab called.

I got in and we were off. The driver wanted to know where I was heading. I came back with just about anywhere. That suited him fine.

"Hey, you just stink of gas!"

I told him that I'd got some grease on my pants and cleaned it off with gas. He let out a hell of a laugh. He went on to say how way back home when he was a kid his ma used to take a whole lot of stuff, pants coats and so on and put them in a tub of gas in the back yard. That got them real clean. Then one time, his grandpappy was out there warming his old bones in the last of the sun before the fall. There he was, swinging in his rocker and smoking that old pipe of his. He struck a match to get the baccy going and flicked it away. It landed right in that tub of gas. The whole lot just went up. His ma went crazy.

We drove on for quite some time heading east. The sun was well up. The colours of the fall were touching the trees. I got to itching for a canvas and paint. We pulled into a truck park and headed for this joint where you could feed. I paid for his tray. He got through his mighty quick and said he had to be off. It suited me. I took my time figuring out my next step. Where the heck was I going? Where to stay? One thing was pretty clear. There was no going back. I was just faced with a mighty big blank canvas. Whatever I was going to have to fill that great white space with something. But what the hell? I gave a great laugh out loud. The truckers looked right round at me and then got back to eating.

I headed off the highway and hit a small township somewhere or other. It was one of those nice little places with some pretty old dwellings and so on. Everywhere looked pretty good. It was a nice homely sort of place where folk smiled and said hello. A place to pitch my tent for a while? Maybe. I got myself a burger at a kiosk and sat for some time in this park. It had a small lake and reminded me of the one back in Chicago where Rebecca used to take me. God, I could use Rebecca around right now. But now it was just me with a darned great rucksack on my back with just about all I had zipped up inside.

Some old guy staggered along the path. "Mind, son?" He threw himself on the bench. He looked a real nice old guy and gave me quite a smile. He took out a copy of *The Herald Tribune.* "Hey, just look at this!" Right there on the front page was a heading *Ad man's daughter shot.* The whole of the page and inside was taken up with copy and pictures. Wagstaffe was cited as a witness. A mug shot of me was printed headed ***Wanted***. The old guy squinted at me and reckoned it looked just a bit like me. He got up leaving the paper in my hands and shuffled off. I guessed I ought to get myself right off the campus mighty fast.

I made straight for the highway and picked up a truck heading east. It dropped me off somewhere that didn't look too fancy. I figured I'd better keep out of motels and started sleeping rough, curled up in my sleeping bag. I had quite a wad of dollar bills but reckoned on keeping spending low. I ate at wayside places and hid away in farmsteads and woods. Somehow, it was okay. I felt free. I kept away from towns. My beard grew pretty big and I guess I got to looking like some bum who had been on the road for one a hell of a long time. So that's just about how it was. I shacked up just about where I could. I got used to living rough. I tried a motel now and again but got shown the door mighty fast. I guess I'd got to looking not too good.

I just lost all count of time. But somehow, I got to sketching here and there. When I left my studio, I packed some of my stuff. Two or three cartridge blocs, pencils and conte crayons. So, when I got to seeing something that caught my eye, I just sat down and sketched. Sometimes folk would come up and watch. I'd get offered a few bucks for whatever but I made it damned clear my stuff was not for sale. I guess I just didn't need their dough. I still had plenty stashed right away at the bottom of my backpack.

Then came the time when I met the Man. It came about like this. I was making my way through some small township when I hit upon an optometry. What the hell did I see there in the window? There she was in T & G butterfly frames looking right out at me from the display – Rosa with the slogan *Guys date dames* in T & G. frames. It had faded. But there she was, Rosa, smiling right out at me through her fancy frames. Somehow, it shook me. Okay, she was one hell of a bitch. She'd treated me real bad. There was no getting away from that. But somehow, something stirred right deep down somewhere. Tears burst right out. I sobbed. She was a big, fat, sad and twisted kid who'd got snarled up somehow and she just didn't deserve that slug in the head from that asshole Wagstaffe.

I wiped my eyes with the back of my sleeve. It had got mighty dirty by now. The light was going. I looked back into the window. It was then that I saw him reflected back from the glass. It was this old guy with one hell of a beard. He didn't say anything. He never did. But somehow, I picked up whatever it was that he was getting over. He shook his head to one side and indicated that we should team up. Well, guess that after being alone for God knows how long, I was not too sure. But I said okay. So that's just how the Man became my buddy. We teamed up and went around together. He kept quiet and didn't get in the way. So that suited me fine. It was kinda good to have company. So, I didn't have to feel so lonesome. I got to talking to him about whatever. He always listened. Maybe he'd come back with something or other in that strange way he'd get to getting his meaning over.

Times we'd be sitting together on some park bench somewhere or other. I'd get around maybe to art or something like that. Well, I guess he'd not thought about that before but I figured he was an intelligent guy who could work things out and come up with a comment that made some sense. Anyways, we tramped around the Catskills, a pretty nice place. I took in a lot of Tom Cole's stuff at art school. Now, I could see what he painted way back in God knows when. A hell of long time back. Anyways I liked his stuff and got something out of it. And here I was, tramping around making it up mountains and squinting down the Hudson making its way into the landscape. So, I got out my pad and did a whole lot of sketching as the Man sat by.

Sometimes we ran into folk taking in the landscape and passing by on a track some place. They'd call out, "How de," and give a grin. At times, they'd stop and chew the rag just a bit. Maybe I'd open my pack and show my sketches. They'd comment and say they were damned good. One guy knew about art and we talked about Tom Cole. That was great. One thing I just couldn't figure out; these folk never took in the Man. He just stood there and kept his trap shut.

So, time went on and it started to get somewhat chill up and around the mountains. So, we moved down into the small townships. I got to looking into a place that kept stuff for hunters and such. They sold guns, knives and tackle for fishing. The Man gave me a nudge and moved me to the door. We went in. The guy who kept the place gave me a look. There was a whole lot of stuff around the place. Hunting guns, fishing rods, handguns and knives. The knives got me. I had Wagstaffe's fancy gun in my pack but I could use a knife. I picked out one with bone handle and a blade that meant business. The guy came over. "You want that buster?" I paid him his dollars and we got out. I fingered the blade, slipped in into the sheath and eased it into my pocket. The Man grinned his approval.

So, in the late Fall, we got to hanging around the small townships. Sometimes we got into a low-down hotel. Sometimes they just wouldn't take us in. So, we just had to find some place where we could hunker down way out of the chill wind. Somehow the dollars made out. I must have picked up a mighty big wad when I got out of the place at Lake Forest. It so happened that we were moseying around this little old place and came upon this gate. We went into a back yard someplace and hit on something of a shed. So, in we went. It was full of stuff, tools and so on. But I got out the sleeping bag and hunkered down. By this time, it was pretty dark and pretty cold. I'd just got off and felt okay. Then the door came open and some guy beamed in a flashlight. "What the hell?" he yelled. What the hell? I felt for the hunting knife and got to my feet. The guy came in and started yelling, "Get the hell out of here." I guess he just didn't get to see the knife. I lunged forward and knifed him somewhere or other. He yelled out holding his arm and calling me an asshole. He disappeared into the yard. A woman called out, "You okay, Herb?" I guess we'd need to get the hell out of this place real fast. I got together my stuff and beat it with the Man.

We made it out of town and headed back into rough country. Up a track leading up a hill with a mighty lot of trees and stuff around. A pretty heavy movement made us stop. A moose got up and made off fast. We got up to this high point and looked back down to where we came from I picked up the sound of a siren. Cops? The Man moved his head in the way he does. So, we got going again up, up into the Catskills and well away from wherever.

So, we went on making out as best we could. Sleeping rough, booking into some cheap dosshouse where they were not too particular. I carried on sketching the country that got Tom Coles going. Maybe I was on the run from God knows who or what. But Ben Traumann still had an eye and could move his hand to put down this great landscape. We came across this place with a waterfall pouring down into the Hudson. I did what I could with conte crayons but I itched for oils. Maybe sometime I could work up a canvas. Maybe.

So, it was damned good hoofing around the Catskills. It got me seeing. It got me thinking. I went back to Rebecca who did just about everything she could do for me as a kid. She taught me to be a good Jew. She taught me to be ME. I thought back over those times with the Bible. She knew the Book inside out. Those pages about God. Blessed be He, created just about everything. So, as I looked around up here in the Catskills, it all came right home. How the heck did all this and everything get made? How did God put it all together? We artists know how to paint. We see something that grabs us. We set up our easels and canvas. We rough out whatever and then get going with colour. And what about guys like Michelangelo and his fantastic sculpture of David? How did he take a damned great block of marble and bring out something that gets folk standing there with open mouths? God, that's one hell of a mystery. I guess that there are a whole lot of issues that just can't be made too clear.

I guess that hoofing around in great empty places gets a guy doing some pretty deep thinking. Back in Chicago with the razzmatazz of God knows what things get blotted out. You just get caught right up in making dough and getting your name up in lights. I guess that's how it was way back in the agency making a name for myself. But all that's past and here I am with the Man up in the Catskills. So, in spite of it all, am I beginning to find myself? Maybe? I remember Rebecca unpacking a mighty strange struggle of Jacob with some strange being, was it an angel or God? It's then that he got a new name, she told me it was Israel and that we Jews had to learn to struggle. I'm beginning to cotton on to what she meant.

Sometimes, I get to fingering that fancy gun of Wagstaffe's. On one side of the grip, Adam and Eve munch into an apple and on the other, Cain is finishing off his brother Abel. Strange stuff. Somehow it came back to something that Rebecca told me about how Adam and Eve did wrong by eating apples. How come? Why did God say that this was something he didn't want them to do? Why the hell? Why kick them right out of the garden and so get a real bad time? It didn't figure. How could God say He loved us and then give us a damned good hiding? It just didn't stack up. And then Cain killing Able? Had Cain eaten just too many apples and something bad had got right into him? How come we get to killing each other like Wagstaffe putting a slug into Rosa? Had Wagstaffe eaten just a few too many apples?

Then I got round to thinking about this guy someplace who got to telling me about the time he was in the US air corps back in the war. He had a pretty bad time. They made him an air-gunner up in the nose of a B17 Flying Fortress. Over some place, they dropped a whole lot of bombs, killing, I figure, a whole lot of innocent folk. Then the crate got hit and he had to bail out and landed in a tree someplace. They got him and put him with whole lot of our guys into a hell of a strange place he called Dresden. So, he told me that it was a place near the market where some stallholders cut up meat for sale. It was called Slaughter House Five. So, they were all packed in. Not too much comfort. Then came flights of US planes dropping leaflets telling folk to get out. Then they came back, this time with the Brits and bombs. What he could see of the city was pretty neat. It looked easy on the eye with places that had been around before Noah had got into the ark.

So, this guy had to hunker down in the slaughterhouse and just hope that a bomb didn't come their way. It didn't. But that damned nice place was made a fireball. They got mighty hot down there. When things died down, the German guards got them out. They were mighty sore and treated the prisoners mighty rough. They put them to do some clearing up. The guy told me how he had to pull a woman, burnt up with her young kid in her arms, out of the rubble. He brought up his last meal. All this was way back in early 1945. Okay, I had got to hearing something about this sometime back, but to hear this, and more from a guy who'd been there? What the hell can one say? Sometimes you just have to keep your mouth shut.

It got me thinking real hard. **Real hard.** Here we are, we humans, walking on the face of this planet of ours, breathing the air, taking in whatever. All this is mighty good. We make a pretty good life for ourselves. We build mighty good townships. We set up universities. We create fantastic paintings. We write good books. Then we get to beating the hell out of each other just like Cain beating the hell out of his own brother. How come? How come? You know how it is that you pick up this and that as you live your life. It came back to me how some old Greek fellow said, "Wonders are many, none is more wonderful than man/humanity." Maybe he didn't get to seeing too much of the damned awful things we do. Maybe.

Moving around the Catskills, you get to meeting some pretty nice folk. One day, we came across this small place. It had a real nice friendly feeling with homesteads and something of a shop here and there and folk going around their business with a ready smile on their face. We sat on a bench alongside a pond with ducks paddling around. A dame came along with I reckoned to be her daughter. They threw crusts of bread to the creatures. That done, they came and joined us on the bench, gave a smile and got to talking. She said that a real nice place it was to live. The kid joined in too. It made me feel mighty good. The Man listened but said nothing. They went on like they just were not seeing the Man. But that's how it is. Then she made the suggestion to come and have a little something at her place. So off we went. She sat me down and fried up something that smelt real good. And when she put that plate down in front of me – boy! Wow! Back up the track, I had quite a spring in my step. That dame had done something I needed badly, something I've heard some folk calling tender loving care. Yup, that's it, tender loving care of the sort that Rebecca gave me when I was a kid. I've just never forgotten that.

As we made our way along the Hudson, I turned over a whole lot of the stuff stored away deep between my ears someplace. All the bad things that had hit me as a kid and since and all the good things. I guess that's how it is for most. Life's a mixture. Some get a whole lot of the bad and some a heck of a lot of the good. That's how it is. Now, if just about everyone everywhere on this little old world of ours got to treating each other real well, like that dame who fed me, I guess it would just be like heaven. I can't remember too much about the Bible but what struck me is that there was a whole lot about being mighty kind not just to us Jews but everyone. So how is it that a whole lot just don't get the message and just give others a mighty cold shoulder and sometimes worse? Figure that out. It gets me foxed.

A song of sorts welled up from the depths. It was sung by the crooner Bing Crosby way back. It went something like, "Eliminate the negative, accentuate the positive and don't mess with Mr In-between." I figured that there was just too many around messing with that Mr In-between and maybe a darned sight too many not getting round to eliminating the negative. I rated myself in that direction. So that's how it was. As I tramped around with the Man, I guess that for the first time in my life I felt really good inside. I took great lungs full of the good air up there in the mountains and felt it was damned good to be me. Yes, damned good to be Benjamin Traumann, the kid of two young Jews who got the hell out of Germany way, way back. I felt real good. Mighty good. And I guess that was not all – like Tom Cole way back I could paint and draw and had been taught by just about one of the best art teachers around, Abe Grosnevski. A damned fine teacher and a mighty good friend. I guess that I'd got some pretty good cards in my hand.

As it happens, my mind went back to the Chicago Art Institute and a painting that hung there by Marc Chagall. Chagall, a Jew, beat it out of Paris to the States when it looked like things were going to get pretty bad if the Nazis came to town. Anyway, I spent a hell of a long time getting into this painting. It's called the White Crucifixion. It shows that old Jew Jesus on the cross. All around, Jews are getting to a hell of whatever. Flames flare up from a synagogue. At the foot of the cross is the Jewish menorah giving light to us humans, Jews and goys. By the painting was a word from the artist, "My thoughts represent not the dreams of one people but of all humanity." He went on, "I painted Christ in pictures of the ghettos, surrounded by Jewish troubles, by Jewish mothers running terrified with their little children under their arms." That painting and all it meant got me really churned up. It sent me back to Cain and Abel and why the hell we human beings got to treating each other so damned badly and so on. Somewhere I picked up something about, "Man's inhumanity to man." How it was, God knows, how many of us Jews got sent into the gas chambers at Auschwitz? Inhumanity? It shuts the mouth right up tight. What the hell can you say about the god-awful things we humans do? God, GOD, **GOD?** Why the heck don't you step right in and stop us?

But then the amazing beauty of the Catskills with the Hudson sparkling way down below floods in and gives a whole different view of things. Cain fades away like a ghost and you get grabbed by what you see all around and all the wild creatures. Right now, as I take all this in, some bird nearby with a red head [cardinal] perches itself on a branch and sings a song that gets my ears tingling and heart beating just that bit faster. I get to feeling that life is damned good in spite of the way we louse things up. That's it, life is right damned good. That's what grabs me.

So, I get going with the Man lagging behind. Somehow, I've got a spring in my step. I could almost skip along as I did way back when Rebecca took me into the park as a kid. Yes, I felt like a kid again with the song of that bird ringing in my ears. Way, way ahead I got to seeing this peak in the hills. It pointed up like a finger through the trees right up into the sky. Somehow, it drew me. I just had to get there and maybe scale that peak tight up to the top. That's what I just had to do.

So, we went on a hell of a long way on through the trees. A bobcat eyed us from a way off. We came to the foot of the peak. A rough track seemed to go up. I guess I'd sweat a bit getting to the top. Then I got to seeing this little old shack of a place. A good place to rest up a while? Then I spied smoke coming from a rough chimney. So?

Anyways, I made for the shack and tapped on the door. No answer. I pushed the door just enough for a mouse to sneak in. I peeped in. I just made out some guy just sitting there. I pushed the door open and said, "Hi." The guy motioned us to come in. It was a relief to warm up with the stove throwing out quite a bit of heat. But it was not too easy to see the guy in the gloom. As my eyes got round to adapting to the half-light, I could just make out the guy. He seemed to be a redskin and had a large feather in his hair. I'd come across these folk once in a reservation. So, we just sat there. I noticed he had on what appeared to be something of a table what might have been a tomahawk. So, we just sat silent for a hell of a long while. What was there to talk about? Then he started talking of a sort. It was not too easy to get his meaning. But I picked up that way, way back Chief Nashotah decided he'd got enough paleface scalps and he'd smoke a peace pipe with Colonel Bright of the US cavalry. So, the chief with his braves, sat around on top of the peak with the pipe ready for the colonel. They waited up there in silence. So, it happened that the colonel, with his men, crept up through the trees. They raised their carbines and started shooting down the braves. Then the colonel drew his sword and ran Nashotah through. The chief gave one hell of a yell and died. It seems that at times Nashotah's yell can still be heard if you listen carefully. That's what this Indian guy seemed to say.

We sat silent as I took this in. It came to me that this was no more than just another case of how we human beings knock the shit right out of each other. My gut went tight. Then it happened. The guy stood up with the tomahawk in his hand and gave out one hell of a cry. I got just a bit scared. The Man moved his head toward me. My hand reached for the hunting knife. I kept it behind my back. The guy rushed toward me with his tomahawk raised high. I gripped the knife hard and thrust it into the guy real hard. He yelled, collapsed and twitched there, where he fell and then went still.

So, what now? I guess that I just had to torch the place just as I had torched the place back in Lake Forest with Rosa's body. Somehow, I managed to get some of the logs out of the stove and threw them around. They soon got the dry stuff around the place in flames. I got out mighty quick before it went up and headed for the track up the peak. I looked back to see the shack going up with flames just about everywhere. So, I got going fast up the track. It became hard going near the peak but I struggled on to the top. I threw myself down on a rock near the edge. The Man stood nearby. I looked down to see smoke rising up from the shack and imagined that old Indian sizzling away as the flames burnt up his body. Maybe I caught something the Man was saying. I could never be certain of anything he said. It may have been, "Life's pretty tricky – pretty tricky." Something like that, maybe. Then a bug under a rock seemed to pick it up, "Pretty tricky – pretty tricky." Then the bugs over the whole peak picked it up, "pretty tricky – pretty tricky – pretty tricky …"

So, I sat up there on Nashotah Peak where the chief and his braves got gunned down. Life was mighty tricky for them. So, what had they on mind? Just to make peace with us palefaces. What do they get? A bullet in the gut. What did Abel get from his own blood brother? He got the shit kicked right out of him. And that's about how it is. I guess that wherever you look in that damned great storybook of what we humans have done on the face of this mighty good earth, there's just a bit too much of what Cain did to his brother. Man's inhumanity to man? Okay. Okay.

So, I just sat up there on the Peak turning things over and watching the smoke rise from somewhere down there. I reckon that the Indian guy was by now reduced to ash. Okay, I knifed him. But what the hell could I do? Get that tomahawk slicing my head in two? A guy has just got to protect himself? Isn't that so?

Then, I heard things way down at the foot of the peak. Bells of sorts. Then I could make out a fire truck heading for the shack with a squad car behind. The car stopped. I could make out two cops getting and looking up to the peak right where I was.

One of the cops started climbing up the face. Maybe he just hadn't figured the track. Perhaps he just liked something of a challenge. But on he struggled. I watched him getting closer. He looked a pretty good climber. Then he got just too close. He yelled something. I got edgy and started to finger Wagstaff's gun. The cop drew his gun and fired a shot way off somewhere. The Man gave me the nod. I pulled out the Wagstaffe's fancy gun and fired near the cop. He yelled, let hold his grip and started to tumble back down. I threw the gun over the edge where it went down and disappeared. I could just make out the cop getting fixed by his buddy. Then they drove off back down the track to the highway.

So, I sat up on the peak, listening to the bugs under their hot rocks. Some great bird started circling around making one hell of sound sending creatures scuttling away to get their heads right down. I guess that tracking around in the Catskills time, whatever that is, just doesn't get to have too much meaning. The Sun comes up and brightens up the landscape, then it goes down and all goes dark and we switch off. So, I sat up there with the sun more than half way across the sky. Then came another sound shattering the peace of Nashotah. Not that damned eagle or whatever but something way up there. I listened, putting my hand to my ear. There it was. An aircraft? Then I got it, a chopper.

So, I just sat there. Listening to the chopper getting nearer. It was coming right this way. Why the heck? Then it came in sight, too close. It hovered right over the peak and circled round. I got somewhat worried. The peak had a pretty flat place on top. The chopper came down. I got to wanting Wagstaffe's gun or maybe my hunting knife. I started heating up. Then they came. Two cops and a guy in a white coat. The cops grabbed me. The guy in the white coat stuck something into my arm. I hollered out and then, I suppose, I just went right out.

I guess things got almighty confused after that. It seemed I was in something of a dream. I just had no clue as to who I was or where I was. Folk were around. Doors banged. I, whoever I might be, was pulled around. I reckon they must have doped me up a hell of a lot. Then things got somewhat clearer. I sensed I was being taken some place. What was happening, I just couldn't make out. Quite a racket was going on. Lots of folk were talking. Some guy started talking to me but no way could I figure out what the heck he was saying. Then whatever it was, quietened down and two guys took hold of me, led me out of the place and eased me into some sort of van. Or so it seemed. I guess that wherever we were heading was some place off. I guess I was damned glad to get out of that van and back on my legs.

The guys led me up some steps into this mighty big place and into some sort of reception place. They did quite a bit of talking and handed me over to a big guy in a white coat who took me into a room. I had to strip off while this guy ran things over me, weighed me, looked into my eyes with something and made notes. Was that it? He rang a bell. These two big guys in some sort of outfit got me to my feet and called me "buster". They got me into an elevator and took me up somewhere. They led me along some passage. Here and there, guys in some sort of uniform were hanging around. The two guys in uniform opened a door into some sort of room. One said, "Here you are buster. Home sweet home!" The other came in with, "Here's your D.J.!" And threw me some damned strange outfit. He told me to get dressed for dinner. I threw off whatever I'd been wearing and struggled into the outfit. They got out and slammed the door hard. I looked around and figured it was a mighty strange apartment. A pretty rough bed, a hard chair and a john and faucet. It was somewhat basic. Light came through a small window way up with bars. I guessed they'd brought me to a hell of a strange place.

I sat on the bed and got to turning things over. Where the heck was I going? Back to the Catskills or some place? My apartment door clanged open and one of the staff came in. He threw me a rough white gown and told me to get my things off and into the gown. I asked why. He didn't like that and told me to get a move on. So, I did what he asked. As he led me out, he muttered something about getting cleaned up in the shower. So, he got me padding along the long corridor down the shower room. There were a whole lot of guys under the showers making a hell of a racket. A number of staff stood around keeping an eye on things. I got off the robe and made to get under the shower with the rest of them. One of the staff came over and ran his eye over me. He looked pretty tough. Not the sort you would want to get into a tangle with. He yelled at me, "Jew boy. Dirty filthy Jew boy!" and gave me a push. I went flying over the wet floor. He then gave me a mighty heavy kick in the ribs that brought tears to my eyes. He followed that up with a kick in the groin. That made me gasp. The guy who brought me to the shower came shooting over. He yelled, "Just stop that right now. Quit that or I'll get you up in front of the governor." He got me to my feet and put his hand on my shoulder. "He's new," he explained and made it clear that no way did he go along with that sort of thing. I got the feeling he was an okay sort of a guy. I asked him if the governor was the proprietor of the hotel. He gave quite a smile, and said, "You could put it that way."

So, it went on. I just couldn't figure the place out or what I was doing there. The guy on the staff would get me out with a whole lot of others in the apartments and take us down to the dining room. We had to line up with trays for whatever and then sit at a bench with the other guests. I couldn't figure that we all wore the same outfit. I asked this guy if he had some other stuff to wear. He gave me an odd look and asked about myself. So, I just learnt to clam up and not ask questions.

The time was that the staff guy told me that they needed to see me in the medical room. He took me on the elevator and down to another floor. So, we got to this place with a red cross over the door and handed me over to what I reckoned to be an orderly in a white outfit. He checked through some stuff, stuck something into me, weighed me and that sort of thing. He then rang through somewhere, said okay, and led me through into a small room. A dame in a white coat got up, shook my hand, smiled and pointed me to a really comfortable chair. She seemed real friendly. She told me she was Lucy Fordrinier, a staff doctor. Then she got me talking about myself. She seemed real interested and listened carefully. No one had treated me like this since Rebecca. Somehow it made me feel real good.

So, she listened and just made a comment here and there. She was interested in how the Traumanns and Grossmanns came to the States. She explained how it was that some women like my mother got into a bad depression after having a kid. And so on. It so happened that I got to seeing the doctor just about every week. That was fine. I itched for the next time. I asked her if I could call her Mom. She smiled and told me to go right ahead. So, she became Mom. I could tell she really cared. I told her about the Man and couldn't figure out where he'd gone. She reckoned he was pretty good at looking after himself and not to worry too much about him. But I still felt it mighty strange that he was no longer around after the hell of a long time getting around in the Catskills with him.

Mom was sure interested when I came to telling her about the Catskills and how Tom Coles had done some pretty good paintings up there. She had quite a regard for Coles and had some reproductions of his work. She got quite excited when we got on to art especially when I got on to my time at the Chicago Art Institute. Before too long, we got on to Chagall's *White Crucifixion* and how the artist, a Jew like me, picked up the Christian icon to get over Jewish suffering. I mentioned his words, "Christ has always symbolised for me the true type of Jewish martyr." So, we got round to thinking about how it is that we humans get to beating the hell out of each other just like Cain giving the KO to his kid brother. Mom reckoned there was no easy answer to all this. Anyway, she suggested I might get back to doing some sketching and that sort of thing. I thought that a pretty good idea. I warmed to it. A day or so afterwards, the staff guy brought me the pack I had up in the Catskills with my sketches and stuff. I was right glad to get it back. So, I got to going through my stuff liking what I saw. If I could get back to having a studio to work some of these sketches up in oils maybe. It was then that Mom fixed something up. Somewhere in this place, not too far from my apartment, there was a room with some light. They took me along and gosh – an easel was set up and a table with paints and a canvas or so. They told me to go ahead and do what I wanted. They went off and left me there. I just couldn't believe what I was seeing. I guess Mom had fixed it. So where to start?

I went through my Catskill sketches and hit on Nashotah Peak rising up through the valley with the Hudson sparkling down below. That was it. So, I got down to it laying down an outline. It flashed through my mind that maybe my old skill might have fallen off. That somehow hand and eye wouldn't quite work together. I was wrong. It all came rushing back. Hand and eye still produced the goods. So, the brush applied the colour just right and my heart beat just that much faster. I felt a thrill going right through every part of me. I was creating something damned worth looking at. I guess the same thrill must have taken over Tom Coles way back. I just lost myself in working up the canvas. Time passed and the light outside started to fall off. The opening of the door gave me a start as the staff guy came in. He stood with open mouth as he viewed the unfinished canvas. "Gee – gee that's…!" He just couldn't get his words out. He put his hand on my shoulder and told me he'd be taking me here each day. He led me out and down to the eating place. I felt so spaced out that I just didn't fancy what was on my plate.

When I was taken back to what I thought of as my apartment, I just couldn't settle too much. I walked up and down the small space. Then I threw myself down on what passed for a bed and rolled around until, I suppose, light went off. So, day-by-day, I got down to what became my studio while I worked on the Nashotah canvas. Then one day, shortly afterwards, Mom slipped in. She was pretty impressed with my canvas that was nearly complete. Somehow, I knew she had fixed things to set this up for me. She said it might be a good thing to set up an art group. She was pretty certain that some of the guys in this place might benefit. But someone would have to head it up. I didn't quite figure what she might be getting at.

Anyways, it so happened, one or two guys came trickling in. Somehow, a few donkeys appeared. Just in case you don't know what they are, they're a long seat with an easel at the end, that's an art donkey. Extra art material appeared. Then somehow, before too long, there were six or so guys pretty keen to get going. So, somehow I took over and showed them how to get working with charcoal pencils. I set up simple still life with boxes, vases and that sort of thing. Basic stuff. I'd get round to looking at their work, commenting and correcting. It went well. Mom put in an appearance from time to time. Then I got her to pose. She had an interesting face and we all got down to her portrait. I must confess depicting the human face is not too easy. I had studied anatomy at the institute and knew about bone structure and the muscles of the face. So, I got round to correcting the work of the other guys. Mom took away my portrait of her.

So, it went on, until ten or more filled what had become the art studio. Some were producing some pretty good stuff. I took them on to oils but kept off watercolour. It so happens that's not an easy medium. You make a mistake and that's it. You've worked damned hard with the work coming on and then? Hell – it's a mess and fit for scrap! So, I kept them on to pastels and oils.

Then one day, Mom brought in a pretty important-looking guy with some others. He was introduced as the governor. I chipped in, "I suppose that means you're the proprietor of this establishment." The other guys tittered. He came back, "I suppose you could put it that way." Anyways, he went round, looking at the stuff the group had put together. He came round to asking me about my time at the Chicago Academy. He went on to thank me for setting up the art group and talking about an exhibition.

I went back to my apartment feeling pretty good. Somehow, I'd got something mighty worthwhile going. I felt pretty sure that my old friend Abe would be mighty pleased too. Abe? Abe? Yes, Abe. I guess he'd wonder what the hell had happened to me. Somehow, I just hadn't given him a thought. Looking back Abe had given me a whole lot of backing. He guided me through the academy and then stood in as something of a father, with me living at his place. Yes, I reckon I'd owed a whole lot to Abe and I had just stopped giving him a thought. But somehow, I bet he'd kept me in mind. So how do I get back in contact?

Then things got going. An Expo was set up somewhere downstairs in a pretty imposing room. With Mom and some other guy, we went through the work done by the art group. We made our selection. The stuff was properly mounted and hung on expo boards. It all looked mighty good. If Abe could just see this! Then came a day for opening. A whole lot of folk were there and a TV crew. This governor guy gave quite a speech and put it over that the idea of an art group came from me. Hell, did it? He said how it had improved the lives of what he called the inmates in the art class. Inmates? Then Mom came in and said how occupational therapy was important for rehabilitation. I couldn't quite make that out. A whole lot of clapping went on, flashlights were going off and the TV crew were doing whatever. The governor got me going along with his group to explain what they were seeing. I felt pretty easy. So, I went back to my apartment feeling that I,

Bennie Traumann, was a somebody. That's how it was. I walked tall so tall that my head nearly touched the ceiling!

Some days after I got a letter through the mail. This was mighty unusual. I sat and fingered the envelope. The handwriting and so on. I turned it over and over. Then I carefully unsealed it and slowly withdrew the letter. The paper felt crisp to the touch. It was good paper and cream in colour. I shut my eyes while I opened it out. I wondered who would be writing to me? Then I looked and there was Abe's signature! I'd like to put down the contents but maybe not. Abe had seen the expo on TV and all that had been said about me setting up an art group and the value of therapy and so on. He felt damned proud of me. Damned proud. He then went on to say he'd got a medical problem of some sorts so he was confined to his apartment and so on. It did me a whole lot of good to hear from Abe. I'd be sure to get down to writing back. I turned over the good folk who'd helped me along the track – Rebecca, Abe and Mom. I guess that in some ways I'd been dealt a pretty good hand at times with an ace or two. What the heck would I have down without these great folks who'd kept me on track? And right now, Mom. Yes, Mom down there at the medical centre who'd got me to write all this stuff down and got behind setting up the art group and so on. I guess that without these folks, I'd just have faded right away into just about nothing. They made me who I am, Bennie Traumann.

But that was not the end. I got called down to the place where you could see folk. A member of the staff took me down. There was a guy who wanted to see me. He was pretty old with grey hair around his kippah. So, I knew right away he was, like me, a Jew. He motioned me to sit. He looked at me for quite a while. He then leant forward with a smile and took my hand in both of his and said, "Remember, once a Jew you're always a Jew. We Jews walk tall!" He introduced himself as Rabbi Joseph Cohen. He had a synagogue in a township not so far off it seems. Then he got round to the publicity about the art expo and Chagall's stuff and *White Crucifixion*. It seemed he had a copy in his study. It was good to chew the cud with him. Somehow, we hit it off.

That was the first session with Rabbi Cohen. He came pretty often and got down to talking about life and what a heck of a mystery it was. He went on to say that the word "mystery" came from the old Greek for that which shuts the mouth. I could see that and told him a few things about my time up in the Catskills and how amazing it all was. He agreed and said that in his younger days he did a whole lot of trekking up there and he was nuts about the work of Tom Coles.

Mom was pretty glad that I was seeing the Rabbi. I got a hunch that maybe she'd fixed it. So, we got round to thinking about this and that and what is meant to be a Jew and all that God, blessed be he, had passed on through Father Abraham and so on. The Rabbi said that our people had their eyes and ears wide open so they could cotton on to God's will. I didn't mention Wagstaffe's fancy gun with Cain beating the hell out of Abel. But I aired how it is that we humans did some mighty bad things like the Holocaust and so on. He stroked his chin and thought round it. He said that throughout history, the story of Cain and Abel had come up just too many times. So often the goys had treated us Jews real bad. So, I put out, "Why then doesn't the Almighty stop all this sort of thing? Make us behave well?"

Rabbi Cohen stroked his chin and looked at me deeply. He came back with, "You know what our Creator did when he made us humans? Did He make us automata so all He had to do was to push the right button and we'd toe His line? No, as we read in Genesis, He made us in His own image. What does that mean? It means He has given us the freedom to make our own decisions. So, we can go ahead and love our fellow beings as our brothers and sisters or we can treat them badly just as Cain treated Abel. You get it?" I got it. Did Wagstaffe have to shoot Rosa? I guess not. Okay he'd feel mighty sore over what he'd read in her diary. Who wouldn't? But to put a slug into her and pass the gun over to me and get out of the joint mighty quick? What the hell? Did he have to do that?

The Rabbi went on to say that we Jews, unlike Christians, did not believe that somehow Adam and Eve had infected the human race with sin. No. But we came with a blank sheet. On one side we could choose the good and the other side the bad. It was right up to each one, Jews or goys, to make our own decisions. I bought right into that. That guy Wagstaffe made a real bad decision and made things pretty bad for me. So it seems.

So, things were not so bad. I ran the small art group. That was fine. I had some of their work and my stuff hanging in my room. I spent time with Mom. She was damned good at listening and feeding in a question now and again. Then these sessions with the Rabbi. He brought me back to my Jewish roots. That was good. He unpacked a whole lot in our Jewish faith that somehow, I hadn't quite got hold of. That was pretty good. It got me back to reading our Bible and picking up again some of the things that Rebecca had passed on to me. I got down to studying the work of Marc Chagall in some detail. What a guy! He gets you going right down into the depths of our brains. He makes you think hard about what the hell life's about. For God's sake, we're not robots but **thinkers** – feelers – beings that create whatever and just about whenever. That's what we are!

So, time slipped by as the earth turned round and made its way around the sun. So, what the heck is time? Can you catch yourself a bit of time, hold it in your hand and say you've caught it? It's about as slippery as a well-oiled eel. It slips right through the fingers, slithers across the floor and right out under the door. It's gone. And what would you do if you caught just a bit of time? What would you do with it? Could you use it to paint a picture or put some music together? Well, I reckon I'm not going to trap that bit of time and lock it away some place no way.

So, life went on. I painted pictures with the art group. That was good. Some of the guys shaped up real well. They'd make passable artists if they stick at it. Then the sessions with Mom. They were good. She'd listen to me and then, as she did, make a point here and there. Then Rabbi Cohen came in every so often and we talk over Jewish things together. That was okay. It made me think over where we had come from and what it really meant to be a Jew. It helped me to walk just a bit taller.

Then came a day – THE day. This guy from the staff came in and got me getting my stuff together. Somehow, I thought he was moving me to another apartment. No, I'd got it wrong. He got me into the elevator and down to floor level and into an office. I waited. Mom came in and smiled, as she always did. She reached out and touched my shoulder. I sensed something was going to happen. My hands started to get sticky. Then Rabbi Cohen came in and greeted me in Hebrew, "Shalom aleichem." Somehow, I couldn't quite get out Aleichem shalom and gulped out "Hi!" So, we sat for some time. Then in came the man I had come to recognise as the governor. He had two others with him. The governor guy looked around then directly at me. I wondered what I had done. I mopped my brow. He said, "This is an important day for you Traumann. We've decided it's okay to parole you. I think we all agree that you have made a pretty good contribution to your section. You've set up the art group and the men in the group have improved a lot. That's thanks to you. So, with Dr Trish Goodson and the Rabbi, we agreed to release you on parole."

I gulped and mopped my brow again. My head went into a spin. Parole? Parole? Out there some place? I just couldn't figure it all out. They could see that I was in a hell of a whirl. The governor turned to Mom and asked her to explain. "Bennie," she started, "this comes as something of a surprise. But we're not going to turn you loose on the outside world. You will need some support. This is where Rabbi Cohen comes in." The Rabbi picked things up. 'Bennie, I'm going to look after you with Mrs. Cohen. You'll be fine with us. We'll see to it. Don't you worry. You'll be okay you'll see."

It was at this point that things started to happen. Something welled right up inside me. I lost my breath. I started to make some damned awful sound. I started to sob and thrash around. It looked as if Mom fished something out of her bag. They rolled up my sleeve and Mom stuck something into me. I calmed right down. The governor leant over and grasped my shoulder and said he'd leave it to Mom and the Rabbi and to trust them. That's how it was. Mom and Rabbi Cohen took me out and got me into his auto and drove me off. I guess I was in pretty much of a whirl. Then I got to recognising places. The route followed the Hudson. Then we came into a pretty big place with a lot of places that had been around for quite some time. It was easy on the eye. Mom whispered it was Catskill and we not too far from the Rabbi's place. Somehow, I got to feeling that this was going to be okay. It looked like a nice homely place where folk were friendly.

We pulled into a parking lot by some sort of place with one of those timber-framed dwellings. It looked okay. The Rabbi turned round, smiled, and said that we'd arrived.

A homely looking dame came out and greeted us. She made a great fuss over me and gave me quite a hug! I couldn't place her accent but that didn't matter. "So dist ist Bennie," she said, "Bennie ze arsist. Yah? Velcome Bennie. Velcome." We went into the place. It was pretty spacious. It had a good feel about it. I noted the mezuzah fixed to the doorpost. I touched it as I used to do when Rebecca had one fixed way back in Chicago. The Rebbetzin smiled and patted my shoulder approvingly. I knew that somehow things were going to work out. I was at home in a good Jewish household like Rebecca tried to get going. I felt like doing a Hassidic dance and singing god knows how many halleluiahs.

So, I could go on. It was like a party. Even although Mom was a goy, she joined in and was part of it all. I reckoned I was a damned lucky guy. Did I plan all this? No. Somehow it all just came together in a big way. It looked like Mom was going to stay over and the Rabbi was to take her back wherever in a day or two. She seemed pretty happy about that. That was good.

It so happened that Shabbat was coming on as the Sun started to go down somewhere in the west. So? What now? Mrs. Cohen started setting up the table. It brought back memories of Rebecca and how she set things up. I missed all that. From the kitchen came a good smell from the past, the baking challah bread. My mouth watered somewhat. I'd forgotten how damned good it tasted. So, there it was. The Shabbat table set up, candles ready to be lit and the Kiddush cup all ready. It started to come back to me. It made me feel mighty good. This was a real part of me. I belonged to all this. This was where my roots were going back to Father Abraham and all that. It got my heart pounding and getting me walk mighty tall. So, the amazing wheel of life had made a heck of a big turn in my favour. I had a deep feeling in my gut that it might stay that way.

So, we sat down to our Shabbat meal. Mom came too although she was a goy. Did that matter? The Rebbetzin got this going by lighting the candles and saying the prayer, "You are our light, O Lord, and our Salvation. In your name we kindle these Sabbath lights. May they bring into our household the beauty of truth and the radiance of love's understanding. On this Sabbath eve and at all times, let there be light." The words came rushing back into my mind. I could say a big amen to all that. Of course, Rabbi Cohen found a cappel for me to wear. Even Mom, goy that she was, was given a psalm to read, "Those who sow in tears shall reap with song of joy." Yes, YES, **YES**, I wanted to shout out. But I felt it deep down. So, it went on. Rabbi Cohen blessed the challah bread and the cup of wine. I felt I had come right home and it was always going to be like that. Something good tingled through the whole of my body. Wow! We then got down to the meal that the Rebbetzin had been cooking. And boy was I hungry!

Later, we all retired. I was taken up to a big room at the top of the place. It looked fine. I snuggled right down into the bed and slept the best sleep ever. Next day, we went off to the synagogue next door. It had been a long time since I'd been to a synagogue. I now felt in something of a whirl. Gosh, was all this really happening to me? It was like a damned good dream so good you just didn't want to wake up. But this was for real – for *REAL*. Here I was, a real Jewish man, listening to the words from the Torah, moved by the tones of the cantor and so on. I felt like jumping up and doing double somersaults and shouting out hallelujah.

I got back to the Rabbi's place after synagogue. Mom was at the door with a packed case and the Rabbi brought his car round. Mom placed both her hands on my shoulders. I caught just a glimmer of a tear in her eye. She just said, "You'll be brought to see me." Then she was off. I owed a hell of a lot to Mom. I guess she had something to do with keeping an eye on guys' health and so on in some place somewhere. What was the place? How long was I there? How did I get there? It was just an almighty great blank except for Mom and the art group. But some great sea change had come about and I was right here in Catskill town with the Rabbi and his wife. I got round to calling them Ma and Pa in time. So that's how it all was, but somehow, I was okay and going to stay that way. I'd come right home to my promised land and I guess I couldn't do better than that.

So, there it was. What more could a Jewish guy like me want? I settled down to the life around me with Ma and Pa it seemed all so natural. It felt like it had always been just like this. I had quite an apartment right at the top of the house. It had all I needed. It was a fine studio with a window of some size with a view right over the housetops to the Catskill Mountains. Somewhere up there would be Nashotah Peak. So, I got round to setting up my apartment as a studio. One of the synagogue members ran an art shop in the town. It seems like a whole lot of people came to the Catskills to sketch and that sort of thing. He fitted me up with an easel and whatever I needed. So, I worked up some of the sketches I'd made when I tramped around down by the Hudson. He took the finished stuff and sold it off in his shop. It worked well. I'd got myself a life and it was mighty good.

So, there it was. Ma and Pa took me into their lives and I took them into mine. We became a family and that was more than good. I took myself up into my studio and worked away at portraits I'd taken from sketches of the folk who came to synagogue. I took a few trips back into the mountains and made a whole lot of sketches that got worked up into watercolours or oils. David Rubenstein, who kept the art shop, would take them and sell them on commission. So, I started making a living and able to send a buck or two in the direction of Ma.

Somehow, I still wrote up the journal just as Mom advised way back. I guess I didn't put in all the detail but just an outline like I did when preparing a painting. I got through reading some of the things that had happened. The notes on the family way back in Mainz and the optical business of Traumann and Grossmann. They were bringing in the bucks and living a pretty swell life-style. Then Kristallnacht, when all hell was let loose and things fell apart, the synagogue got torched. Maybe that's when Ma and Pa somehow got unhinged. The Grossmanns saw the writing on the wall and, with the Traumanns, headed for New York and on to Chicago. Then I got to wondering if any of the family disappeared in the holocaust? Something I'd never get figured. Just thinking over what happened at the holocaust makes me want to scream just like the guy in that work by Munch.

So that's about it. I've got down to writing up something of my life so far. This was Mom's idea and I got down to it. I guess if I'd got myself a crystal ball, I might just get a peek into how my future might pan out. But I just don't have a crystal ball. But right now, things are just okay living here in Catskill with the folk I call Ma and Pa. Here I am doing what I'm pretty good at, painting. I'm living a good Jewish life, wearing a cappel, touching the mezuzah, using the phylactery. So, I guess I've become a real Jewish man and that's got to be good. I reckon I'm just going to stay that way until I get sent to Abraham's bosom.

Okay, okay so I've been dealt a mighty good hand. I've reached the land flowing with milk and honey as God, blessed be He, promised us Jews way, way back. We got there and dug our heels in. Life was mighty good after a hell of a long time out there in the wilderness. So, we got as much milk and honey as we wanted and a whole lot left over. Then other folk wanted to get in on the act and made things mighty tough for us Jews. Things were bad but deep down we were dead sure that Yahweh would see us through even when the Romans fired the Temple and smashed up Jerusalem.

So, looking back that's just how my life's worked out. There were times when things got rocky but somehow there was always someone like Rebecca to see me through. Then that hell of a time when Wagstaffe finished that poor kid Rosa and passed the buck on to me. That's when I got going around the Catskills with the Man, whoever he was. If that was the wilderness, I got a whole lot out of it, a whole lot. Then things got a touch blank and I found myself God knows where. That's when Mom got hold of me and got me to set up the art group. That was good. Then the Rabbi puts in an appearance. He has sure done me a whole lot of good. So here I am right now, living with the Rabbi and his Rebbetzin now my Pa and Ma!

I have to say I got a whole lot out of Rabbi Pa. Just to give a sample. In his study, where we get down to thinking about this and that, he has this repro of the Jewish sculptor's *Jacob and the Angel*. Wow! It goes back to Jacob getting into a tangle with an angel. Not the sort of thing anyone in their right mind should do, I reckon. Anyway, Jacob comes off pretty bad. So, Epstein shows Jacob who is shattered being held up by this mighty big angel. So, what's that all about? I talked this over with Pa who reckons it's something to do with the struggle of life. Maybe – maybe?

So, I'm right here in my Promised Land just about overflowing with a heck of a lot of milk and honey. What more could a Jewish guy want, or for that matter, a goy? Okay, things might get to falling apart – maybe. Isn't that just what happened to our people way back in Judea? There they were nice and cosy taking in their fill of milk and honey figuring that it was just going to stay that way but what the hell happens? In come the Greeks and take over. Then in come those Roman guys and things get real bad. So, there's a heck of a lot of trouble and fighting and the holy Temple gets burned down and our people kicked out of the holy city. So, I figure that there's no reason why I should sit right back and take in the milk and honey and think it's going to stay that way. No sir! But somehow, no matter how it pans out, just as the Lord took pretty good care of our people, I guess He'll fix things for me that's what I figure. So right now, with Ma and Pa here at Catskill, it's mighty good. Mighty good. I guess I want it to stay that way for a hell of a long time.

Before I sign off, I reckon that writing up this journal, just as Mom suggested, I reckon is just about the best thing I've ever done. Some guy or other, so I'm told, got to saying that we get to living this life of ours forward but understanding it backwards. I guess that's just how it's worked out for me. Okay, looking back, some dammed good highlights like the time at the academy and so on. There's been those times when I've just been the dumbest cluck that ever clucked. So, I guess my eyes have got just a bit sharper and I'm not going to get taken on rides no more. No sir!

So that's about it. The movie's ended, the curtains down, the lights have dimmed; it's time to close the book!

FINISH